A STRENGTH SUMMONED

A Novel

Book 2 Of The HOLD FAST Series

CYNTHIA HARRIS

For my friends at
Prestonfield House —

ISBN: 9798365376021

Cover art and design by Jared Frank

Printed in the United States of America

For all who have

summoned the strength to

carry on after the profound pain of loss

Trigger Warning:

This novel deals with themes of sexual assault, miscarriage, and the mental health struggles in the aftermath of such trauma and loss. While the author has taken great lengths to ensure the subject matter is dealt with in a compassionate and respectful manner, it may be triggering to some readers.

CHAPTERS

ONE
Calder Revealed

Edinburgh, Scotland
November 1766

The days started blending together on our never-ending visit to Edinburgh. I tried to stay busy running the house with Missus Douglas, though I was only useful for approving spending for shopping than anything of consequence. I have learned that I have no actual role here as mistress of the grand house on Canongate, other than owning the building.

I often sat at Father's desk to write letters to Laird Graham and Grant. I even wrote a letter to wee Robbie to tell him how much I loved him and missed him. He certainly knows by now why we left Skye in such a rush. I felt bad for not telling him the truth of our departure, but I know he will feel special getting his very own letter in the post.

I have tried to avoid seeing William, not because I did not want to see him—I did. I thought about him and his kisses constantly. The memory of them makes me as weak as I felt on that very night. The few times we have seen him at the tavern, we remained quiet with each other, often just staring and smiling occasionally at each other across the table. Our words remained short but cordial.

One afternoon, he was seated next to me and softly touched the side of my hand under the table while Duncan was telling a story and I smiled, but I could not look at him or I would certainly betray myself to my uncle. Duncan got up to see about the whisky situation, and I laced my fingers with his and looked at him. Both of our eyes were filled with love and longing. His touch was light and tender, and as our fingers caressed each other, I could barely breathe for his touch... that *and* the fear that my uncle could discover us at any moment.

Duncan has not asked me a single question about our supper, but has waited for me to tell him about it on my terms. I am afraid if he sees me and Will together too often, he will see that things have shifted in my heart. What I really want is Will to return to Macleod House on Canongate. I believe his propriety will not allow it. Luckily, the MacLeod's have made the White Hart Inn a daily stop under the guise of looking for Allan Calder, so we get to see each other nearly every day.

"Are ye unwell, lass?" Duncan asked when he returned to the table with a fresh bottle.

"No. I am fine. Why?" I asked, suddenly startled that he was back at the table and his direct question.

"Ye look flushed, lass. Yer face is bright red."

"This fire behind me is warm, I suppose."

"Here, then sit on this side of the table," he said, standing up and moving around to take my seat while offering me his.

Now, seated across from Will, his stare made me blush even more. He was grinning from ear to ear at me as he brought his glass to his lips and asked slyly, "Is it cooler over there? Ye still look flushed, lass."

I know my face and chest immediately turned an even deeper shade of red. Duncan was busy filling glasses, and I gave Will a wide-eyed look, silently willing him to stop teasing me. I could tell he was amused with himself for making me blush such that Duncan noticed.

+++

I joined Elizabeth at the law office, where we wrote the last of the letters to the remaining clients outside of Edinburgh. We let them know that upon Father's death that we released them from any contractual obligations and recommend the transfer to Master Forbes or their own choice of legal representation. We had a standard text Master Forbes drafted and the two of us split the list of clients to copy and customize for the letters.

"This has gone so much faster with yer help, Alexandra," she said as she sealed her last letter.

"It is good to have a task. I am not sure I expected to be in the city this long, but if I am helpful to my father, then it is worth it. I have tried to volunteer at Canongate Kirk when I can, but this makes me happy and fulfilled as well."

"Master MacLeod talked of ye all the time, and when he last saw ye on Skye, he was *so* proud. He was beaming when he came back and told us of all that happened there! A woman as clan chief is extraordinary, lass!"

"Everyone we have met on this journey has reminded me of how blessed I am to be the daughter of Alexander MacLeod."

She just smiled at me on the words and changed the subject. "I had a wonderful time at yer supper party. Master MacCrimmon seemed to need to have his voice heard."

I laughed and said, "I suppose we both did!"

"Master Forbes told ye that ye would make a fine advocate and I believe ye would!"

"I guess that comes naturally, but I am verra sorry the debate interrupted our evening. The tone of the discussion got a little out of hand for such a festive occasion."

"Och, no. I could see what was happening... *we all could.*"

I stopped writing my letter and looked at her across the desk, confused, as I asked, "*What* was happening?"

"The lad wanted yer attention," she said plainly, setting the wax seal on her letter. She looked up at me and said, "He *loves* ye, lass!"

I knew what she might say based on Duncan's revelation that night, but I wanted to hear Elizabeth's opinion on the matter as a woman. She does not know what William and I have said to each other since, but I am sure the look of shock on my face told her I did not expect her response. I have never really had another woman as a friend, and it feels good to speak openly with someone who understands what I might be feeling.

"It was plain to everyone at the table that Master MacCrimmon wanted your attention, and it was not to debate his all too male opinion on the future state of women's rights in Scottish law or society." I laughed and shook my head as she continued her observation. "I believe yer opinion on *not* marrying—or only marrying *for love*—was a dagger to

4

the poor man's heart. He feared that ye not only disagreed with him, but that he was not one that *ye* could love. He was going to fight ye on it, though—even in front of others. I am uncertain he convinced ye, however."

"Och, Elizabeth! I keep learning that everyone can see what I cannae."

"Ye will see it when yer ready to."

I nodded my head at her and smiled, thinking about my conversation with Will and that I had made the first step toward letting him into my heart. Perhaps I am slowly and silently becoming ready.

"William and I talked. He confessed he loves me, and he thought we could make each other happy."

"I knew it! *I knew it!* What did ye say back to him?" she asked excitedly as she sat up in her chair, eager to hear my story. I wanted to tell her what I have found myself unable to tell Duncan.

"I told him my heart was open, but that I could not lose myself along the way." Elizabeth nodded, but did not say a word. "I am of an independent mind, and I will be the next chief of my clan, so I will not be the typical wife he may expect. If he can accept me and my responsibility... then I want to be with him."

"Alexandra," she said, touching my hand, "that is such wonderful news! Master MacCrimmon is a verra handsome man and would be a fine match."

I smiled and nodded in agreement at her assessment. William MacCrimmon is indeed a handsome man and a fine match.

"He kissed me, and I couldna move. I didna know what to do," I said, laughing and hanging my head in embarrassment at my inexperience.

5

"Lass, it will come to ye naturally," she said as she placed her hand on mine. "When ye love someone, ye will connect with each other in a way that is just *yers*. Aye, there are the basics, but two people learn each other."

"Thank ye, Elizabeth," I said, turning red at the thought. "I am surrounded by men, and my mother died when I was young. I had my aunt to be sure, but have never really had women as friends to talk to."

"I understand, and I am here fer ye to talk anytime ye want."

I smiled at her offer, but changed the subject. "This is my last letter," I said as I finished and handed to her to seal.

"All done!" she exclaimed as she set the hot wax with Father's seal.

"If it is alright with ye, I would like to send a letter to Laird Graham, so may sit here a bit more. I would like ye to put in the post with the others. Just give me a few more minutes and I will complete it for ye."

"Take yer time and call fer me when ye are ready. I have more work to do upstairs fer the files that need to transfer to Master Forbes and we have two hours to make today's post coach."

She left me alone in the room and I wrote to my uncle. I had not even finished half of it before I heard the door open again. Thinking it was Elizabeth walking into the room, I said over my parchment, "I am so close, Elizabeth! I just need a few more minutes."

There was no response from the person who entered the room, so I looked up and caught the icy stare of Allan Calder.

It shocked me that the elusive man, who has avoided us for months, showed his face here and now. I then marveled at the wonder of how, in the damp and rainy weather of Edinburgh this day, the man did not have black streaks down the sides of his face and neck. This is a mighty resilient grease! His skin was ruddy and pocked like someone who had fought spots as a young man, but also does not care for himself. He is incredibly thin and his all-black wardrobe, along with the black grease slicking his hair back, depicts a dark and menacing figure. He is a specter on this threshold and one that I was uncertain I wanted to encounter on my own.

One of the first things I noticed about the man when he accompanied my father to Dunmara Castle was that his hands were bone thin. His skin was so light that you could see every vein running through them, making his hands look blue. Blue and cold. A thought further supported because the man rubbed his hands together constantly. One could only think it was to warm them up.

His demeanor is still as slick as his hair. If I knew anything, this man was not to be trusted. He followed my father around as his shadow and I have seen no hint of a brilliant legal mind or even good judgement. Being here now told me that much. Somehow, he made a name for himself under the tutelage of my father and under the respected MacLeod name here in Edinburgh. I may never understand what my father saw in him at first, but celebrate that he knew he could not carry on with this practice. To do so would have been a travesty to Alexander MacLeod's reputation and all that he built here.

"How can I be of help, sir?" I asked him, while trying not to show the shock I felt seeing him standing before me.

"I would like to know why I have not been paid my wage."

"Ye have not received a wage, because ye have done no work since my father died and this office is, sadly, no more."

"Ye have no right, I have clients to support," he tried to argue.

I remained calm, "Master Calder, ye have no clients. My father removed ye from all active clients."

"Not true, lass. I have Master Hugh as my client and am expected to help him with his case."

How dare he call me lass?

"Ye can support anyone you wish, but will not take any action here, Master Calder, on behalf of this office," I said with a harsher tone than I intended, but this debate and his increasingly dismissive attitude frustrated me.

Allan Calder seems hellbent on challenging the decision my father made and now seems even more determined by taking away business from a widow with children to feed. I find this stance offensive on both sides.

Master Hugh was the chief dressmaking rival of Master Scott, the deceased husband to Missus Helen Scott, who made my wonder of a dress for the Advocate Society. From what I can tell, the man probably harassed his rival into an early grave and is now trying to put his widow and children out on the streets.

"There is absolutely nothing to be gained by taking on this petty and personal feud. Master Hugh has held this grudge for many years against his rival Master Scott and is trying once again to punish his competition—even after death—by dragging the man's widow through the mud in the papers and now the law courts. I dinnae want us to get in the mud with him. This is not a complaint I would hear in the Great Hall at Dunmara Castle, let alone the halls of justice! What the man is doing to Missus Scott is *shameful*!"

Master Calder said nothing, but suddenly there was a hint of color rising in his ghostly face. He clearly did not care about my opinion.

"Let me also add that I dinnae have confidence that Master Hugh can pay us for what would be weeks, or perhaps even months, of work to investigate and take before the courts. And for what? Just to harm a woman with immense talent trying to feed her own family and honor her husband's good name?"

I am not just trying to support another woman in this moment, I am actually repeating my father's own words from his notes. He knew Master Hugh was a false client with a false accusation and did not take him as a client multiple times.

"Yer wrong, lass!"

I excused his dismissive use of the term *lass* once again for a moment, but he had better not say it a third time. I cocked my head and looked at him, almost daring him to say the word once more. I waited, but he made no other attempt to persuade me on additional thinking or rationale why this was a legitimate client for the firm.

"That is yer opinion, sir. But we will not be taking on this false client," I said definitively. "And this is no longer a debate! As I said moments ago, the law office of Alexander MacLeod, Esquire, is no more."

He grumbled something I could not hear under his breath as he turned toward the window. It was clear he did not agree with my decision and was clearly frustrated having to debate it with me. My guess, however, is that he is more concerned with his wage than with the principle of the argument.

He regained his insolence and turned back around to me and said loudly, "I do not take orders from *ye, Alexandra*!"

I gave him a half-smile of indulgence on this thinking, but then said, "Ye mistake yourself, sir! First, ye will address me properly—and respectfully—by my title, *Lady MacLeod*. Dinnae call me by my given name or *lass* again!"

His mouth was ajar in shock at my direct reproach. Only a man with so little respect for women could seem stunned that one might set him in his place. I will not stand for his disrespect, and definitely not in my father's own office.

"Second, that is my father's name on the brass plate outside the door, and this was *his* business. One left to me upon his death and one we have closed. If ye had come to work, ye would ken that."

"All well and good, *Lady MacLeod*," he said, emphasizing my title with great contempt. "But yer father is *dead*... and ye are sadly nothing but... *a woman*."

Impertinence aside, this is the one position that the great slick eel of a man, Allan Calder, will never recover from. His belief in my ability is based on the short-sighted thinking inherent in too many men of today. Surely, there is no way a woman could be capable of running her own business. The one exception being a brothel. Men never seem to mind a woman running a brothel.

"Ye think what you wish of me as a *woman*, but I am no fool!" He rolled his eyes at this, but I did not flinch. I stared him straight in the eyes, unwilling to back down. "Do ye not think that I ken that George Hugh has tried on three occasions—just this year—to have this firm represent him in the same petty grievance? And every time, my father refused him and his absurd claim for the same reasons I have said to ye now."

He looked at me, shocked I would know this, but said nothing.

"Och, aye! Surely you would ken this as well, sir! It makes little sense that we would waste our time with Master Hugh and risk not being

10

compensated for our efforts at the same time. I cannae for the life of me understand why you are continuing to push it. Perhaps you have no respect for my father's opinion, or..." I said, leaning in and searching his eyes for an ounce of truth from the man, "perhaps ye have made *yer own arrangement* with Master Hugh."

The look of shock on his face showed I would know these details were worth every word I said. But the consequence was that my challenge clearly added to his very visible anger and frustration boiling over to where I stepped slightly back toward the desk should he be brave enough to touch me.

This was the first time in this exchange that I thought about my physical safety. The man stood before me dumbfounded and still wringing his hands furiously. Now I suspect it has less to do with keeping them warm and more to do with his own nervous temperament or trying to settle his anger and emotions.

He laughed heartily at this statement. "Yer father!? Yer father had but one goal and it was to see ye married, *lass*! He saw the succession as a lark to support yer laird in a moment of clan weakness!"

Ignoring the intentional sneer of *lass* once again, I said, "You ken nothing of my father, my family, *or* my clan."

Laughing heartily and with an added layer of anger and resentment, he said dismissively, "Och, ye are so naïve! Ye must ken that the entire show at Dunmara was not for ye, but for yer future husband."

I thought for a moment about the reasons the man before me would try to provoke me with such a lie. My head was spinning thought the interactions I had with the council of brothers and immediately remembered the words Duncan said to me during the succession planning at Dunmara Castle: *Men with thwarted ambitions can be a danger. Do not give in to your own emotions and inclinations to fight them, lass.*

I reminded myself this was about Allan Calder's ambitions. It meant nothing to him that my father was dead, or that I was a woman. All he could see is his own goal to stay aligned to this firm and live off the work, reputation, and prosperity Alexander MacLeod built here in Edinburgh. He had been successful in doing so... until now. His cruelty to me was because I was his only hope to keep any semblance of his own perceived power and influence. His ambitions were now being thwarted by *a woman*. I am an obstacle in his path. Duncan's words rang in my ears. I had to check myself here and find a way out of this conversation—and quickly.

"Och, aye! I know all about the marriage contract and the work yer father was doing to negotiate an advantageous marriage for ye, as the future *Lady MacLeod*."

I looked at him, trying again to keep my emotions in check and off my face. If he were trying to bait me with such accusations, I could not give in so easily.

"Do ye not believe me, then? Look here," he said as he walked to a shelf filled with books behind Father's desk and pulled a leather portfolio from the wall. A portfolio I had not noticed before. He took a parchment from it and turned it around on the desk, facing me.

I walked closer to see the document fully. It was as I feared. Before me was the missing marriage contract, presented to the Fine. But now this document had a name filled in for the bridegroom under my own, clear as day.

At the city of Edinburgh, on the _____ day of _____ in the year _____ it is contracted, agreed, and matrimonially concluded betwixt **Alexandra Flora MacLeod** *the only lawful daughter of Alexander Ewan MacLeod, Esquire and the deceast Flora Catherine MacAskill, now ward and heir of her guardian the* **Laird Graham Malcom MacLeod of MacLeod** *of Castle Dunmara on Skye on the one part and* **William MacCrimmon** *on the second part.* **That is to say** *that the said partys execute betwixt them a* **Contract of Marriage** *which binds an obliges each of them to the Terms, Conditions and Stipulations forthwith in manner and to the effect following...*

I stopped reading at the mention of William's name in a script as large as my own. I stepped back away from the desk slightly on my heels and yet still tried to keep my face from showing the shock I immediately felt from what this paper may reveal to me—which would be a monstrous betrayal by the men I love and trust the most. My mind raced.

Everything Duncan has been doing to push me and Will together as of late made me uncertain. I needed to collect myself. I could deal with the other men in my life, but I just had to get this specific man out of my sight before I risked my personal safety or Elizabeth's. Master Forbes was in court today and could not help us.

"This parchment means nothing, sir," I said, dismissing the evidence before me and crossing my arms defensively in front of my chest. "My father and my uncles agreed I would make my own decisions about my future and reassured me it would be so."

"It means something, Alexandra. This is a legal contract and represents yer father's wishes for your future husband. If ye understood the law, ye would know that!" His dismissiveness and continued informality in addressing me were overflowing at this point.

"Ye misjudge me again, sir! The document has a name in addition to mine, but it is not his full name, and the document is not signed or dated. It is a shell of a legal document. It means *nothing*."

I could not fully speak to the legal binding of this contract before me under the laws of Scotland as I am not legally trained, and Calder knew it. But I am intelligent enough to know, as Alexander MacLeod's daughter, that this contract is not complete. The only difference is the odd inclusion of William's name. I held my ground, hoping my instincts were correct. I had so many questions!

Could the council of brothers have betrayed my wishes and my heart?

Could the last few months with Will have been a plan put in motion by the men I trusted?

Was Will a participant in this scheme? Did he truly love me at all?

My silence, however, opened the door for Calder to keep talking while my head and my insides swirled. His nerves showed a bit at my rebuke of this document. He walked all over the room, muttering to himself and twisting his hands together over and over. I could not make out a single word he was saying. He would come stand before me and start to say something, only to turn back to the window or the fire to think about it more. His manner made me nervous when he would come close, and I could feel my relief when he walked away, but I could not find an opening to end this misery for us both.

Finally, softening his tone and revealing his true intentions, he said, "There *is* one way around this. *Ye could marry another.*"

He stepped forward and walked around the desk, getting a little too close to me once again. With his awful breath on my face, he said with a newly discovered tone of praise, he reached out with his icy fingers to stroke my forearm still protectively crossed before my chest, and said, "With yer natural business sense and charm and with my legal mind, we could make this firm the most successful in all of Edinburgh. All we have to do is *destroy this document.* As ye rightly said, it is not signed. I dinnae ken what yer father or his brothers meant by putting the poor stable lad's name on it, but no one *ever* needs to see it again. Ye could toss it into the fire without consequence."

With his blind ambition showing even more, he leaned in and whispered in my ear, *"We would want for nothing in this city, Alexandra."*

I clenched my jaw and pushed every ounce of repulsion at this advance down in my gut to avoid provoking this miserable creature here alone by punching him in the face or being sick on his boots. Duncan's advice about *men with thwarted ambitions* were still ringing in my ears. I am standing here alone, but alone and angry. I did not hesitate in my response, but tempered my tone so as not to provoke this man any further.

"Och, Master Calder, I completely agree with ye," I whispered. He stepped back slightly as I advanced forward and kept smiling at me as if I were actually about to accept his outlandish offer. His eyes lifting for a moment in hope, as I continued, smiling at him as he smiled back, "This *could have been* the finest, most successful law firm in Edinburgh. But regrettably, my father, the lifeblood and soul of this practice, has died, and it is no more. Alexander MacLeod's clients will be supported by the men—and women—who not only represent the laws of Scotland, but represent the honesty and integrity worthy of his name and legacy. That, sir, means that we have sent all of our clients the option to sign with

Master Forbes or seek their own counsel, and we will carry forward that plan without the need of yer service."

I walked behind the desk and continued professionally but quickly, "We will send ye any personal items you have left on yer desk upstairs, so ye will want to let me ken now if Mistress Hay has note of the location of yer current lodging. If not, ye will want to let me know where to send yer possessions."

He said nothing. I took the void in the room to tell him, "Then, sir, I will ask ye to leave these premises immediately and never return. I will make it clear to everyone who works here, and I will alert Duncan and Angus MacLeod who serve as security for this office, and Master Forbes, who owns these buildings, that ye shall never be granted access here for any reason."

He charged at me forcefully, enraged, though I did not move in response. Just a step from my face said, spitting on me, "*Ye have no right! Ye have no right... ye stupid whore!*"

I am grateful that he did not touch me in anger, as I am not sure what I had at my disposal to defend myself other than my own hands and the point of a quill on the desk before me. I could likely take this weak twig of a man, but add this to the many times I have not thought through what I need to be safe. That thought did not stop me from laughing slightly at his insult, as it was, in fact, probably the best he could do at the moment. Bless him.

"Call me what ye wish, sir. Yer services are no longer required, and it is clear to me that yer *ambitions* can be better achieved elsewhere. To that end, we willna be providing ye with a referral letter. My father left none fer ye in his will. Here, let me walk ye out, sir."

Trying my best to keep the tone civil and professional, but motioning him toward the door with my arm to end this conversation. Thankfully, he did not resist me in this move. I walked slowly and cautiously behind him down the hall, trying to keep him moving forward and keep some distance between us should he lash out at me physically. I thought for a moment that I should have called for Elizabeth, but I did not. I did not want to put her at risk, as well.

He was fuming, but made his way to the front door before speaking to me again. When we arrived, he turned and said with a smirk, "Yer father was not alone in his assessment. Yer nothing but a stupid, misguided woman and will only serve the purpose of the ambitious men in yer life... *as ye have until now.*"

His words stung, but I told myself that they were the same as the others he spoke this day—and are simply not true. These were mere insults born from his own rejection and anger. I opened the door for him and waited for him to walk across the threshold.

"Ah, again you have read it all wrong, Master Calder," I said, leaning in just enough to push him back further onto the stone landing so that I could close the door. "Have ye not thought that perhaps these men are *serving my ambitions*, sir?"

His mouth was ajar in disbelief at the strength and commitment behind this assertion, and said, "One day, ye will regret this! I will see to the *reckoning* myself! I promise ye that!"

"I doubt that verra much," I said as I shut the door in his face before he could respond again. I locked the door immediately with the key and waited with my ear to the door until I heard his footsteps down the stone stairs to know that he was gone.

Exhausted, I bent over with my hands on my knees. I sought to catch my breath in deep sighs of relief, but I knew I could not stay here long. I had to get home and talk to Duncan, and quickly. Allan Calder knows where my father's house is located and, for all I knew, the man could be on his way there now. I had to get there first, and I had to uncover the truth of this marriage contract and how William's name was suddenly added to mine.

+++

I shouted up the stairs, "Mistress Hay! Erm, Elizabeth!"

"Aye? What is it, lass?" she yelled back as she peeked over the banister at me.

"I need ye to call fer Jonny. I have to get home straight away!"

"Of course," she said back to me.

I ran into the office and as I put on my cloak, I stared down at the marriage contract upon the desk. Deep down, I could not believe that the men I love the most could betray me, or that what I have grown to feel for Will over the last several weeks could be based on a falsehood. But I had to get to the truth of the story I just heard, and I desperately needed Duncan's reassurance. I took the paper and placed the contract and my unfinished letter to Laird Graham back into the portfolio and headed out to the front door.

Mistress Hay was waiting for me in the front hall. "The carriage is here!"

"Och, that was quick!"

I turned to her and grabbed her by the shoulders with both hands. "This is important. I just let Allan Calder ken he will not be paid and that his services are no longer needed."

18

"The man was *here?*" she asked, touching my arm with great concern. *"Alexandra!* Ye were with him *alone?"*

"Aye, he came in while I was writing my letter, looking for his pay. I let him ken he no longer works here, that the office is no more. I also told him he does not have a letter of referral and all clients are being given the option to move to Master Forbes or find new counsel."

"Ye should not have been on yer own with him," Elizabeth said, shaking her head.

"Look at me! That man is *never* to step foot in this building again, for *any* reason. I told him ye would send any of his personal effects to him. Do ye understand?"

"Aye."

"I also need ye to lock up important files this verra moment and every evening until we transfer the last items to Master Forbes."

"I can keep messengers from coming and going freely by locking the doors. Master Forbes will support that, especially when he and his staff are in the law courts."

"Aye, the door is to remain locked. I will try to enlist some help from my uncle for greater security for us tomorrow."

She touched my hand and said, "Are ye alright, lass? Did the man hurt ye in any way?"

"No, but why do ye ask me that?" I said, now even more concerned that I confronted the man on my own.

"Master Calder is filled with bitterness and spite. I told Alexander many times that I did not feel safe alone in his presence. I could see the cruelty and ambition behind the man's eyes. He has ice in his veins to be sure and ye should not have met with him here alone! It troubles me so that ye took such a risk!"

I nodded slightly in agreement and recognized personally that she noted his *ambition*. I touched her shoulder and said, "Then we are of the same mind. Please lock the front door the minute I walk out, put everything away under lock and key that should be kept private, and go home." She nodded to me in agreement. I grabbed her hand and said, "Be safe. I will send new instructions to yer home in the morning. Dinnae come here until ye have heard from me. I must talk to Duncan first."

She seemed touched by this acknowledgement of concern for her and others and replied, "Jonny is waiting for ye with the carriage." She smiled as I walked out the door, only to turn to me once more, as she had something to say. I waited as it took her a moment, but she said contemplatively, "Yer father would be so proud of ye."

She leaned in to kiss me on the cheek and caught herself at the moment that maybe it was inappropriate, but despite a quick pause, completed the task anyway. Her words and this sign of affection comforted me. She has never said the words, but I believe she loved my father, and she has shown me nothing but kindness, respect, and even *love* from the very minute I walked into this building. Elizabeth Hay has become a welcome and treasured friend on this trip.

I heard the door lock behind me. I ran down the front stairs. I told Jonny, "Thank ye for bringing the carriage so quickly, sir."

"We were expecting ye to leave about this time and had everything sorted for ye in advance when we saw the signal from Mistress Hay," he said as he helped me up the steps of the carriage. I had not realized until now that there was a flag raised from Elizabeth out the back window to the stables beneath. That is how they knew to come around. The workings of the busy city continue to amaze me.

20

Before he shut the door, I touched his arm and said, "Jonny, it is essential that I get home as quickly as possible. Can ye make that happen?"

"Aye," he said with a smile and a tip of his cap, "we will take the back way."

TWO
Alliances Forged

I nervously looked out of both sides of the carriage, praying that I did not see the ghostly face of Allan Calder along the way. He knows where MacLeod House is, but surely, would also know that Duncan, Angus, and William could be ready to meet him there.

I hope he would not think of coming to the house today. But if he dared to in his anger, I had to get there first. The carriage moved at incredible speed across roads that were not forgiving. I raised my hands to the ceiling of the coach more than once because of the constant bumps and jolts on the rough roads, but I never felt unsafe. Jonny is a master of the carriage! I do not know what those on the ground thought of us barreling our way through the damp and muddy streets of Edinburgh, but we arrived in the courtyard close in mere minutes.

I thanked Master Jonny for his safe passage and went straight into the house and then for the whisky in the parlor, knowing that I would likely find Duncan there as well. As I turned into the room, I saw him sitting in front of the fire with Angus.

"Well, well," I said sarcastically. "Fancy meeting you two here!" I filled my glass to the top and then, after a quick drink of it all, filled it once again.

"There ye go, mi'lady!" Angus said, nodding his approval at my double-pour, by raising his own glass again to me in tribute.

"Angus, how is it I can understand ye when I drink whisky?" I asked, taking another large sip.

"I dinnae ken, mi'lady! The mighty *uisge beatha* 'as many 'ealing properties, but I dinnae ken it improves 'earing... in fact, I found it does quite the opposite."

"Long day, lass?" Duncan said, as they both laughed and raised their glasses above their chairs in tribute. In fact, that is all I could see before me were two whisky glasses hovering over the tops of the chairs. This display of drunken solidarity would have been comical had I not been incensed from the events of the day.

I moved to stand right in front of the fire and right before them, "I will get right to it. *Why would ye all lie to me?*" I said as my initial angry accusation subsided into disappointment. "I dinnae ken how those that I love so dearly could *betray* me so!"

Confused by the sudden formal accusation, they both stopped their glasses at their lips and looked at each other, confused.

Angus spoke up first and said, "A nod's as guid as a wink tae a blind horse, lass!"

23

"What he means is—we dinnae ken what yer talking about! Yer going to have to tell us more than just the accusation, Alex," said Duncan, leaning forward in his chair, and matching the confused look on Angus' face with his own.

"I got to spend my afternoon at my father's office with Master Allan Calder, Esquire."

After all this time looking for him, the shock of my words rendered Duncan mute. He shook his head but there was no response until Angus finished his glass with a gulp and said, "Then ye earned yer glass... miserable chancer, no? Slick as an eel, the man is. Imma man o' the battlefield. Y'ken to connect wi' the men who will save yer life and ye theirs. That man licked yer father's boots but told me in every way 'e was oot fer 'imself!"

I turned to Duncan and said through my teeth in anger, "I understand, but this miserable chancer may have verra well shown me this afternoon that I am surrounded by other *miserable chancers. Liars* no less!"

Still confused, Duncan, with his brows furrowed, stood up from his chair and said, "Ye saw the man?" He knew we had been looking for Calder for months and seemed genuinely concerned that I was the one to encounter him on my own.

I ignored his question, went to my bag, and pulled out the marriage contract and held up to Duncan's face. "Do ye have anything ye wish to tell me, Duncan?"

Grabbing the paper from me, he said, "Ye found the marriage contract?"

"The marriage contract found me, as I talked to that horrible man," I said, staring at my uncle's face for any clue as he read the names just as I did.

He looked up at me with what appeared genuine confusion, "Wait, it has Williams's name on it!"

"Aye, it does! Master Calder let me ken the current state of the contract this afternoon. Is that not *interesting?*" I did not give him a chance to respond and continued my attack. "Were ye in on this scheme? Did ye and my father arrange this match? Is William aware? Is he a party to this deception?"

I was fuming and continued my litany of unending questions, *"How could ye?!* Are ye just playing with my heart? Is this entire love-match based on a lie that ye, Laird Graham, and my father planned from the beginning? And fer what gain? Fer Clan MacLeod or fer something else?"

Angus quickly retreated to the whisky bottle in the back of the room, silently taking Duncan's glass, which needed refilling along with his own. Duncan remained calm as each question and accusation was loudly hurled at him all at once. He held the contract in his hands, and tried to make a joke by saying, "I believe that is a first fer ye, lass! Ten questions in a single breath."

"Och! Stop it! I am not playing the question game today. I am too angry! Ye have been pushing me into the arms of William MacCrimmon for weeks, uncle! *Why?*"

"Now just hold on! I havena been pushing ye to anyone," he said, looking to Angus for support when he brought him a refilled glass.

"The lass and Will are *finally* together, then?" Angus asked, seemingly oblivious to the conversation that had just happened before him.

"We are not!" I yelled angrily at Angus, who stepped back and sipped his glass almost apologetically without saying another word. He does not know what is happening here at this moment, and neither of the men before me deserves to know more than I am willing to share about what William and I have discussed. We will solve only one mystery this evening.

Duncan still seemed somewhat confused by the accusations, which I took as silent confirmation that Calder was exactly what I thought he was—*a liar.* But I needed these men—these men that I love—to fully convince me of the fact.

"Aye, I will leave ye to talk," said Angus, trying to back out of the room, and with the bottle of whisky. That point alone would not be acceptable to me or Duncan at this moment.

Duncan and I shouted to him in unison, *"No!"*

"Ye should hear all of this, Angus, because if ye have had any part in this rogue scheme, there will be hell to pay for ye as well!" He knew I meant what I said and did not challenge me. In reality, I am certain we were both protecting the drink from going out of the room with Angus more than anything.

Shrinking back, he put the bottle on the table and stood quietly, sipping his own glass. He said a soft, *"Och, well damn!"*

"I dinnae ken why William's name would be on this document," Duncan said. "I saw the contract the last time ye did... at Dunmara. We both ken that the contract only had yer name that evening. And yer father brought it back to Edinburgh." He could see that I was still uncertain and seething at the prospect of being lied to, and grabbed me by the shoulder, "I have *never* lied to ye, lass! And I *never* will! Tell me everything that slick eel told ye."

26

I relayed the entire conversation and final scene with Calder. Duncan and Angus took in every word. They were as shocked by this story as I was repeating it. I became emotional thinking about how I felt in the moment. I tried to pull myself back together.

"I dinnae want to believe it of ye, but is there any truth to this man's story? Have ye arranged a marriage to William MacCrimmon without my consent?"

"I have done *no* such thing!" Duncan said, shocked by the accusation. "I have words fer ye confronting this horrible man on yer own, but I will save that fer another time. I believe that ye are correct that the name means nothing on an unsigned document, but what I have told you about William MacCrimmon has been the truth, lass. I have only told ye the truth!"

"If you are unaware of this, uncle, is there any possibility that William could be fulfilling my father's wishes—or even Laird Graham's—without yer knowledge?"

Duncan stared at me, unsure how to answer.

"I had to ask the question."

"Aye, ye did," he said as he took a quick sip of his newly filled glass, "but I cannae answer to what I dinnae ken. I see that this information, considering our recent conversations, looks coordinated. I can tell ye that I dinnae believe for one second yer father signed William's name on this parchment! First, I dinnae believe he ever met the man, and second, he wouldna go against yer wishes. I *ken* he wouldna! Never!"

"But why would Calder..."

Duncan interrupted my question and asked his own, "Why indeed?"

My uncle understands the true nature of men and seems to be thinking about the ulterior motives that may swim in the mind of a man trying to make this allegation for his own personal gain. I could see his mind trying to work out what those motives might be. This is the man who gave me the clear advice when I was named heir about men with thwarted ambitions.

We all stood quietly for a moment. Duncan came to me, took my hand, and reassuringly said, "We will have to uncover the truth— together."

"Aye, *together*," I said, with a weak smile as I nodded to him in agreement. I could not stay mad at Duncan for long. He is one of my last *fathers,* and I trust him more than anyone else in my life. With his hands on my shoulders, my uncle kissed me gently on the forehead and placed his arm around my shoulder. At that moment, I knew everything would be fine, and I released my fears and worries instantly.

He turned from me and directed, "Angus, man, go ahead to the White Hart and find William to meet with us!"

I reacted immediately, pulling from his embrace, and yelled, "*Wait! No!* I dinnae want to talk to William! Not about *this!*"

Angus paused at the door, uncertain of which order to follow.

"Trust me," Duncan said. I relented with a slight nod of my head in honor of the complete trust I had in my uncle. I was still fearful, but I have been learning to get out of my own way—at least a little. Now, might be one of those times I need to let trust the men who love me.

Turning back to Angus, Duncan continued, "Go, man! We are right behind ye."

He then turned to me and said as he drank the last of his glass, "We need to get to the truth of this, and quickly. The four of us. Get yer cloak and the contract."

I became increasingly nervous at the thought of seeing Will and discussing of all these things—like marriage contracts—so early in our secret courtship. A courtship that could be exposed to Angus and Duncan this very night. I hope Will does not betray our secret. I challenged him once more on our walk to the tavern, "I dinnae ken how involving William helps us solve this."

Duncan grabbed my hand resting by my side and smiled at me as we kept walking. "I ken it is awkward. But the man is involved whether ye want him to be or not. Ye asked a question I cannae answer... *is William fulfilling some ask from yer father or Laird Graham?* I dinnae believe the lad is, but we need to uncover the truth. Do ye trust me?"

"Aye, I trust ye with my life."

"It will be fine. I promise," he said as he squeezed my hand and opened the door to the White Hart Inn.

+++

Duncan has a habit of walking into a room and stopping at the threshold. He surveys the room to see who he knows, or to find the best seat—and I have determined—to wait for the acknowledgement that he has *finally* arrived. This is an acknowledgement he feels he deserves. Jacob obliged him once again.

The exclamation of our names greeted us on the way into the tavern, thanks to Jacob, the barkeep and owner, *"Dun-can! Alex-an-dra!"* He always welcomes us with the sing-song articulation of our names for all to hear. He always makes us feel special—like the most important people in town finally arrived at his tavern.

Jacob rushed to Duncan immediately and shook his hand. Looking at us both, he said as he motioned us to the back, "Angus and William are already here, and I have ye all in the back room so ye can talk *privately*."

"Thank ye, Jacob! I hope all is well with ye this evening."

"Ah 'tis, mi' lady, we are glad to see you here and we already have yer drinks waiting for ye at the table."

"And how is Hilary, sir?"

"Och, she is braw... ye ken that the wee bairn will be here any day," he said, smiling as a proud new father-to-be.

I grabbed his hand and made him stop for a moment so I could say, "Aye, I do. Tell her to stay strong in these last days, sir. I am so happy fer ye both with the gift of this new life, and I cannae wait to hold the wee bairn myself!"

"Thank ye, mi' lady," he said, sending me forward with his arm to the back of the tavern. Duncan and I walked to the very last table where Angus and William were seated and waiting for us.

We sat beside each of them. Duncan with William and me with Angus. I nodded and smiled at Will, but tried not to look at him after that. I was determined that my face should not fully betray my heart to my uncle. That would be a feat considering the topic we were about to discuss.

"I should have stood fer ye, Alexandra," William said apologetically. Since Prestonfield House and Master Garrick's silent instruction, William has kept some formality in standing for me occasionally, but even more so since our conversation. It is sweet of him to show such respect to me.

"No need for formalities here tonight. We have some things to clarify and need yer help. Thank ye for meeting us here this evening."

"I didna have to go far *and* to be honest, Angus didna give me much of a choice." We all laughed at this, as he continued, "He told me just enough to bring me down from my bed and said that ye and Duncan would explain the truth of it."

Before I could say another word, Duncan spoke loudly, "We have a *liar* amongst us!"

Every head at the table turned to him sharply and he nearly spit out his drink, laughing at our reaction and his mistake. "Sorry, sorry... no! We have *lies* amongst us, friends. *Lies! Lies*, that I believe only the four of us can uncover the truth of, so I ask each of ye, as MacLeod kinsman, to be honest and truthful at this table."

Duncan raised his glass to the middle of the table. We all nodded in agreement to his ask and raised our own glasses and ale pots to each other. "*Slàinte!*"

"Alexandra, lass," Duncan looked me earnestly in my eyes and asked, "please tell us all the story of what happened at the law office today with Allan Calder? I am sorry to ask it of ye, but William needs to ken what occurred and it woudna hurt for me and Angus to hear the tale again."

"Ye found Calder?" William asked, now sounding concerned and sitting upright in his chair.

"Aye! Well, in truth, the man found me."

I told the entire story from beginning to end. No one interrupted me and let the words all soak in. I could see Will's reactions out of the corner of my eye—especially when I mentioned his name was on the marriage contract. He said nothing, but seemed genuinely confused at this admission and stared at the document before us on the table. I kept my gaze on Duncan, seated across from me, in relaying the facts of the story. The only interruption was from my uncle, at the end, when he reminded

31

Angus and William that the marriage contract was designed for my succession to counter Clan MacLeod objections. He also reminded us that the original document presented before the Fine only had my name on it. The document returned to Edinburgh with my father, and this was the first any of us have seen of it since.

"I ask all of ye at this table and upon the words Duncan said at the start—please tell me that ye had no idea of this change to the contract or other plans for my betrothal with my father or Laird Graham."

All three men at the table said they did not, and I believed each of them. While I still could not understand the reason Calder would change the contract, I did feel some relief.

Outside of his confirmation that he was not part of any betrothal plan, William was silent through our explanations. He spoke finally to say, "Alexandra, I admire yer ability to handle this situation with the horrible man, as ye did."

Angus, who had not uttered a word since we arrived, nodded his head in drunken agreement and said seriously, "Aye, verra strong!"

I just looked at him from the side, but none of us said a word. William gulped the last of his drink and looked me in the eye and asked, "But I have to ask ye—did Calder *touch ye or threaten ye... in any way* during yer meeting?"

If I did not already know that Duncan MacLeod thought that William MacCrimmon was the right match for me, the man just proved it with this question. For he just asked the one thing neither Duncan nor Angus did earlier, and I could see that my uncle respected him for it immediately. It showed on his face, as he looked at the man and raised his shoulders in anticipation of my answer.

All heads turned to me, and I nodded, while choking over my response and staring into the bottom of my glass. "Aye, the man *threatened* me."

The mood at the table shifted on the faces of the men before me. Duncan and Angus both seemed crestfallen with this acknowledgement. Not just that they had not asked this question themselves, but visibly reacted to the truth of the answer by bowing their heads. William's instincts were correct that Calder was the type of man who would have threatened me, and they all hated that it was so.

"I need to ken exactly what he said—or did—to ye, lass."

"I will tell ye," I said, taking the last sip of my glass for courage. "Master Calder told me outright that I was *nuthin' but a woman,* and ye all ken how I feel about that line of thinking!"

Angus nodded and said, *"Miserable chancer!"*

"Then he decided that was not enough of an insult and called me a *stupid whore* and I was just here *serving at the mercy of the men around me and that I would pay for this decision,* and he would see to *the reckoning* himself."

Speaking about this point caused Duncan to lower his head in shame and disbelief once again. I saw the look on their faces, but before they could say a word, I tried to dismiss the awful words myself, as many strong women do. "This man has nothing over me, and ye all ken it!"

Jacob refreshed all our drinks swiftly and quietly, almost without notice. Angus, Duncan, and William exchanged looks with each other, before William finally said to my uncle while looking at me directly, "That is a threat, is it not, Duncan?"

Duncan just nodded his head slowly, still in disbelief and regret. It was a threat, and he was sorry for it.

William said plainly, "He has threatened ye, Alexandra. I dinnae care what ye think of the man, or what we believe to be yer ability to take care of yerself, but Allan Calder has now made himself a danger to ye, and an enemy to me. We need to get ye away from the city and quickly... at least for a little while."

"I agree on the threat, lad, but we should not be so hasty on such a retreat," said Duncan.

Will turned to Duncan and was forceful in defending his response. "This man kens where she lives in her father's house and the law office is an even easier target. I will be honest, sir, I am concerned about the safety of *both* Alexandra *and* Mistress Hay. What should we do?"

Duncan sat quietly for a moment and instead of responding to William, said to me, "We have more to do here to wrap up Alexander's affairs before we can go back to Skye. But perhaps I can send ye to find out about this *country house*. It is yers now. Ye can decide if ye want to sell or keep it."

William and I looked at each other, slightly unsure of this plan forcing us together for the ride to an uncertain destination in what were the earliest days of our undeclared courtship. Duncan is not ignorant of what is happening around him, but does not know the extent of the discussions Will and I have had. If he were, I doubt this would be his first suggestion.

"Angus and I can protect the house here in Edinburgh until ye are safely on yer way. We will see what we can uncover about Master Calder, now that he has emerged from the shadows, and I can make my decision about the brewery in Leith."

It was in my nature to protest being directed, but I knew what Duncan was asking me was in my best interest. The reactions from telling these men that Allan Calder had threatened me showed how much they all care for me. I knew they were all trying to keep me safe, and I needed to trust them in this moment. Laird Graham told me at the outset of this journey to listen to my uncle and I must.

"William is right to worry fer Mistress Hay. I need someone to look after the law office for a bit of security for her as well. Can Angus take on that task for us?" I turned to him and said jokingly, "Actually, what is yer role here in the city, man?"

"That there is a fair question, mi'lady!" He sipped his glass as we all laughed, breaking the seriousness of this evening's discussion.

Duncan said, "Aye, Angus can help Mistress Hay tomorrow. My guess is that Calder will actually leave ye alone because he kens ye have us all around ye, but he could try to take advantage of the situation and retrieve things from the law office that we are unaware of."

"Thank ye. I agree. I worry he may try to come back for client files or more. We are safe for Clan MacLeod, but the other files are still moving to Master Forbes. I left Mistress Hay this afternoon with instruction that she put everything under lock and key and that Master Calder should no longer be allowed on the premises. She deserves additional support to make that so. I told her when I left, that I would send instruction tomorrow morning and I can tell her to expect ye, Angus. I will ask her to move faster about transferring everything to Master Forbes. I believe she will be safe once we get her finally into his office."

"Aye, I wi' be there," Angus said with conviction and a drunken nod.

"Alexandra, Angus, and I will get you home this evening. Can ye and William be ready to ride to Glenammon House by mid-day tomorrow?"

William and I both nodded silently to him in agreement.

Duncan asked, "Lass, do ye ken of any pending cases for the firm?"

"No sir, but we have a handful of clients outside of Edinburgh who kept Father on retainer. Mistress Hay and I wrote the last letters today to let them ken of his death and provided them the option to move to Master Forbes or choose new counsel. It will take time for those letters to arrive and for the clients to decide. There was, however, the *false client*, a Master Hugh, that Calder somehow thinks he represents. But he has paid nothing, and Father rejected him as a client three times. So, I dinnae care if he thinks Master Calder was representing him. He is not on the ledger for this firm."

"Then the doors are officially closed. Come to think of it, ye should go with us to the office in the morning to help direct Mistress Hay, since ye ken more about the office and clients than we do. Angus and I will go with ye at ten o'clock. Send notice to her straight away, Alexandra."

"Aye, I will send by Petey first thing in the morning."

Duncan smiled to me and added, "I will let ye and Will ken what to look for in evaluating the house and will send word to the estate factor, Master Cameron, by messenger, first thing as well and tell him to expect ye both by end of day."

William took over the planning from Duncan as they seemed aligned as he said to me directly, "Ye tend to the office with your uncle and Angus in the morning and I will arrange our transportation to Glenammon House with Jonny. We will leave at mid-day tomorrow."

"I will be ready," I said with a weak smile and nod to a man I was starting to love. William continued in a way that I truly admired. It was not just in managing details and planning for our exodus from Edinburgh. I felt his intention, protection, and love from across the table. I wondered if Duncan and Angus could see what I suddenly could.

"Duncan and Angus, our next step is to *go home*," Will said. "I ken that we have more to figure out to do that, but we will as kinsmen, as *family*."

His last words warmed my heart in a new way. *Family*. Not just the family into which I was born. Not just my kinsmen or my clan. But *my family*.

It startled me how this escalated into a hasty retreat from Edinburgh. Three of the most important men in my life are seated with me at this table and all of them only want to protect me. Duncan did not balk at William's sentiment or direction. Perhaps he agreed completely with the direction, or he just saw William taking his own role in my life going forward. Either way, he willingly let the man lead.

THREE
Together In Exile

Glenammon House
Near Blackness, Scotland
November 1766

On the banks of the River Forth, sits Glenammon House, the country estate of Alexander MacLeod. Wee Stirling knew we arrived at our destination before William and I did, as he suddenly bolted toward the small cottage at the edge of the tree-lined lane, the instant we turned off from the main road outside the village of Blackness.

At the estate factor's lodge, we met Master Cameron, an older gentleman who looked weathered, as a man who has likely worked every day of his life outside should. His voice matched his look. It was low and gruff and had tinges of a Northern English accent. But his eyes and welcoming smile told me underneath this hardened exterior he was warm and kind man.

"Aye, 'ello there young'uns! Welcome t'Glenammon! Can I be of 'elp t'ye?" He said, welcoming both of us as dear friends to this house and land.

Will took the lead and said to the man as he left his horse, "Master Cameron, I believe? I am William MacCrimmon, and this is Lady Alexandra MacLeod. Ye should have received word from her uncle, Master Duncan MacLeod, to expect us both here this evening."

"Aye sir, indeed! *Indeed!*" Master Cameron said as he rushed to me instantly and taking my hands in his. "Lady MacLeod, I feel I already know and love ye. Yer father talked of ye often, lass, and ye look the absolute spit of 'im." He released my hands to take off his cap in a show of respect and continued, "It 'urt me and the missus to 'ear of 'is sudden passing. In complete shock we were! Such a young man with 'is life still ahead of 'im. But I can tell ye lass, yer father was a kind man and fair master. Ne'er 'ave I worked for another gentleman that trusted me so! I 'ad the full liberty to tend to the manor 'ouse and grounds as I saw fittin' to do."

"Aye, sir, I thank ye. While I regret the reason for being here, it has mended my broken heart to hear such words of love and respect from all the people my father had in his life." He nodded his head in agreement and *smiled* at me. "Ye should ken that while I am mistress of this house, ye shall have the same freedom. Father instructed that even if we sell this grand house, ye and Missus Cameron will keep yer roles here as a condition of the sale."

The man smiled and embraced me tight with nothing but pure gratitude and relief. Even after death, my father's kindness and respect were once again showing in his care and support of those around him—of those that have been loyal to him.

"Aye! Master Forbes visited us just last week and let us know of yer father's kindness and generosity! We thank God Almighty for 'im in our prayers. My missus and I 'ave cleaned and stocked the 'ouse fer ye both," he said, before he caught Stirling nipping at his boots. "My wee laddie, I 'ave missed ye! Welcome 'ome!"

Master Cameron rubbed the dog's ears before the excited lad ran off again in celebration of his regained freedom to run the vast lands of Glenammon at his leisure. Surely this has to be better than being confined to the courtyard behind MacLeod House on Canongate.

"The lad kent he was home down at the bottom of the lane," I said, laughing at the large dog running wildly up and down the hill between the lodge and the manor house above. If we have done anything right on this trip, bringing wee Stirling back to Glenammon House is one of them.

"Stirling belongs here and not in the city," William said, looking at me and Master Cameron as we both nodded in agreement. We were thinking the exact same thing.

"Leave yer 'orses wi'me and I will take them to the stables," Master Cameron said to William. "I 'ave the keys 'ere. Do ye want me and the missus to come up and show you around the 'ouse and warm the supper waiting for ye?"

I spoke up on this ask, as I was in no mood for formalities today, "No sir, tending to the horses is a big help after our ride today. Master MacCrimmon and I can fend for ourselves this night. But tell Missus Cameron that I will come back down here to yer cottage at mid-day tomorrow."

According to father's will, Glenammon House was in fact mine now, so the man willingly handed the house keys to me as the new mistress of the house.

"I just need a moment to speak to my horse and then we will leave you for the evening."

Master Cameron looked at me, confused by the request, and then looked at William, who just said softly, *"It is their thing."*

I walked over and grabbed a few sugar lumps out of my saddlebag and offered them to my trusted friend, before William took my bag to carry inside. Munro nudged my cheek and grasped the treat as his reward for another job well done.

"Thank ye, my dear sweet Munro for delivering me safely to another unexpected destination. I leave ye in the care of Master Cameron for the evening, but will see ye soon, my love."

Once I handed the reins to Master Cameron, William and I walked up the rest of the lane to the large manor house together. Upon entering the grand hall, we realized we were getting another glimpse of Alexander MacLeod's life that neither of us expected.

I could tell the house had been closed for a while, as the smell of dust still lingered in the air along with the hint of burning wood from the fires. Thankfully, the Camerons already lit the fires for us throughout, and the large house was warm.

I felt the same as I did walking into MacLeod House on Canongate for the first time. It is a grand house, but it is *country grand*, if that is such a thing. My father had the same taste in fine art and furnishings, but here there are more stag heads on the walls and more plaid in the fabrics. A lot more plaid, in fact. The colors also seemed brighter, reflecting the greens and browns of lands surrounding us and complimented by blues to match the river behind the house and the bright sky above.

I stood in awe in the grand hall and took in the new clues to who my father was. Perhaps sensing that I was overwhelmed, William placed his hand gently on my elbow and said, "Let us see what Missus Cameron supplied fer our supper, then we can explore the house."

"Aye," I agreed, knowing he must be as hungry as I was.

Will sat the bags down at the foot of the stairs and we walked to the back, hoping to find the kitchen and instead found the dining room first, with the table set and food covered on a sideboard table. We also found a sweet note from Missus Cameron telling us where the ale was in the cellar below, and the layout of the kitchen stores should we need anything else before morning.

"Bless her."

"Ye check everything here and I will tend the fires," William said as he walked back to the front rooms.

I filled our ale pots and made plates with the incredible offering before us of a roasted venison and potato stew. While slightly cold, we enjoyed every delicious bite.

+++

William stood from his seat and helped me take the dishes into the kitchen. I cleaned each plate and washed in the water bucket provided. He dried each dish and set to the side. We did not know where everything belonged just yet and as it was getting dark, so we decided we were satisfied that at least our plates and cutlery were clean for the following day and for Missus Cameron.

"I ken we are both tired, but perhaps we talk a bit," William said as he took my hand and walked me to the front room, where the fire was burning. He stoked it once more and placed another log on to ensure it was roaring in an instant.

We were tired, but even in the short time we have been here, I love being alone in this house with him. We did not have to think about how to behave before Duncan and Angus, and we did not have to think about decorum. I felt the freedom of being together immediately. Every part of me wanted to know when we would kiss again. But mostly I just wanted to keep talking with him.

We filled our ride this afternoon with conversations that helped us learn more about each other and connect even more as friends. Some of it was idle chatter on the conditions of the roads and the fine weather or what wee Stirling was doing as he led us to the country house. Our conversations also told us more about who we are as people, what we like and do not, and what we each want for our future.

I had known William as one of the summer lads at Dunmara for many years, but did not know him well. Our paths crossed rarely and if they did, it was usually when I was in the company of Grant on the castle grounds or on the rare occasions I needed a horse from the stables.

"What are ye thinkin'... being here at the country house?" Will asked as we both fell exhausted, with full bellies, into the two chairs facing the fire.

I thought about my answer, as I did not really know how I felt. Finally, I said looking around, "Honestly, I dinnae ken what to make of it all. It feels much like when we walked into the house on Canongate. It is unexpected and grand, but it just adds to the mystery of the life my father had on this side of Scotland. Duncan and I didna ken he even had a country house until we arrived in Edinburgh."

"Is that so?"

"Aye! So some of the clues to his life are painful, not because they are unknown, but because it appears he wanted to be here and not on Skye."

"I understand. It is another verra grand house. Perhaps by being here, ye will learn even more about his life."

"Perhaps," I said, smiling across my chair to him, "or it could just deepen the ongoing mystery of *Alexander MacLeod, Esquire*."

We both sat quietly for a moment before the fire. William said, "We have work to do tomorrow to learn more."

"Aye, Duncan has given me plenty of direction on what to do," I said, laughing a bit at my uncle's detailed instructions provided before we left the city. "He told me to evaluate what I wanted to keep and take to Dunmara, and he told me to make certain we secure any papers and letters here, especially if they have anything to do with the clan. He also hoped that we could inventory everything else in case the value of the house was too low, as Master Forbes already suggested."

"Aye, that seems fair."

"Do ye ken I never once asked him how long we would be here in exile?"

"I did! He said probably a week but would send us word or may just come here to retrieve us himself."

"Ye mean to inspect our work."

"Aye, that verra well may be the case. Should we look at the rooms upstairs and settle ourselves for the night?"

"We should! I can barely keep my eyes open and if they lit the fires upstairs, they will surely need tending."

William replaced the candle in the lantern on the mantle to light our way. We walked toward the stairs, where he picked up our bags. Once at the top, we could see that the next floor had many rooms. I took my father's chamber, the largest on the back corner of the floor, and Will chose the room immediately opposite on the long hall overlooking the entry hall below. He restored my fire before leaving my room with a polite nod to me.

"Good night," I said from my door.

From his own door across the hall, Will said, "Good night and sleep well, lass!"

Missus Cameron had expected our every need. She had wood for the fires, water cauldrons, and fresh linens. I put another log on the fire for good measure and turned the latch to move the small cauldron of water over the flames. I wanted to wash the road from my face and hair as much as I could, while the flames could keep me warm. There was no custom copper bath here, but there was a separate room for washing and dressing. I was certainly getting used to my father's life with these remarkable bedchambers.

A restful night, away from the noise and the pulse of the city, was also welcome. I slipped into the warm embrace of feathered pillows, soft linens, and wool blankets. I fell into a deep sleep instantly.

Then came *the storm*.

+++

I woke in the dark, in an unfamiliar room and an unfamiliar bed, to the sound of roaring winds. A raging winter storm was lashing the house with wind and snow with a fierce strength I have never heard before in my life.

There was a large oak tree outside my window that kept hitting the glass panes, making such a racket that I did not know which would go first—the tree or the glass. I was afraid, but was also freezing beneath my linens. I peered above my blankets to see what I expected—my fire had completely gone out. There is no telling how long it has been dormant. I sighed loudly and contemplated whether it was worth leaving my bed to restart it or not. Instead, I threw my blankets over my head. Perhaps my breath could keep me warm underneath my covers for a bit until I could decide what to do in the lingering haze of sleep.

Just then there was a large loud crash. I could not tell if a branch of the tree outside my window crashed to the ground or if the whole tree was felled. I jumped out of bed onto the cold floor and walked across the hall, hoping to find some reassurance. The roaring sound and fury of this storm scared me.

"William?" I asked as I knocked lightly on his door just as another tree beside the house fell at the same time. I knew he could not have heard me through this racket or if he was asleep through it all.

"William?" I said again, louder, as I opened the door to his room slowly.

He sat up in his bed immediately and said, "What is it? Are ye alright, lass? It is a gale out there! I have heard nothing like it in my life!"

Another large gust of wind whistled around the house, and I could see the snow blowing sideways against his windows. I shuddered and said, shaking before the door and almost in tears, "*No sir!* I am *not* alright. The tree outside my window crashed to the ground from the raging storm, and my fire has gone completely out, so I am freezing!"

"Och, come here," he said, lifting his covers open to welcome me to his bed. I leapt inside and put my back to him. I could immediately feel the warmth of his room compared to mine. He must have known better than I to tend the fire more than once during the night. He brought himself to me so that I could also feel the warmth of his own body.

"Ye are solid ice," he said as he rubbed my left shoulder quickly with his hand, trying to stir up some heat under the covers.

I said through my chattering teeth, "I woke to the raging storm and then found the room to be freezing. There is no telling how long my fire has been out. I have never heard the wind so fierce. Perhaps it is because we are surrounded by trees here. At Dunmara, it just whistles as it whips around the stone walls. The wind sounds dangerous here. It makes me afraid!"

"This is a mighty storm to rival all storms to have such gusts and snow like this. It takes work to keep the fires going. I should have stoked yours when I did mine. I didna think."

"I should have known better to tend it more than once in a house this large, but I was sound asleep after our journey, and I had no idea it had faded until it was too late."

I stopped shaking eventually but realized that was because his body was very close to my own. His warm, solid body was *very* close to mine. He released me for a minute to get up and restore his own fire for us. The light of the fire in front of him revealed the outlines of his form beneath his shirt. I watched his strong and graceful hands as he added more wood to the fire until it was raging and warming the room again instantly. Or that could have just been the heat from my cheeks burning red at the thought of being here in his bed.

When he returned, he put his arms back around me and said behind me, "I cannae have ye freeze to death in yer room, but I would also verra much like not to be murdered by Duncan MacLeod."

"Have we not declared that we love each other?"

"We have, *but...*"

"Then I care nothing of Duncan's opinion this night," I said as I nestled myself back into him just as another gust of wind rattled the windows and the sound of a tree falling to the ground shook me again.

"Settle yerself, lass. The storm will pass and ye will be just fine. This is a solid house."

I felt the warmth of the room, of Will's body, and his steady breath in my ear. I let all three lull me back to sleep despite the raging storm outside. The last thought I had was that I am falling in love with this man more and more every day.

+++

I finally woke at first light. It appears I did not even move from my right side. The stiffness in my shoulder and neck told me that much. I turned to my left, toward William, and opened my eyes to stare directly into... *pillows. A wall of pillows!*

Overnight, this man built a wall made of extra pillows to separate us. It has to be the most ridiculously honorable thing I have ever seen! I raised myself up on the top of his new barrier to look down at the man on the other side. Will was wide awake, with his hands behind his head, staring at the canopy of this grand four-poster bed. He looked nervous, but proud of his achievement.

"Have ye actually barricaded yerself behind a wall of *pillows?*" I asked, almost laughing at the spectacle of it all.

"Aye," he said flatly. I waited to see if he would elaborate and he finally did, "I had to... to keep from touching ye and I shouldna touched ye when ye came in the room last night. I was wrong to do so, and fer that, I am verra sorry."

"Why do ye think I dinnae want ye to touch me?" I asked, throwing the first of the pillows off the bed. His eyes grew wide, watching the pillow sail past him and land with a soft thud against the floor.

"Duncan is right, ye do like a question." I gave him a stern look with a tilt of my head, and he corrected himself quickly and said with defiant conviction, "I will keep ye warm, but I will not take yer virtue, lass!"

"Do ye ken that I have thought about being in yer arms ever since that night at MacLeod House?" I asked, as I tossed the second pillow to the floor with the first.

"*Alex*," he said with a tilt of his head this time, giving me his soft warning while I continued breaking down his chastity wall built of feathers.

I did not respond and threw the last pillow on the floor with the others. He did not dare move as I got closer to him and laid my head on his chest and wrapped my arm around him. I could hear his heart pounding, and he took a deep breath and sighed. Eventually, he pulled his arm back and wrapped it around me with his hand landing heavy at the bend of my waist. We remained quiet for a bit, holding on to each other. I raised my head up to look at him across his chest. His nervousness made me smile for a moment.

"How is it we traveled all the way here and are in this grand house alone, and ye have not kissed me again?"

He seemed shocked and a bit embarrassed at the directness of my question. He opened his mouth for a moment but said nothing. I laid my head back down on his chest and his heart was beating faster. I smiled briefly to myself that I stirred him so, albeit with a total lack of propriety.

He moved his hand up to stroke my hair and said in a whisper, "I want ye more than ye ken, but ye would not respect a man that did not honor ye as a maid and I would not respect myself if I dishonored ye so."

I sat up in the bed again, flushed in the face at the thought of being with him and that I, too, wanted him more than he could know. I looked at him with admiration and compassion at the restraint and reverence he was offering me at this moment.

"I respect that, Will. I do."

I stood up out of the bed and walked to the door. I thought to myself that I hoped the morning sunlight through the windows offered him a look at my silhouette under my shift, the way the firelight did for him the night before. He raised himself up on his elbows, uncertain of what I was doing. I turned back to him and said, "I want ye to understand one thing! The next time I am in yer bed, there will *not* be a wall of pillows between us!"

He smiled at me before I slammed the door behind me in mock-anger. I laughed all the way down the hall to my room with my hand over my mouth to keep from making a sound.

We met each other downstairs for breakfast. Missus Cameron came in early this morning and left us warm bread and fried ham. I now suspect that the miracle of fried ham was at Father's direction, not that of Missus Douglas. I smiled, thinking that one of the beloved clues to who my father was on the eastern side of the country was this breakfast wonder. Even if it's just for special occasions, I hope we can recreate this at Dunmara.

One thing I know how to cook on my own is eggs, which I made for us on the fire. Neither of us spoke of this morning's conversation as we ate breakfast together. It may have been because of our own embarrassment, or the natural trance brought about by the breakfast bounty.

I finally said, "We will evaluate the contents of the grand house today. We will go room by room, and I will record what we want to keep. Then we have to inventory everything else that will be sold in the house. And I think we can just assume from the start that we are not considering taking any furniture back to Skye, so at least that is easy."

"So, no ye dinnae want to keep the house, then?"

"Do ye see *us* leaving Skye to cross Scotland to *our* country house?"

We just smiled at each other as we realized at that moment that I spoke of *'us'* and *'our'* for the first time. Much like the more familiar use of our given names, it was another sign of me accepting and thinking about us being together as a couple.

"No, I dinnae think *we* would. Do *we* want to set aside the items *we* wish to keep in the front hall, perhaps?"

"I dinnae think so," I said, smiling and silently acknowledging his first mentions of *we*.

"I am hoping Duncan will come here and we can tell him what we recommend. And if he doesna, then we may have to think about how to transport items to Edinburgh. As I think more about it," I said, looking toward the window, "the sale of the house could actually depend on Duncan."

"How d'ye mean?"

"Depending on his decision about the brewery, I could sell Duncan the house for when he needs to come back. It is not close, but could serve as a comfortable base for him after a cross-country trip."

"Aye, it is not a long ride to Leith," he said, "and it is better to have this fine accommodation than a room over a tavern at the docks when ye need to be on this side of the country for a while."

We washed the plates and cutlery together again before setting out on our task. I grabbed parchment, ink, and a quill from the desk in the study, and we started in the front parlor.

"Remember, Will, we are also looking for a carved wooden box that holds Father's gold watch and other family treasures. So far, we have yet to find it at the house in Edinburgh. Perhaps it could be here."

"Aye."

"Like I said yesterday, we need to gather any of my father's personal items and papers relating to the clan to take back to Edinburgh. Those we *will* set aside."

The evaluation of the front room took us the entire morning. We opened every drawer, spoke about every trinket and book, listed all items in the room, and inspected every painting. In this entire parlor, we decided that maybe one painting of the Scottish countryside with a distant Glenammon House on the horizon was worth preserving in memory of this house and that some books could be donated to the school on Skye—if we want to cart them all the way home, that is.

"This house will take us forever at this pace," I said with exhaustion as I threw myself into one of the chairs in front of the fire. William looked just as exhausted as he landed in the chair next to me. "We just spent three hours of our lives inspecting every item in... *one... room!*"

"Aye," he said with a sigh and wiping the sweat and curls from his brow.

I took a deep breath, stood up, and said, "Ye rest a bit, Will. I need to meet with Missus Cameron. Any special requests for food or drink while we are here?"

"No," he said, smiling up at me before grabbing my hand as I passed his chair, "but I like us cooking and cleaning up together."

"Aye," I said, squeezing his hand in mine, "like it is our verra own house."

I smiled all the way down the hill to the Cameron's cottage, walking in the fresh snow still covering the ground. I imagined Will and me living a quiet life at Glenammon House. This remarkable fantasy was sadly not destined to be a reality based on my commitment to serve Clan MacLeod. I was met on my winter walk by a very happy lad. Wee Stirling proudly escorted me for the rest of my journey.

+++

Missus Anna Cameron was a tiny, older woman who shared her husband's kind smile and distinct English accent. In one short day, I was already thinking of the Camerons as the grandparents I always wish I had. They were a comforting pair of kind souls. I enjoyed their company and welcomed the warmth they offered me here.

We discussed what food and drink we may need for her next round of meals and potential shopping. I reinforced that Will and I could tend to ourselves for the most part. I assured her we would always need wood for fires and water for caldrons, and food, but little else. We agreed on a schedule for linens and general cleaning. I let her know we welcomed fresh bread, butter, and fine food regularly, but we were not looking for formal service in this house. She seemed appreciative of a hands-off approach at first, but became uncertain if she was doing her duty. I assured her she was serving us perfectly and that Master MacCrimmon and I were not accustomed to such formal staffing arrangements that Father had here and in Edinburgh.

I wondered what she might think of two young, unmarried people tending to themselves alone in the grand house, but she said nothing. She was willing to be of service to us however we needed. Glenammon is my house now, and as mistress, she would not challenge my accommodation or my requests.

Master Cameron joined us and confirmed all was well with wee Stirling and the horses. He also gave me an account of the property after the storm. The oak tree outside my room was not felled but lost two large branches, each of which he was breaking down for firewood. That would be added with a large tree that fell across the lane leading to the house, another tree outside Will's room, along with too many within the woods surrounding the house to count. Thankfully, no other damage on the property, beyond scattered limbs and leaves, was recorded. The one exception was we have lost a small fishing boat that became unmoored from the dock during the storm.

I returned to the house with the promise of a venison pie to be delivered for our supper. William just has to light the brick oven above the fireplace in the kitchen for us to make ourselves. He has already proven to be a master at tending the fires in this house, so I think we will be just fine.

+++

Will and I walked the property to see remnants of the branches and entire trees lost in the storm last night and made our way to the edge of the River Forth for the view. Even in the frosty November air, the snow was already melting in places under the light of the sun, revealing the lush lands underneath. The riverbank itself was beautiful and had a very small dock built off the shoreline. This was where the small boat lost in the storm was previously moored. I said nothing to Will, but standing there on the dock, I could not imagine my father fishing. I would bet Master Cameron had been in the missing boat more than my father ever was. The thought made me smile.

Will took my hand to help me step off the dock and kept it in his all the way back to the house. Much like his escort from Cairn's Point, I loved how his large hand wrapped around my own. I also noticed that I stand taller and more confident when his hand takes mine.

After supper, we sat on the floor in front of the fire, just holding on to each other. He had his arms around my shoulders and his chin on top of my head. After reading aloud from my book of sonnets, we sat together quietly. I closed my eyes, welcoming the heat from the fire in front of me and from his body behind mine.

"I love being here with ye like this," he said in my ear and breaking the blissful spell he had on me at this moment.

"I am afraid that if I open my eyes again, ye will be gone."

"I will always be here for ye, lass," he said as he kissed the back of my head and grabbed my hands in each of his and held them tight. I opened my eyes as he said, "I have loved ye from a distance fer many years. Ye didna ken me well, but I tell ye this day that ye hold all of my heart in these verra hands."

I smiled back up at him and felt his arms tighten around me as he kissed my cheek. Then he stood, and with his hands outstretched, lifted me up from the floor and said, "From this point forward, I dinnae want to be anywhere else than by yer side... if ye will have *me*."

I did not want him to be away from me, either. I wanted this man by my side forever. I feel safe. I feel strong and confident with him. I feel loved.

"Will, are ye asking me..."

Before I could continue with my question, he said, "Aye, lass! I suppose I am. Alexandra MacLeod, will ye be my wife? I ken I am nothing but a stable hand, but I love ye with all my heart! I will do everything I can to keep ye happy and I will do everything I can to support ye in yer service to the clan."

I breathed in deeply. I left my words in the silent conflict between what I wanted and what I thought I did not want. What I told myself I *did not want*. What I told myself for years, I *did not deserve*.

"*Will,*" I whispered as I put my hand on his cheek and kissed him gently on his lips. "Aye, sir!" He hugged me tight in celebration and lifted me off of the floor and spun me around, as I whispered again in his ear, "*I love ye.*"

"Och lass, ye must ken that I love ye more," he said with a sweet smile. I have spent a lifetime resisting having a William Lachlan MacCrimmon in my life. But the man is here, and I will never let him go.

+++

We spent a few days in romantic bliss enjoying each other's company. We worked together to inspect the rest of the house in between walks on the grounds and cozy embraces in front of the fire. We lamented not finding the wooden box, but I confessed to Will that I never thought it was here to begin with—especially if it had the gold watch. It *must* be at MacLeod House on Canongate. I am certain of it!

One evening, after reading from the book of sonnets, I asked, "Will, if we are going to marry, why do we have to be apart?"

He whispered into my ear, *"I told ye I have too much respect fer ye, and I told ye that I have no desire to be murdered by yer uncle."*

We laughed together on the valid point the poor man has made more than once. As much as I love my uncle, he would kill William if he thought he touched me. In fact, Duncan would not like us sitting before the fire together like this, let alone sharing a bed as we did on our first night during the winter storm.

However, ending the evening together and talking or reading together made it even more painful to retire to our separate bedchambers on opposite sides of the landing overlooking the front hall. I could almost forgive a wall of pillows to be where he was and could not help asking the same question each night, hoping the man would change his answer. He never did, and I admired him for it. He was right, of course—even if I did not want to admit it.

We sat together in silence, each smiling at the thought of marrying so that we could be together. I laughed to myself as I thought that this has to be the first time that a large, cold house was a blessing. The chill in this house keeps Will close to me when we are together, but for a purpose, he believes is proper and one that I welcomed at the end of each day.

+++

FOUR
Betrothed

MacLeod House
Canongate, Edinburgh, Scotland
November 1766

Duncan did not retrieve us himself, and instead sent word by
messenger that it was safe for us to return to Edinburgh. We
finished evaluating the entire house at Glenammon and carried only a
few personal items back to the city.

Master Cameron secured a sweet Shetland pony, Hettie, to help us
carry some papers, belongings, and two small paintings, including one of
my mother, back to the city. My father had the painting on his bedside
table. It was a lovely surprise when we took an inventory of his
bedchamber. I stared at it for a long time, thinking about how I did not
remember her face and it hurt me.

I had the inventory list if we wanted to take back more from the house before selling and would just have to retrieve these items before returning to Skye. It was difficult to leave wee Stirling behind, but we did so with the assurance that the lad was truly home at Glenammon House and that he would joyfully spend the rest of his days chasing deer and freely roaming the countryside where he belonged.

We said our farewells to Master and Missus Cameron and thanked them for their service to my father and to both of us during our stay. I asked them to write to me on Skye if they ever needed anything. I also told them that Master Forbes would keep them informed on the sale of the house and grounds.

As we rode into the city, and turned onto Canongate, I said, "Will, I believe I should be the one to tell Duncan about our engagement. Ye should be there, of course, as ye will need his blessing and his help with Laird Graham."

"Aye, ye ken him best. I will do as ye ask."

"He is going to be happy for us, but he is going to panic that we have been together for a week in the same house... *alone*."

"I had thought little about that because of the reason we were there. He asked me to protect ye, and I did so. Not to mention the restraint we both had the entire time."

"Aye, but he is going to think the worst at the start! Then he will blame himself for sending us together on his orders, and then... he *may* try to kill ye." William looked at me sharply, unsure that what I just said was true. I said, "I never told him anything about our conversations, but he kens well enough that we talked when I had ye come to the house for supper alone."

"I thought ye told Duncan *everything*," Will said, now shocked at the thought that Duncan did not know we were courting.

"Aye, I do, but I kept our conversation and the fact that we kissed to myself."

"That explains the secrecy in the tavern when we were with him. I tried to follow your lead on how to behave. I thought I betrayed us by talking about family at the tavern the night before we left Edinburgh and hoped he didna notice."

"I am sure he did, but he would have never let us go to Glenammon House together if he truly questioned it. Now I am returning home betrothed. It will take him a moment to understand how it all progressed so quickly *and* how I changed my mind about love and marriage."

A half-smile appeared on the corner of my mouth as I sensed his dread, and I admit I enjoyed seeing Will so nervous. But the truth of it is that there is no telling what Duncan may do to the poor man. I tried to reassure him, "I promise, he will come around... *eventually*. We just need to give him some time."

"When I returned to the White Hart that night, Duncan, and Angus asked me many questions, but I told them to talk to ye. I was so happy, and I am sure it showed, but, like ye, I wanted to protect what we had for a moment myself. I said nothing to them other than Missus Douglas prepared us a fine meal, that we resolved the argument we had at yer supper party, and were friends again."

"Aye! Duncan kens me well enough that we came to some understanding that night. He just does not fully ken what that understanding is. Let him react, but Will, he respects ye and believes ye are a good match. He was an advocate fer ye at the verra start."

Will said nothing, but seemed shocked by the thought of Duncan supporting him. Perhaps he remembered his drunken confession to Duncan at the White Hart and wondered if I knew about it. Of course, I did, but would not tell him that just now.

"One more thing," I said with a smile to my betrothed on the horse next to me, "proper or not, ye are staying in this house from now on and not at the tavern. Ye should not be spending yer coin when ye have a comfortable bed and fine food here. If we can be proper in one house, we can be in another."

He smiled and nodded to me on my order, and said, "Aye, my lady."

Jonny welcomed us back to the stables and Missus Douglas came out from the kitchen to greet us as well. Duncan soon followed her. I nervously looked at him in anticipation of the conversation we will have, and I searched his face for any clue if he could sense a difference between me and Will already.

"Well, well!" he said to us as he patted Will on his shoulder. "How was yer holiday retreat at the *country house*?"

Will and I looked at each other and I said, "It is another grand MacLeod house, and we have much to share with ye."

Missus Douglas had left us some food on the table that would hold us until supper. Duncan sat with us while we ate. Missus Cameron had sent us away with buttered bread and dried venison, but neither of us would turn down anything Missus Douglas provided.

"The house is lovely and grand. It sits just off of the banks of the River Forth," I said. "It is like this house, but much larger."

Will spoke up and said, "Aye, two more bedrooms, a much larger dining room and parlor, and Master MacLeod had an entire room dedicated to his library and study."

I continued, "It is just past Blackness village and is surrounded by almost one hundred and fifty acres of woodland, gardens, and meadows. Aside from the main house and the estate factor's cottage there is a hunting shed, a small dock by the river where he housed a small fishing boat, and a large stables. I believe he had hunting parties there as he had room for more than his own horses."

Will spoke in agreement, "Master Cameron said the lands have nearly two hundred head of deer, not to mention fine fishing on the river."

"That explains all the venison suppers from Missus Cameron," I said, laughing.

"Aye, we did eat a lot of venison," Will said, smiling at me.

From my bag, I pulled out the inventory we recorded of the house and passed it to Duncan across the table. "We noted everything in the house to sell and this mark here on the left indicates the other items we might want to consider keeping. That is... if we want to go back to retrieve them and cart all the way to Skye. Otherwise, we let it all go. We have brought the most important items with us today."

"Well done, you two! Well done! Perhaps we should do the same here at Canongate and see how much we are talking about taking back to Skye."

I nodded. It was a good plan to conduct the same inventory here and said, looking at Will, "Surely, that would not take as long as Glenammon House!"

"Aye, I suspect we will need to return with a cart. I do not see yer wee pony taking all we currently have to Skye. The question is, how big of a cart?"

"I loved being there, and the Camerons are fine caretakers, but I do not see keeping the house. The exception could be if ye decide to stay involved in the brewery and would have to come here during the year. It could serve as a home for ye."

"Aye," Duncan said, thinking about all the decisions we still have before us. All the decisions that mean we were not any closer to going home. "Let us get out of Missus Douglas' way for supper and move to the front room."

We followed him, and I immediately filled three whisky glasses for the second part of this conversation. I handed the men their drinks, and I sat in the chair next to Duncan and Will stood in the space between me and the hearth.

"Duncan, there is more we want to share," I said, looking at him directly as he sipped his glass. "Will and I... are *betrothed*." He sat silently before me with a blank stare on my words, so as usual, I continued talking. "We are *engaged* to be married, sir."

I could see William out of the corner of my eye, and he was either standing tall and proud at the declaration of our love or bracing himself for what may come for him at any moment. My guess is the latter.

He did not have to wait long. Duncan stood up immediately and yelled as he charged at Will, "I ken verra well what *betrothed* means, Alex! By Christ, man! If ye *have touched her*, I will kill ye, right here and now, in my own brother's house!"

"Duncan!" I said, now standing between the two of the most important men in my life.

"No sir, I *have not*," Will said calmly to a man, turning purple with anger, who had his fist formed in front of his face.

I tried to put my hands up to calm the masculine rage before me, and repeated William's assertion, "No sir, he *has not!*"

"I shoulda kent better than to send the two of ye alone to the country with a *budding romance*," my uncle said, seething. He was angry at himself for dispatching us to Glenammon as he is at the thought of us together in that house. "I thought I was doing the right thing to protect ye, lass! And I failed ye."

As I predicted, Duncan's anger soon became his own grief. I thought to myself that if he only knew how much personal restraint and a wall made of pillows protected my virtue, he would respect Will even more!

"Stop this, now! I have *never* lied to ye," I said, still standing between them and forcing my uncle to look at me. He let me finish my thought, "I have *never* lied to ye, Duncan! We have declared our love for each other but have only kissed and held hands. That is the truth of it. Our *budding romance* went no further than that."

"Och, but it has! It has gone all the way to *betrothal*!"

I too thought about how fast it has all progressed. I nodded to him in agreement and confessed, "Will has respected my virtue from the very beginning, even if I sometimes wish he wouldna."

Duncan gave me a stern, fatherly look as I immediately turned red in the face with the admission. I could hear Will shift his feet on the floor behind me, perhaps wishing I had not added the last part, and likely thankful that I did not confess about the night of the storm when we shared a bed to stay warm. But my words were the truth. I asked the man many times to let me return to his bed, and he would not allow it.

He spoke before I could, "Aye, I love and respect Alexandra fer who she is. I honor her role in our clan. I would verra much like to ask fer yer blessing, sir, because I respect ye as a man and I ken how important ye are to yer niece and she is to ye."

Another thing to know about Duncan MacLeod is that he likes a compliment and clearly, Will has figured that out. I turned to look at him and smiled in admiration for his words. I moved to stand next to Will and took his hand in mine and said, "We both would like yer blessing."

Duncan stood quietly and stared at us, before finally smiling to himself and releasing his anger. He walked forward to shake William's hand before he kissed me on the forehead. He stood there with his arms on both of our shoulders.

"Ye have my blessing, and I will send word to my brother, fer it is truly the laird's blessing that ye need to marry."

"A Yuletide wedding, it is!" I said, trying to lighten the mood even more now that the threats of violence in the room have subsided. I knew in my heart that Laird Graham would welcome the thought of a marriage between me and just about anyone. He never said the words to me, but I knew from the moment he made me his heir and successor that he had a fear that my belligerent independence could leave me in the same situation that he was in—childless. He would see this betrothal as a welcome blessing for me *and* a prospect for preserving the future of the clan.

"*Slàinte*," we said together as we brought our glasses together.

"I should go help Jonny with the horses and I will also get the bags," Will said as he backed out of the room with a quick and loving touch on the back of my arm. I assume he wanted to give me a chance to talk to Duncan alone, and we both appreciated him for it.

"Are ye happy, lass?"

"Aye, sir," I said, wrapping my arm around Duncan as we faced the fire together, "verra happy. I have been taking yer advice about getting out of my own way and letting people love me... and I thank ye."

"I can tell he loves ye and to be honest, the lad always has," he said. I looked up at him. "Aye, his confession in the tavern aside, the lad has *always* loved ye."

"You could see what I could not," I said, still somewhat astonished that I was so blind to Will's affection and intentions for so long.

"Anyone near ye both can see it in his eyes when he looks at ye every time ye speak, or smile, or laugh... *especially* when ye laugh! Ye did not *want* to see it before, but I am glad that ye can now."

Tears started forming in my eyes as I looked up to him and said, "Ye ken Will and I talked weeks ago, but I did not tell ye what we said because I was trying to understand why my opinion on love and marriage was changing. I think I wanted us to figure out if being together could work before I said anything. I didna want to make things awkward with ye and Angus. I ken he committed to escort me back home to Skye with ye both."

"I can understand that. Will swore an oath to his laird, as ye said. And a relationship should have elements that are private. If I may ask, what made ye change yer opinion?"

"Erm, yer words made me think more about why I wanted to keep everyone at a distance just to protect myself—to protect my heart. I thought about all I was missing in life by doing such a thing and remaining blind to the love that surrounds me."

Duncan nodded, as he was proud that his words had an impact on me, and that I listened to his advice and counsel. "My opinion on marriage changed because when I opened my heart to Will, I found I love and respect him as much as he does me. And both have only grown. Love *and* respect." I stopped to think about what I just said and smiled. "I will say it again because it makes me so happy! *I love him!* Will makes me feel stronger and I know that having him by my side as I become clan chief will only help me—just as Lady Margaret did for Laird Graham."

My uncle kissed me on top of my head and hugged me tight in his arms, presumably in agreement.

"Duncan, I told Will that proper or not, I dinnae want him to spend any more of his own coin at the White Hart. We have plenty of room in this house and Missus Douglas' fine cooking. He should take his room here at MacLeod House and be with us as he was before."

"I will support ye on this. Ye are mistress of this house."

I know he wanted to say more. Perhaps he wanted to channel the voice of my father and remind me about propriety and restraint, but he did not. He trusted me and that what we told him about how we behaved at Glenammon House was the truth. I also believe he did not want Will to spend the little money he had at the tavern, either.

After a moment of quiet, still holding on to each other, I said, "Will has been an unexpected blessing in my life, Duncan. One I was convinced I didna deserve."

"Och, my dear lass, we all *deserve* love," he said as he kissed the top of my head again.

+++

Duncan wrote his letter to Laird Graham, and I wrote one of my own to let my uncle know I was happy. I expected it would confuse him how my opinion of marriage changed in such a short time away and that he should hear from me directly.

William returned to his room at MacLeod House, and it was just like when we all first arrived in the city. Meals were a chance to laugh with each other and plan or catch up on the events of the day. Duncan and

68

Angus let us know that Allan Calder has all but disappeared from the city. They were intent on doing their duty, searching all the inns and taverns in Edinburgh, and waiting for him at the law office, but the man has not been seen again. In fact, when Mistress Hay tried to return his personal items, the messenger brought them back to her straight away, saying the man no longer lived at the room she had on record.

Laird Graham wrote back that he was most pleased and granted his blessings on us both and our marriage. He wished we would be married at Dunmara Castle, but said if we could not wait, they would have a celebration for us when we return. He granted Duncan permission to sign the marriage contract under the expectation that Master Forbes would ensure we both understand what is in it before we are married.

+++

The black door opened, and the warm smile of Mistress Elizabeth Hay met us.

"Alexandra!" she said as she came to embrace me tight.

"It is good to see ye again, Elizabeth. Are ye well?"

"Aye, verra well, and happy here," she said, absolutely beaming with her new position in Master Forbes' office. "What exciting news!" she said, hugging me again. Then she shook William's hand and said, "I am so happy fer ye both! Come in, please."

"Thank ye verra much, Mistress Hay," William said.

"So good to see ye again, Master MacLeod," she said with a smile as she placed her hand on Duncan's arm, ushering him into the room. He nodded to her as he took off his hat. He was always shy around Mistress Hay and said nothing. "Master Forbes is waiting for ye all. Please, follow me."

We walked into the office to find Master Forbes at his desk. He stood and came around to give us an equally enthusiastic welcome. We talked of the happiness of marriage and our brief thoughts on our evaluation of Glenammon. Then it was time to talk specifics about the reason we are all here.

"Master Forbes, I brought the marriage contract we retrieved," I said as I placed it before him on his desk. "We believe Master Calder altered it, but ironically, the names are in fact correct."

"Thank you. I recreated the contract from the version we had in our files from the last meeting I had with Alexander. There may be other things Calder changed in this document, and I believe it is best to use this new version. It will also allow us to record William's full name."

Duncan said, "On behalf of Laird MacLeod, I agree to that, sir."

Master Forbes folded the old document I presented, tore it in half, and set it aside on his desk as Duncan continued, "It is important that we not only sign the marriage contract today, but that Alexandra and William completely understand and agree to the terms within it."

"Aye, sir," Master Forbes said as he put his glasses back on and began explaining to us all the structure of the contract. The first part was the fairly traditional language used in contracts across Scotland. The words at the start were in line with what I had seen before in the false contract. The space for the names of the betrothed on this version still only shows only mine.

"I will not read the entire contract to you. You are welcome to read it yourselves here, but there are three main areas that you both need to understand and agree to before signing."

"First, William, you will gain no title or Clan MacLeod leadership responsibility with this marriage beyond becoming a new member of the

Fine. You will become a part of the elite gentry of the clan because of your marriage to Alexandra and eventually as the father of children in the line of succession. You keep that position until yer own death."

"Upon Alexandra's death, only the children you have together, or a designated MacLeod heir, will be in line for succession. You nor anyone in your own family or sept line of MacCrimmon can inherit MacLeod titles, lands, or property by this marriage."

William nodded his head in understanding, and I am sure thinking that such a notion was easy to accept, as he has no family left to inherit anything. Also, this was never his intention. I looked at him, but he kept his eyes straight ahead, focused intently on Master Forbes.

"In the case of a legally designated heir instead of your own child, it will require the approval of the Fine, and some additional legal protections," he said looking over his glasses at me, "not unlike what you just experienced yourself, Alexandra."

It was my turn to mark my understanding of the rules with a nod of my head. Becoming the heir and successor to my uncle was safeguarded by legal protections under the laws of Scotland. I hoped Will and I would not have to do the same, but I understood how the law could protect us.

Looking back at William he said, "Second sir, you are not entitled to any income from Alexandra's estate or her trust upon her turning twenty-one, or upon her death, beyond what she wishes to give you throughout the course of your marriage or in her own will and testament."

I looked at Will as he took in these words. He still kept his eyes intently focused on Master Forbes. I have not told him the extent of my inheritance in any of our conversations and believe it will shock him when he learns all that my father left me. He is aware of the houses, of course, but not the money in the bank or how profitable Glenammon

Brewing has been. There can be no doubt of his intentions in marrying me, as the man does not know about my newfound wealth. We have never discussed the details of my father's will or my inheritance.

Taking a pause once again, Master Forbes looked over his glasses at William, and said, "Lad, the expectation is that you will find a suitable position on the clan lands to occupy your time and you will of course, be a support for your wife in her service as chief and for your children."

"I understand sir, I worked in the stables at Dunmara before and have no problem doing the same again. If Master Knox will have me, that is." He put his hand on mine and said, finally looking at me, "And I will always be the support my wife needs in her service to Clan MacLeod."

I could not help but smile at the thought and took his hand in mine. He held on to me as I did to him.

Master Forbes continued, "Once again, upon her death, should that be before your own, her estate will pay off any of her personal debts, debts of the clan, and then sustain her children and heirs. That said, Alexandra, I can help you draft your own will and testament to leave William a sum of your choosing when you are ready."

"Aye, sir! I would verra much like to keep ye on as my personal advocate and will take ye up on that offer."

Duncan spoke up, saying, "Aye, Laird MacLeod has also instructed that we would like to keep yer services as a clan, sir."

"Great news indeed," Master Forbes said, pressing forward with the focus of today. William would not be without he just has no claim to gain title or money simply by the act of marriage. Of course, I will see to my husband being taken care of.

"And finally, there is the matter of a dowry," he said as he pulled out another parchment from his leather folio and turned it to face us. "It is only a mention in the contract and exists as its own document."

This was unexpected. Duncan and I looked at each other, confused. Clearly, neither of us read the contract fully because we had little time with it on Skye.

"Alexandra, your father instructed that if the marriage contract was presented and signed, this document would also be presented to you and your betrothed."

We looked down at the new parchment as Master Forbes began telling us what was in it before we could read it ourselves.

"William, the dowry left to you includes £3000 pounds sterling," he said. William's mouth was open, unable to speak, as he looked to his left to me and then to the right to Duncan with genuine surprise at this declaration. A gift that could set him for a quiet life on Skye, even without my own bequest.

Master Forbes then unlocked a drawer in his desk with a key he had in his pocket. He pulled out a small black velvet pouch, where he emptied three stones on top of the parchment. Diamonds. Now all of our mouths were open.

"Alexandra, your father offers these diamonds he bought in Antwerp for your wedding ring, lass," Master Forbes said as I immediately bent over and started crying with my hands over my eyes. William stood up to place his hand on my back, uncertain what to do to help me try to catch my breath. Duncan handed me his handkerchief across the chair that William just vacated.

My uncle tried to make me smile by saying to Will, "Lad, yer going to have to use part of yer dowry to buy yer wife her own handkerchief, as she never seems to have one when she needs it!"

I immediately laughed at him through my tears, and said, "I am just so touched that he thought about this *at all*!"

This was just another clue as to who Alexander MacLeod was and I was going to have to explain my outburst of emotion to the men staring at me. I finally caught my breath and said, smiling through my tears, "Master Forbes, I spent most of my life swearing that I would *never* marry, and it is clear my father didna believe my independent declarations for one second!"

"Aye, lass. He had *hope*. Your love is here, and he would be most happy for you both. Do we all understand the contract and dowry?"

"Aye," we all said in unison. I settled my emotions and Will returned to his seat.

"I will date the document and add William's full name," he said as he put the quill to parchment, "and then Alexandra and William will sign the bottom of each page of the official contract and the copy draft you will take with you. Duncan will sign each at the end on behalf of Laird MacLeod, and I will sign as a witness. Lad, your full name, please."

"William Lachlan MacCrimmon, sir."

Once Will and I signed each of the pages, Master Forbes handed the quill to Duncan. "You can see that I have noted that your signature reflects approval from Laird MacLeod at the bottom."

"Aye," Duncan said, as he took the quill and signed both documents.

With Duncan's signature on the contract and then the copy, Master Forbes signed as our witness on each and handed the bank note and pouch of diamonds to William and then contract folio to me.

We were done. All of us sat across from each other with huge smiles. This was a moment I will always remember.

"Thank ye, Master Forbes. I would verra much like to invite ye to our wedding reception. I will invite Mistress Hay as well, and will send her all the details for the occasion."

"It will be my honor to celebrate with you, and most hearty congratulations to you both."

+++

We all sat in the White Hart beaming at such a fine day and a sense of accomplishment on settling the marriage contract once and for all. Will seemed quiet and pale. I wondered if the language of not inheriting anything put him off, but that was never his motive in marrying me.

Jacob brought us the bottle of whisky and three glasses.

"Merci, Jacob!" I said.

"*But of course,*" he said in his mock French accent back to me.

Duncan spoke up and said, "We are celebrating a betrothal, man."

Jacob put both of his hands on the table and leaned toward me to say, "Master MacCrimmon can tell ye, I told the man months ago he would marry ye!"

"He did indeed," Will said, nodding his head in agreement.

"Ye never told me that!" I declared. Jacob was just another that could see what I could not.

"I will send over oysters fer ye as our gift fer the celebration," he said.

"Thank ye, sir," I said, smiling at Jacob for his kindness and friendship, "and I will send notice to ye and Hilary to join us fer cake and wine on the day once we settle everything."

"We will be honored to join ye in celebration."

Duncan poured the glasses and Will leaned in and whispered to us, *"I feel nervous sitting here with this bank note and gems in my pocket."*

"Ye will be fine, man!" Duncan said. "Just keep yer mouth shut about both and we will be home shortly. I will take ye to the jeweler tomorrow and the bank if ye want. With that amount, I would encourage ye to create an account of yer own."

"So much to decide," Will said, looking bewildered and confused by what had just happened.

I raised my glass and said, "Aye, but first, we celebrate. *Slàinte!*"

I smiled over my glass at Will, and he smiled back at me in such a loving way that he made me blush. I could tell that we were thinking the same thing at this moment.

We are one step closer to being married.

FIVE
Blood Of My Blood

MacLeod House
Canongate, Edinburgh, Scotland
December 1766

My wedding dress arrived at MacLeod House, and it was another masterful work from the talented Missus Helen Scott. She helped me think about what I wanted for my special day and already had the perfect dress started that became my own. We spent time together over the past week to make it perfect.

At my last fitting, I stood before the mirror and cried tears of joy. Much like the first dress she made for me, her handiwork for this most special dress made me feel beautiful. I thought about my mother and then Lady Margaret. I wished more than anything that they could both be here with me, to share in the joy of this moment and this dress, and to guide me at this very important time in my life.

The dress was made of ivory silk with an embroidered pattern resembling plaid on the bottom of the skirt. The stitching was intricate and beautiful, crossing ivory silk thread upon ivory silk fabric. The corset was so snug, I could barely breathe, but I was convinced this design feature was intentional to bring my breasts up even higher than normal and to accentuate my waist. I assume these were two elements designed to entice my beloved even more. For that, I could not complain.

I talked her into reducing the frill in the sleeves and make them taper all the way to my wrist with small silk-covered buttons, much like the ones she already had along the back of the dress. I think she was thrilled at the prospect of creating a dress to rival any from a Parisian modiste, but it involved more work for her to remove the lace that had been part of the bodice before. I told her I wanted to do a smaller hip pad underneath, as I felt I already had enough hips naturally, and we kept the skirt longer than normal. She tried to argue with me on the last, but I wanted to keep as slim a figure as I could.

Missus Scott added a small silk square on the breast for me to pin the MacLeod broach on the front of my dress without damaging the silk in the dress itself. The dress was gorgeous! I could not wait to show it off and I could not wait for Will to see me in it.

"Missus Douglas, do you want to see it?" I asked her proudly, holding the large box from the courier.

"Aye, verra much," she said, with a big smile, "and we should hang it quickly, so the fabric doesna bend."

We went up the stairs together and unwrapped the box and paper surrounding the dress. I held it in front of me so she could imagine me in it.

Missus Douglas had tears in her eyes and said, "Och, Mistress Alexandra! I have never seen a dress so beautiful!"

She helped me hang it on the wardrobe door and we smoothed out the skirts. It will hang for several days, but Missus Scott's preparation with the paper and laying it flat for the short trip down to MacLeod House ensured it was in excellent form.

"I will need yer help with these buttons," I said, showing her the back of the dress.

"Of course, I am here to help ye however ye need. But we need to talk about flowers. I have to order some flowers for the house and the cake. We have an existing order for our annual greenery for the Yuletide, which ye already approved, but if ye need any more, I can place that for ye."

"Aye! I will need small flowers for my hair, as I plan to put it up. And I will need a small bouquet that I can leave at Father's grave after the ceremony. I would like to see if we can get sprigs of juniper for the men and to go behind my MacLeod broach. Is that possible this time of year?"

"Juniper is part of the request for Yuletide greenery every year. We will have plenty for ye and yer men."

Everything came together, and we settled on Monday, 15 December, as the day William and I would marry at Canongate Kirk. Now, Edinburgh would not just be where my father lived, it would always be where I fell in love and was married. As much as I wanted to return to

Skye, I could not deny that this trip and this unexpected destination would forever be important to me.

+++

The night before the wedding ceremony, Missus Douglas made a feast for our family of roasted beef, carrots, and potatoes. She even made small cakes for us all to preview the larger wedding cake she was making for the celebration.

At supper tonight were just me, Will, Duncan, and Angus. The four of us have become so close on this trip and are honestly the only people I would want to spend the evening before my wedding with. I love these wonderful men and how they love me in return.

Duncan told stories about what a *right pain in the arse* I am most of the time, presumably trying to scare off Will at the last minute. But his attempts were all done with love and humor—not to mention they were true—so I could not be that angry with the man.

Angus paid him back on my behalf, by telling us all kinds of stories about what *a right pain in the arse* Duncan is most of the time. The drinks flowed, and we all spent the evening talking and laughing together until my cheeks hurt.

At one point, Will took my hand under the table, and through a drunken smile, I said, "I couldna asked for a better dinner company this night." I raised my glass with my right hand as Will brought my left hand from under the table, up to his mouth and kissed it tenderly.

"Aye, lass," Duncan said, standing from his seat at the table, "we will have plenty of toasts tomorrow, but I am most happy fer ye both to have found each other on this journey. We arrived in mourning, but we will all leave Edinburgh with joy and a stronger sense of family. To Alex and Will, *Slàinte mhath!*"

"*Slàinte mhath!*" we all said, bringing our glasses together at the center of the table.

"Now, we must all be at the kirk by one o'clock tomorrow," he said, orchestrating us and fulfilling his fatherly duty. "Will, tell us if ye need anything more in preparation?"

"No sir. I am ready. I picked up Alexandra's ring with ye earlier today," he said as he smiled sweetly to me. I could not wait to see what they chose.

I chimed in saying, "Missus Douglas and I delivered sprigs of juniper to each of yer rooms. If ye have one, ye should wear it behind yer MacLeod broach. If ye dinnae, ye should have it with ye somewhere in honor of Clan MacLeod."

Duncan looked at me with a proud smile and then said, "Will, ye and Angus will meet Reverend Gordon before one o'clock and then I will escort Alexandra across the street just before the ceremony."

"When we are wed, we will lay my flowers at Father's grave and then come back to celebrate with friends we have made in the city." They all nodded in understanding of the plan as I continued, "It will be a fine day! I told Missus Douglas to keep breakfast light in the morning because she has much to do for the reception and has to help me with my dress."

"Aye, lass," Duncan said, smiling at Will, "I dinnae think we need a fine breakfast. Just maybe a small bite to calm the nerves."

Will asked, "Mine or yours, Duncan?"

"Both, man!" Duncan said, taking a large sip of his drink to finish his glass.

We all laughed together again, as it was my turn to kiss Will's hand. He keeps proving that he is part of our family. Missus Douglas came in to take our plates. Angus said something we could not understand, and we laughed more. Clearly we are all delirious with drink and happiness!

Duncan said as he and Angus stood to leave, "We all thank ye, Missus Douglas. It was a fine supper."

I finished his sentiment and said, "Again, no grand breakfast for this lot, and I will see you in my room after eleven o'clock."

"Aye, Mistress Alexandra!"

Angus and Duncan made plans to have one more drink at the tavern at the end of the street and then Duncan said, "We will see ye both tomorrow."

I stood up and said, kissing his cheek, "Be safe. Remember, ye both have responsibilities tomorrow."

"We do, and it is our honor. Try to sleep tonight, lass."

As they took the keys and walked out of the front door, I turned to Will and said in a whisper, *"I would like to see ye at the cistern, if ye wouldna mind?"*

He just looked at me and then nodded. He walked out to the back door, and I knew that I would have to get past Missus Douglas, but on the night before my wedding, I had little care for decorum and propriety anymore. Still, I was slightly cautious.

"Do ye need anything, Missus Douglas?" I asked her in the kitchen.

"Och, mistress, I should be askin' ye that question," she said, smiling at the last of her cleaning for the night.

"I am fine and look forward to yer help tomorrow."

"The lad brought up extra water fer yer bath, and if ye need anything else tomorrow morning, please tell me. I will bring ye the flowers fer yer hair when I join ye."

"Missus Douglas, I thank ye and Petey! Truly," I said, touching her arm. She seemed startled at first that I touched her, but she smiled a motherly smile of encouragement before she turned back around to finish her work for the night and in preparations for tomorrow. It was then that I slipped quietly out the back door.

I ran to him in the dark and we kissed each other with a passion that has been building for days. We tried to steal touches or a kiss here and there, but after tonight's supper and in anticipation of tomorrow, I needed his mouth on mine and it appears he needed the same. He lifted me immediately against the side of the building and, in our passion, moved his mouth with a fury down my neck and chest.

"Och Christ! I *want* ye so," he said in my ear as he lifted me more off of the ground and pulling up my skirts at the same time.

"*Will*," I whispered back to him, knowing that as much as I wanted him, we had only one more day. "I had to see ye, but we only have one more day!"

One more day.

The many weeks of longing looks and light touches have taken their toll on both of us. He stopped himself, put his forehead to mine in resignation, and said, "I will meet ye tomorrow at the kirk, my love."

"I will meet ye at the kirk," I said as I kissed him once more quickly before walking away from him backwards and smiling all the way to the corner of the building. Missus Douglas was already gone for the night, and I was proud that I could make it back without detection. Much like Will, I was in a fevered state and needed the calm of my warm bed.

One more day.

I thought about how my life was about to change. I wanted nothing more than to share my bed and my life with William MacCrimmon. I finally fell asleep with the thought that this was the last night I will be alone in my bedchamber.

+++

Missus Douglas came for me with flowers for my hair and a sprig of juniper. I had already bathed and touched my lips and cheeks with bits of the rouge salve she left in my room when we arrived. We worked on my hair first as she carefully placed the smallest flowers throughout the back.

"What do ye think, lass?" she asked, holding the up a small hand mirror so that I could look at the back of my hair in the large mirror on the wardrobe.

"Beautiful! Now we have to deal with these buttons."

She helped me step into my dress and began the long task of the buttons on the back of the dress and then the sleeves. She worked in silence and my nerves started getting the best of me.

I spoke up to try to break the quiet that was tormenting me and said, "What was yer wedding day like Missus Douglas?"

I could see her smile in the mirror before me and she said, reliving the memory, "I was just thinking about it. My husband, Sam, was a kind man. He worked in the stables here before Master Jonny."

"I didna ken that!"

"Aye! I worked for yer father when he had small rooms near his law office and moved here to work at the house on Canongate when I married. Sam and I worked here together for the man who owned the house before yer father did."

"I imagined my father building this house as it is such a reflection of him."

"No, Master MacLeod bought the house and grounds from the previous owner. He changed it to be sure, but it existed mostly as it does today. I was verra glad to work for yer father again!"

She smiled as she continued recalling her memories of her own wedding day. "I also married at Canongate Kirk."

"Did ye?"

"Aye! The thing I remember most about that day was the way Sam held my hand. He had held it before, of course. Under tables when we could, or when we walked together. But after I met him at the altar, he took my hand and did not let it go the entire day. Our vows and the sermon were a blur. It was our hands together that made the connection so. He was mine, and I was his in that moment and forever."

"That is lovely!"

I smiled at her for this sweet memory as she continued, "About a year after we began working for Master MacLeod, Sam fell ill after Hogmanay. I thought it was just the result of the winter chill, but it was more than that, and he died suddenly about a week later."

"Och, I am so sorry!"

"Petey was not yet six years old, and yer father was so kind to me. He gave me all the time I needed to care for my wee lad while working for him and never complained that I often had a small boy with me, hiding behind my skirts, to complete my household tasks."

I admired what she said about his kindness, but I asked, "And ye never wanted to marry again?"

"No. I am content with the life I have and caring for my son who needs me. I had the love of my life and I dinnae need another."

I smiled at the thought of her words, and about my intentions to never marry at all. I wondered if Missus Douglas was truly content with her life or if, like me, she was protecting her heart in her own way.

"Petey found his own Da dead on the floor of the stables and has never spoken a word since."

"No!" I said, turning to look at her and stopping her progress on my buttons. "The lad spoke before?"

"Aye, as much as you can at that age, but never again after that day."

"That gives me hope then, Missus Douglas," I said, placing my hand on her arm.

Still staring at me, she said, "I dinnae follow ye, Mistress."

"I mean... think about it! If the lad spoke before, he can speak again. His being mute is because of the shock of his father's death. I am no healer, Missus Douglas, but I believe in my heart that Petey will find his voice again... *when he is ready.*"

She only nodded to me at this sentiment. Perhaps it was more than she could hope for herself, but I believed in my heart that wee Petey would speak again. I now realized what a gift Father's bequest was to this family and to this lad for his education. This boy will find his voice!

We remained silent for a bit, but suddenly, I just started laughing and could not stop.

"What is it, Mistress Alexandra?"

"Och Missus," I said, laughing even harder, "can ye imagine Will's large hands trying to get me out of this dress?"

She laughed with me and said, "Lass, I was just praying to the Lord above to give the man some patience, or he may have to rip ye out of it and that would be a tragic loss of such a beautiful dress."

We attached the MacLeod broach to the silk patch, and she placed behind it a small sprig of juniper. Missus Douglas turned me to face the mirror. "There! All done! Yer *beautiful*, lass."

I teared up at the sight. This dress transformed me. I felt beautiful in it. Embarrassed suddenly, I asked, "All brides are beautiful on their wedding day, are they not?"

"Aye, but in this dress, ye are a vision. I thought yer dress for the Advocate Society was a work of art, but this is stunning. Master MacCrimmon may need help standing upright when ye enter the kirk."

I smiled and turned to her to say, "Ye have been a tremendous help to me today. I thank ye. And... I am verra glad we had a chance to talk to each other more."

She nodded to me, and we both turned to the door as we could hear Angus and William walk down the hall and out the front door. Suddenly, my nerves returned to me, and I placed my hands on my belly and bent over.

"Are ye ready for me to send in yer uncle?"

"Aye, it is time," I said, taking her hand in appreciation. She kissed me on the cheek and walked out of the room.

Being alone only made me even more nervous. Soon there was a knock at the door, and I knew it was time for us to go.

"Come!" I said, with a shaky voice. Duncan walked in and, true to form, stood at the door waiting for a response. I turned around, but for the first time, he was not waiting for his acknowledgement. He stood with his mouth open and a tear in his eye.

"Christ, lass," he said, walking toward me. "Yer beautiful. Ye took my breath away fer a moment."

"Thank ye, sir."

"Missus Douglas asked me to bring ye the rest of the flowers," he said as he kissed me on the cheek. He handed me the small bouquet. He then handed me a small black box.

"What is this?" I asked him excitedly about the prospect of an unexpected gift.

"When I took Will to get yer ring, I secured a wedding gift for ye myself," he said. I have never seen my uncle look nervous, but I could tell that he was. It was endearing to see this strong man in my life be so loving and tender.

"Duncan!" I said as I sat the flowers on the bed and started opening the box. Inside was a small black velvet pouch. I smiled at him as I reached inside to reveal a bracelet made of Scottish pearls with an ornate silver hook clasp.

"Och my, they are so fine! Such gorgeous pearls! Help me put them on, will ye?"

As Duncan wrapped the bracelet around my wrist and hooked the clasp, he said, "When I saw this, I was reminded about the pearls Alexander mentioned in his letter to ye, and I thought he would want ye to have them on yer wedding day. Since we never found the wooden box, I wanted to give ye yer own pearls. Not knowing yer dress, I thought a bracelet would be a fine addition."

I kissed him on the cheek and said, "They are so beautiful. I have been thinking a lot about Father today. Partly because I am in his room, in his house. But also because I am so grateful for what he did for me and Will. I ken he did not expect William MacCrimmon in my life, but he did not expect me to be alone and for that, I love him even more."

Duncan nodded to me, as none of the brothers expected me to be alone forever. And perhaps it was another clue to who Alexander MacLeod was as a man, that he loved and cared for me so. I see now that despite being here in Edinburgh, he was still seeing to my care. As was reminded again that distance separated us, not love.

"I have also been thinking about my mother, and Laird Graham and Lady Margaret, of course, but I am glad ye are the one with me here on this day. *I love ye.*"

Duncan hugged me tight and said softly, "My darling lass, I love ye and am honored to represent my brothers and escort ye to the kirk this day. The lad is the love ye deserve, and yer the love he deserves. Are ye ready?"

"Aye, I am ready if ye are," I said, taking his arm.

We walked out of the front door of MacLeod House on Canongate, and I felt myself gliding across the street on the arm of my uncle. I am not certain if my feet ever touched the ground. We both smiled at each other along the way, and it felt as if everyone on the street stopped to let us pass. Reverend Gordon met us at the door of the kirk.

"Och, Lady MacLeod! What a grand day! Ye look beautiful and Master MacCrimmon is waiting for ye at the front. I will walk in first to take my place and yer uncle can escort ye in when yer ready. Take yer time. We cannae start until ye get there!"

I laughed for a moment on his last words and nodded to him with a smile, as he left us. I turned to look at Duncan, but my nerves were showing on my face.

"I am so nervous, I cannae breathe," I said, as I bent over slightly and put my hand on my chest. I could not say how much was truly nerves or breathlessness from the corset that seems to have become even tighter since we crossed the street. It was likely a combination of both.

Duncan lifted me up and put his hands around my face to say, "The minute we walk through that door and ye see Will, yer nerves will leave ye in an instant."

I looked at him, with narrowed eyes, wondering how he could know such a thing. Before I could ask, Duncan opened the door, forcing me to test his theory. He was right. The very moment we walked into the sanctuary, I only saw Will at the end of the aisle and every bit of nervousness I felt before disappeared. I smiled at him all the way as we walked to him. He put his hand to his heart and stepped back, telling me and everyone in the room that it pleased him to see me as well. Once again, I believe Missus Scott and I did well on our dress.

I barely remember the ceremony as it was so quick, as I told Reverend Gordon that we did not want a sermon. We did not have many attending us. Duncan stood proudly with us and Angus, Missus Douglas, Jonny, and wee Petey rounded out our small group of witnesses. Reverend Gordon allowed us to have a small portion of the ceremony in Gaelic.

"'S tu smior de mo chnaimh, anns mo chuislean 's tu 'n fhuil
Bheir mi dhut-sa mo chorp, gum bith 'n dithis mar aon
Bheir mi dhut-sa slan m'anam, gus an criochnaich ar saoghal."

"Ye are the Blood of my Blood, and Bone of my Bone.
I give ye my Body, that we Two might be One.
I give ye my Spirit, 'til our Life shall be Done."

When Reverend Gordon announced we were married, Will kissed me sweetly. Our eyes locked, and we smiled at each other through the kiss. For that moment, much like when I walked into the room, there was no one here but the two of us. Our small party of witnesses cheered. I went immediately to Duncan and hugged him tight.

Will shook hands with Jonny and Angus, only to move to proudly to Missus Douglas and Petey and thank them for being with us here today. I smiled, thinking that I have just married the most respectful man in all of Scotland.

Duncan broke the spell I had in watching my new husband to say, "*Happiness* is not always of yer own making, lass. Sometimes it happens upon ye without ye knowing. Ye just have to accept it."

"Not everyone kens what *happiness* is, uncle. That is true. But today *I do. I truly do!*"

After the ceremony we spent some time at Father's grave wishing he were here with us on such a special day—a day he always believed I would have. The new marker had arrived, and it was carved out of a dark stone with a Celtic cross on top and the simple words:

In Loving Memory of
Alexander Ewan MacLeod, Esquire
Advocate

28 June 1726—20 July 1766

Son, Brother, Father, Uncle, Friend
Hold Fast

This was the first time we laid our eyes on the marker as the stonemason took his time filling the order. Master Forbes had to tell him that the man's family would only be here for a short time and threatened to withhold the last payment as long as it took the man to deliver the stone as promised.

"It is noble tribute to the man," Will said, holding my hand. His words were sweet in honor of the man that he did not have the chance to truly know.

Upon seeing the headstone, I thought of Shakespeare's *Hamlet*. I said to my companions the same, "This makes me think of Ophelia's lament in *Hamlet*."

Both men looked at me, uncertain of what I might say. Whether you knew the play or not, the mere mention of the name Ophelia often resulted in uncertainty because of her perceived madness. I tried to calm them, "She is lost in grief, but her song rings in my ears today."

> *"He is dead and gone, lady,*
> *He is dead and gone;*
> *At his head a grass-green turf,*
> *At his heels a stone."*
>
> **Hamlet,** *Act 4 Scene 5,* William Shakespeare

Will just gripped my hand more at the thought of reciting Shakespeare in the kirkyard and the absolute acceptance that my father is gone forever. His sudden passing being the very reason we shared a journey of sorrow to Edinburgh, a journey that brought us together, and to this very joyous moment. In some odd way, it was my father's last gift to me. And I thank him for all he has done for us both.

"Of course, he would place the clan motto of *'Hold Fast'* on his stone!" I smiled at Duncan and Will as I placed my other hand on my MacLeod broach, attached to my gown that said the same words.

"Aye, he was always a proud member of Clan MacLeod," Duncan said with a proud smile of his own.

Suddenly, we heard the voice of Reverend Gordon once again. He said as he handed me a small charcoal drawing of the gravestone, "Lady and Master MacLeod, one of my student volunteers from the university, drew the stone, so ye can take it home with ye."

"Thank ye sir, that is most kind," I said, smiling at the paper he handed me. I handed it to Duncan. "We will treasure having this reminder when we are home on Skye and cannae look upon his marker ourselves."

"I hope ye will join us at the house this afternoon for some wine and a piece of Missus Douglas' cake, sir," William said, finishing my thought and already serving as a valued partner.

"Aye, I was just speaking to Missus Douglas, and told her I will absolutely be there to celebrate with ye. But fer now, I will leave ye and yer family."

After a last moment of reflection and silent prayers for the departed, we walked away from the side of the kirkyard for home. I thought about the emotion of the day. With my left hand in William's, I stared down at the thin, silver band with three sparkling diamonds, and smiled as I glided across Canongate on sheer joy and happiness, just as I had earlier.

+++

MacLeod House was lit with candles in gold lanterns surrounded by fresh greenery and flowers across all the mantles. Wedding or not, it was a festive display in line with what Alexander MacLeod would have expected at this time of year. A small table was set in the front hall with a small cake with flowers in the same reds and greens. Missus Douglas brought out porcelain plates rimmed with gold and an ornate script of the letters 'A' and M' intertwined in the middle. The cut glasses for wine were also rimmed in gold. I have never seen a set so fine and thought that I might take them all back to Skye, as they were clearly made specifically for my father.

Reverend Gordon, who cheerfully talked with Missus Douglas about the fine cake and the wine, was the first to join us. Master Forbes and Mistress Hay arrived at our celebration next. Jacob and Hilary rounded out our party but could only stay for a moment before having to go back to their tavern and the wee Jamie, so we moved ahead quickly with the toast shortly after they arrived.

With Will by my side, we stood upon the first step in the front hall as I raised my glass to the room. "Thank ye, Missus Douglas, for a fine reception. Everything is just perfect, and I know we all cannae wait to have a taste of this beautiful, sweet cake. Yer an excellent cook, and my travel companions have already tasked me to see that we have fried ham at Castle Dunmara!" The room laughed and the men nodded their heads in agreement. We have *all* fallen in love with fried ham. "Madam, ye, Jonny, and Petey have made our stay here at MacLeod House on Canongate most welcome and comfortable. Ye are all part of our family now."

Missus Douglas wiped a tear from her face and smiled at me. This show of appreciation and affection genuinely touched her. I could then see Jonny, cap in hand, nod his head to me in respect. And wee Petey just smiled up at me sweetly as I kept talking.

"Duncan, Angus, and all of our new friends we have made in this city. We thank ye for being here to celebrate this day with us."

Will raised his glass and said, "To our family and friends, *Sláinte mhath*!"

The room returned the toast, and the party broke up so that Will and I could be alone, finally. The last to leave us were Duncan, headed to Leith and then Glenammon House. Angus booked a room at the White Hart. I was happy with the reception, but even happier, with an empty house and my new husband who carried me up the stairs to our bedchamber.

+++

"First things first," I said as Will sat me down on the floor by the bed. I reached across and threw every pillow onto the floor.

As the pillows fell, he turned me around and with his mouth on my neck, said, "Och, ye were clear in yer instruction about the next time ye were in my bed."

He buried his nose in my neck and then my hair as he began taking the last of the flowers and pins out of the back. *"I love yer hair down,"* he whispered in my ear.

"Yer gonnae have to deal with those buttons first, sir," I said over my shoulder as I started undoing the ones on my sleeves as quickly as I could.

He kept trying to undo the buttons on the back of the dress and finally asked while laughing, "Is this a grand dress, or a *device of torture* for a newly married man?"

"I kent Missus Douglas could help me into the dress, and I didna think about ye having to help me out of it! She and I shared a laugh together at the verra thought this morning."

Finally, he succeeded in his task and left me standing in my shift. He removed his boots and breeches as I pulled him from his gentleman's coat. I did not know what to do, but I *did not* care. It seems to be happening without me guiding it. Just like last night, by the cistern.

"*Will,*" I whispered his name as he took his shirt off and stood before me. My husband is the most beautiful thing I have ever seen. I thought to myself that he looks like a drawing of a Roman statue I had seen in one of my history books. He must surely be chiseled out of solid stone, and I could barely breathe at the sight of him.

"Yer so beautiful, lass," he said to me softly as he walked to me. I could not find the words or a voice to say that he was beautiful to me as well. He touched me gently as he slowly kissed me, starting with my neck, then down my shoulders. Every touch made me shiver and burn at the same time. Hot and cold.

"Yer skin is so soft," he sighed, as he sat me on the edge of the bed.

"*Will,*" I whispered when I could finally find my own voice, "*please stop.*"

He did as I asked, but looked confused, breathing heavily in my face. He then said with a sly smile, "I dinnae ken if I *can* stop. It is a well-known fact that if ye do, yer cock will fall off. Ye dinnae want that lass, do ye?"

I started laughing at the absolute silliness of his words and the fact that he said it with a straight face. He tried to put me at ease, and I loved him for it. I said, laughing more, "Ye must be the most ridiculous man in all of Scotland! I have never heard of such a thing!"

He smiled at me and kissed me on my nose, pleased that he made me laugh. His plan was a good one, because I immediately did not feel as nervous as I did just seconds ago.

"I ken this is supposed to be painful the first time, and yer being slow and gentle, which I appreciate verra much, but I am so nervous. If ye just do it, then it will no longer be the *first time*, aye?"

He looked at me and nodded in understanding. He knew what I was asking, and it was not the slow tenderness of making love. We had time to explore and do that later. As much as I wanted him, I wanted to be done with the first time more because I was so scared.

"Are ye sure?" he asked. I nodded to him in agreement. He sped things up and kissed me so that I again could not breathe.

"Have ye done this before, Will?" I asked, panting in his ear.

"Aye!"

"I am yours," I said as he pushed my leg aside further with his knee.

+++

SIX
Marriage Lessons

I looked at my husband lying next to me with a triumphant smile. I have never been this physically close to anyone in my life and wanted nothing more than to be even closer to him.

"How are ye, love?" he asked.

"I am fine," I said as I thought about it all and as we both laid next to each other, still breathless. A tear formed in my eye as I could not truly describe how I felt. I just gave William a part of myself that I have never given anyone else. Not just my body, but the deepest part of my heart. I only wanted his hands on me more, yet I was embarrassed at the same time.

I felt much like I did with that first kiss before the fire. I brought the linens to my chin and shut my eyes tight. My mind raced as fast as my heart, and I could not gather my thoughts enough to say to him how I was feeling in any way he could understand.

I turned my back to him as he wrapped his arms around me and pulled me close to him. The moment between us was awkward at first, but I found comfort in his warm embrace, much like I did during the snowstorm at Glenammon House.

"Did ye love her?" I finally whispered to him over my shoulder.

He held me tighter and asked, confused by the question, *"What? Who?"*

"When ye did this before, did ye love the lass?" I asked, feeling immediately jealous at the thought of my husband lying with another woman.

"No," he said, wrapping his arms around me tighter and kissing the back of my head. "Och, no! My father attempted to educate me the summer I turned sixteen. That means he took me to the brothel in the village. I suppose it saved him the conversation."

Knowing I was likely concerned that he knew what I did not, he continued, "The woman was much older than me but verra kind. She told me everything she could. Some of it I kent from lads talking, and if ye have ever been around animals, ye ken how it works at the most basic level to have a bairn. But some of what she said to me was surprising because she talked of what a lass wants and needs."

I nodded as I reflected on what Lady Margaret told me when I came of age, but it was just the basic premise of the differences between men and women. And like Will said, if ye have spent any time around animals, you understand the basics. Any discussion about marital relations was a quick academic education on how bairns are made in a cryptic speech about *seed* and *vessels*. But most of our talks of what men and women do together sounded like a duty a woman must do because it was something men were owed by being a husband. And it was never talked about being remotely pleasurable or about wants and needs. I think that only added to my fear.

"I wish someone had done the same fer me."

"No, lass," he said, pulling my hand up to kiss my wrist tenderly. "Ye made me so happy this night, and I hope I did the same. We have a lifetime to learn from each other."

I thought about what Elizabeth said and agreed to the sweetness of his comment. She said almost the same words about people who love each other—that they will learn to connect in a way that is unique to them.

"Come, let us sit in front of the fire," he said, standing with some linens around him. I took the other blanket around my body, and we sat together in each other's arms quietly for a bit, watching the fire burn. Being in his arms like this, listening to each other breathe and gentle touches are truly intimate. I thought about our time at Glenammon House sitting before the fire, holding on to each other, and reading Shakespeare's sonnets. We sat quietly for a bit, and I turned my head up to him but said nothing.

"What, is it?" He knew me well enough to know that I had something to say, but had stopped myself.

"I was going to tell ye something, but I suddenly feel embarrassed," I said, placing my hands over my face. "I fear my thoughts at this moment are *foolishness*."

Pulling my hands from my face to hold them in his own, he said, "Tell me what yer thinking, love. Ye should never feel like ye cannae. We must be honest with each other—*even* fer thoughts of foolishness."

I took his words to heart. If I am married, I have to learn to share my hopes, my dreams, and my fears with this man. We have a lifetime ahead of us and I needed to show that I let him into my heart—*even for thoughts of foolishness.* That is an important part of us *learning each other.*

Holding his hand in mine, I said, turning to face up to him, "When I was fifteen, I woke one morning in a pool of blood, unsure of what was happening. But I kent fer certain—I was *dying!*"

"I screamed for Lady Margaret and cried and cried. The pulsing pain in my belly also told me I was most certainly *dying.* She came to me and explained that I was *not dying,* and what it would mean to have my courses going forward. She brought in Missus Gerrard to help us, and she told me I was, at that moment, *a woman.*"

He nodded in understanding of what women must endure, as I continued, "But I believe she was wrong."

William gently squeezed my hand in his again. My voice was clearly shaking, and he tried to reassure me as I spoke to him nervously.

"Erm, no. I mean, I think there is more to becoming a woman. That moment meant I *was a woman,* to be sure. But I also believe that when ye took me as yer wife just now, I also became a *woman.* And I believe I will become a *woman* again when I birth yer bairns."

Perhaps there is more to being a woman than just these physical moments. Moments that not all women share equally in life, but I cannot deny what Will made me feel this night. He made me feel loved and respected. He made me feel like a woman—*his woman.* Sharing the truth of my feelings—even my thoughts of foolishness—made me feel closer to him. I spent so much time keeping myself closed to others that I did not understand how trust and honesty between people is a strength, not a weakness. The closer we are, the stronger we are—*together.*

With dreamy eyes and halting breath after another one of his loving kisses, I said, *"Please, do it again."*

+++

"How is it I have a husband?" I asked, almost in joking disbelief as I looked up at him with my chin resting on my arm across his chest.

"Well, ye did try everything *not* to have one," Will said with a smile, looking down at me.

I laughed with him as I lifted myself up and took his face with both hands and kissed him as I said, "That I did! But ye saw right through my shield and won my heart, anyway. Yer not just my husband and my love, but yer my friend. I never thought that I deserved any of those things in this life. I thought I would be alone forever. I *wanted* to be alone forever! Ye taught me a different lesson and I love ye with all of my heart, Will!"

"Ye move a lot in yer sleep."

I sat up and punched him in the arm. "That is yer response to my confession of love?"

We both laughed, and he said, wrapping his arms around me, "I love ye too, lass!"

This is another thing that I am learning about Will—his humor matches my own. He is serious when he needs to be, but he likes a laugh as well. Between Will, Duncan, Angus, and Grant, I am destined for a lifetime filled with laughter—most often at my own expense.

"Aye! I remember my father telling me when I was a young lass that I always slept like I was a fish thrown upon the shore. I flipped and flopped, as I could never find comfort in going to sleep. My mind raced constantly, and I felt confined by my linens. Even if I could fall asleep, the restlessness continued without my knowing it. I guess I am the same today."

"Well, this bed is too small for that, or I will never sleep again!"

We both laughed at the notion, and I moved my way up closer to say in his ear before kissing his cheek, "My bed at Dunmara *is much bigger.*"

"I tried keeping my hand on yer hip to steady ye," he said as I rested my head on his shoulder, "but that just kept me awake even more."

"Och! I thought you just couldn't keep your hands from me!"

"Aye, that is true, as well! But it was only part of my plan."

"Remind me to read ye sonnet twenty-seven next time we sit together before the fire."

"Read it to me now?" he asked softly. I sat up and smiled up at him before getting up to retrieve Shakespeare's book of sonnets from the table across the room. I was happy when I found the page and that I had remembered the right sonnet for this moment.

I crawled back into bed and propped myself up on my pillows. I brought him to my chest so that I could wrap my arms around his broad shoulders and hold the book before us so that we could both see the words on the page. Kissing the top of his head, I read the sonnet aloud.

"Weary with toil, I haste me to my bed,
The dear repose for limbs with travel tired;
But then begins a journey in my head,
To work my mind, when body's work's expired:
For then my thoughts (from far where I abide)
Intend a zealous pilgrimage to thee,
And keep my drooping eyelids open wide,
Looking on darkness which the blind do see:

Save that my soul's imaginary sight

Presents thy shadow to my sightless view

Which, like a jewel hung in ghastly night,

Makes black night beauteous and her old face new.

Lo, thus, by day my limbs, by night my mind,

For thee, and for myself, no quiet find."

Sonnet 27, William Shakespeare

"Och! I ken that his thoughts of a distant love keep him restless, but *'For thee, and for myself, no quiet find'* certainly describes it!"

"Will!" I yelled, leaning in to kiss the top of his head again. "Yer going to have to get used to it, husband, because I am not going anywhere."

"Aye, and restless or not, I dinnae want ye anywhere else, my love."

+++

I awoke in a fog, feeling Will's hands trace my right side—from my neck, down my side to my hips. I must admit, his movement from one end to the other was not a bad way to welcome a new morning, though he made my skin rise in goose flesh as his loving touch also ushered in the chill of the room. I stayed still to enjoy every minute of it until he moved his hand forward.

"Good morning!" I said, immediately moving my hand to meet his mid-thigh.

"Yer awake, then?" he said as he moved closer to me.

"I dinnae ken how I could sleep... with such attention."

Through gentle kisses on my shoulder, he said, "I just want to touch every inch of this body of mine."

Catching my side glance and silent rebuke over my shoulder, he thought for a moment to correct himself, but instead said, "Ye *are* my wife."

He kept tracing my body—up and down—with his hands and kissing the back of my head, neck, and shoulders. "When I said the words, *I give ye my body, that we two might be one,* I realized it was more than the act that made it so. I realized I should worship and protect every bit of yer body as much as my own. I will respect ye and do everything I can to keep ye happy and safe."

I grabbed his hand just before he went further, "Watch yerself, sir!"

"Well then," he said, trying once more to move ahead, "is this not an area you would welcome yer husband, madam?"

"I am afraid ye will need to earn your access... *there!*"

With that, Will laughed aloud and pitched himself on his elbows, clearly playing along, "Och, ye must be teasing me!"

He was likely confused, based on the free access he has had to my body as of late, but I scoffed and smiled, "Am I?"

After a long silence and then a quick peck on the cheek, Will played along with my new game. He said, "Right, then. What exactly is needed fer... admission, *wife?*"

It took everything I had to keep from laughing at his ask, but I whispered breathlessly in his ear to add to his tension, "*Well, husband, ye will need to show me how much ye want... access. Ye will need to dance before the fire. If yer dance is worthy... then... perhaps we can discuss.*"

My plans were received as intended because he sighed heavily into my ear in anticipation at first, then sat up straight in the bed at the demand, "Yer mad, woman! *Raving mad!* I am yer *husband* and yer my *wife!*"

I found his indignant response at the prospect of not having his way with me laughable. It only helped me carry my challenge forward. "Well then, ye should ken by now that *yer wife* is not a woman beholden to tradition and such entitled claims on her body! Husband or no!"

I wrapped the linens around me tighter in a show of blatant defiance and further restricting his access to my body. Will knew I would not back down now. He knows the strong, independent woman he married. This is a matter of principle!

He fell on his back and cursed aloud, "By Christ, woman!"

His resignation finally showed on his face. Not to be denied, he stood up and moved to stand at the foot of the bed and in front of the fire. He knew this was an utterly absurd request. But my beloved giant of a husband gallantly bowed to me and set about a perfectly formed dance that might have been a sword dance of old, sadly without the swords or the pipers to make it so. But it would have certainly roused the Scots preparing for battle or to impress any young lass at a cèilidh. He finished his dance with an extra shake of his bare arse from under his shirt for me, complete with more cursing, before collapsing back on the bed next to me in a fit of laughter. We laughed together at the spectacle to the point of tears. His commitment to his dance had me grinning from ear to ear.

"Well done! Well done!" I said to him as I kissed his cheeks over and over. He wrapped his muscular arms around me. "That was magnificent! Ye *earned yer right...*" I said as I grabbed his hand and placed it exactly where it was headed moments ago.

+++

106

I woke in the middle of the night to find Will sitting at the edge of the bed. I crawled over to him and placed my arms around him from behind. I kissed the back of his head and then his neck. I turned my head and rested my cheek on his bare shoulder. He was a warm comfort to me, even just sitting still, and I smiled at the thought of him.

"Are ye well, my love?"

He placed his hands on my arm around him and turned his head to the side to meet mine. "Aye, I couldna sleep."

"Was I keeping ye awake by being restless again?" I asked apologetically.

"No, love," he said, reassuring me and patting my arms already tight around his shoulders. We sat quietly, holding on to each other for a moment before he spoke again.

"I arrived in Edinburgh with a broken heart. I loved ye so, Alexandra, but I was nothin' to ye. I was nothin' but a protector and a stable hand assigned by Laird Graham. Then I kent we were friends when ye would tell me stories or read sonnets to me, laugh with me, or even just call me *friend* instead of *kinsman* when ye introduced me to others." I kissed his shoulder again as he continued, "I ached for yer love and each time I was near ye or talked with ye, my heart was lifted and broken at the same time."

I felt the tears forming in my eyes as he spoke because after everything we had been through and the ways we connected physically and emotionally over the last few days and weeks, he was giving me even more of himself. I admired him for his honest confession and hugged him tighter, with my head still resting on his warm shoulder.

"That night of the Advocate Society event, ye must ken that ye took my breath away when ye came down the stairs in yer new dress. But every time I saw ye talking with Master Forbes or the other men in the room, I couldna bear it! I was ashamed that I was so jealous and had no right to be, so I stood in the corner and wallowed in my own misery... that is, until ye came to remind me of the reason we were there. Ye gave me hope because ye said ye *wanted* me there with ye."

"I wanted ye there, Will. So did Duncan. We *both* wanted ye with us."

"I woke tonight because my heart is so full," he said, turning his head to me again, "because ye love me and ye married me."

"I love ye, my darlin' man!"

"I dinnae feel I deserve ye, but I am so thankful and happy. Ye have made me happy. So much so that I couldna sleep. I just wanted to think about how happy I am and thank God fer it."

Kissing his shoulder again, I then reached around to turn his face to mine. "Duncan told me once that *we all deserve* love, but we have both had to *learn*. For ye to have the patience and wait fer someone who was not of the same mind as ye, and fer me to open my heart enough to let someone in at all."

I kissed him and stroked his face, moving his curls away from his forehead so that I could see his bright blue eyes better, as I whispered, *"Thank ye for waiting for me."*

"I was prepared to wait my entire life," he said as he smiled at me and kissed me gently. *"My entire life."*

+++

We finally decided that we needed to go downstairs for some food. Thinking we were going to have to raid the kitchen ourselves, we found instead that Missus Douglas, the wonder that she is, left us cheese, fried ham, and bread and butter on a platter covered with a cloth on the dining table. She also had the ale, wine, and whisky as plentiful here as in our chamber. She even left a platter of olives and dried fruit and nuts in the shape of a heart on another platter.

"Och, she is so kind to care fer us so!"

"Aye, Missus Douglas kens ye with the bread and butter."

"Aye, she does," I said with my mouth already full of both. Will just laughed and shook his head at me and my ridiculous state. The man has made me ravenous, but my only true love at this moment was fresh baked bread covered end to end with salted butter.

"We should have a plate here and take a small one up with us so we dinnae have to come back down so soon."

"I get yer meaning, madam and agree with ye completely."

He sat on one side of the table and made himself a plate. I sat on the other side of the table as he looked at me, crestfallen, and said, "Ye dinnae want to sit next to me?"

"No. I want to *look* at my husband."

After a time of eating and drinking while smiling at each other across the table, we had our fill, and I said, "Will, ye should make the plate to carry upstairs and join me in a moment."

He looked at me with narrowed eyes, unsure of what I was doing, but nodded to me in agreement. When he came into the bedchamber, I met him at the door, took the plate from him, and placed it on the dressing table. Then I took his hand and led him to the small room behind the bed and the copper tub that I had filled for him. He did not notice that I put all the cauldrons over the fire before we walked downstairs.

"Och, this is a surprise! The copper bath!"

"Aye, I thought ye should experience this wonder," I said, indicating to him to take off his shirt. He did as I asked, pulling it from the back and revealing himself to me again. I led him by the hand to the steps into the bath. He stepped in and sat down in the warm and soothing water I filled with the warm water from the caldrons and bath oils.

"Christ above, my love! This is incredible! My entire life, I have washed mostly in icy rivers and lochs. I have washed in cold wash basins at my mother's house or in taverns. But this is *warm*!"

"I kent you would like the copper bath."

I started washing his back and arms with a cloth and soaps my father had. We sat quietly, enjoying the moment together. Will had talked of worshiping my body, but I revere his just as much. He is so strong, but gentle. He is beautiful to me. In washing him, I saw a large scar on the top of his right arm that I had not noticed before.

"What happened?"

"Erm," he sighed as I ran my fingers lovingly over it, "that is one of the lasting legacies of Da's rage."

"Och, Will!" I said before I kissed it tenderly.

"He whipped me with a small branch and cut the skin. Once he did, he fiercely hit the same spot over and over. I have another small scar here on my right hand from the same event."

"I had not noticed them before. I am so sorry."

"Dinnae be sorry. We all carry scars. Some you can see and some ye cannae."

Every now and again he would sigh or shut his eyes as I caressed his body from head to toe with the soap and cloth soaked in the warm water of the bath. He reached for me at one point and kissed me. Making him happy made me happy.

"I can see how yer father would want this. Can ye imagine after a hard day of work having this warm bath to take away all the aches in yer bones?"

"Aye. When Missus Douglas showed it to me on the day we arrived here, I was so overwhelmed by the grand house that I saw it is nothing more than another indulgence of a rich man."

"He is yer father, lass!"

"Aye, but I still thought it was all *too* much. That is until I had my first bath in it the verra next day. Then I was a changed woman!"

"But I gather ye have never had to wash in a cold creek."

"Ye forget our travels here, sir!"

"Yer right, forgive me."

"But aside from our journey, no. Missus Gerrard always tried to keep the cauldrons ready for me, but even then, ye must work at considerable speed before the water gets cold. There is an entire process—and it is quick!"

Will just smiled at me. I am not sure he is all that convinced of my *suffering* with a wash from warm cauldrons, no matter how fast the water turns cold.

"If ye move forward and lean back a bit, I will wash yer hair for ye."

Again, Will did as I asked, and I took one of the jugs and slowly poured the warm water on his head. I then took the lavender soap and began massaging it through his hair with my fingers.

"This is... the *best* feeling," he said, as he moaned with pleasure at the comfort of a tender touch on his head.

I rinsed his hair and said, "There, I am finished."

"Are ye sure? I believe ye missed a spot."

"Really?" I looked confused, but I knew exactly what he meant. Will looked at me with his bright blue eyes and I lathered my hand with the soap and plunged it beneath the water. As soon as we were both unable to breathe, he said, "Hand me that linen and then find yerself in our bed. Preferably without yer shift."

"Aye, sir," I said as he stood from the water and took the linen from my hands and kissed me before turning for the door. I believe we were both going to benefit this night from the warm miracle that is the copper bath at MacLeod House on Canongate.

+++

"Did I ever tell you about Jenny?" He asked, curling my hair around his fingers.

"I *dinnae believe* ye did," I said in a sarcastic tone.

I am not certain I want to hear the name of another woman in my bed, nor do I understand why my new husband wants to share her story with me now. I thought I had escaped the thoughts of other women with the lass at the brothel. But, if I have learned anything of late, Will's stories are about sharing himself. I am starting to understand his method of communicating with me through the telling of them.

"Och! She is bonnie, as ye ken," he said, realizing that perhaps this is not the best start to his story.

"Do I?" I said, teasing slightly, but still wondering where this story was going. He remained silent until I finally admitted, "Aye, Jenny was a bonnie lass. She was part of the lover's triangle with Wesley and Mary, no?"

"Aye, she was, but admit I never understood that relationship." I just shook my head as I felt the same. They were a very odd trio. "But ye have to ken that as bonnie as she was on the outside, she was empty on the inside. I couldna tell if she was empty of spirit. Perhaps she had a rough life at home. Or perhaps felt like she had to be simple and ignorant... that she had to rely on nothing but how she looked to attract a husband, y'ken?"

I could not help myself, and asked, "So ye thought the lass was bonnie, *but* ye felt sorry fer her?"

Will knew he was walking a fine line here with my question. But he continued. I give him credit for remaining honest with me, but this has to be a test of my resolve and the extent of my own jealous nature. Despite him being here with me now, I do not know that I want to think about Jenny pursuing Will or Will pursuing Jenny at any point.

"Ye always tell such great stories, Will," I said, sitting up on my elbows. Looking at my husband, who was laying back with his hands behind his head, staring at the ceiling much like he did when I discovered his wall of pillows. I waited in silence until he finally looked at me. "Ye do! They tell me more about ye and how ye think. But I must ken, why are ye telling me the story of *bonnie kitchen maid Jenny* in my own bed?"

He turned to me, sitting up on his own elbows. Face to face now, he kissed me gently on my forehead and looked me straight in the eyes and said, "Because I want ye to ken why I love *ye*." Will immediately shook his head, trying to remove the words he just spoke aloud. "No. That is not what I meant. I want ye to ken that I have *only* loved ye."

This man has a way with words when he wants. I smiled at this admission. He was taking more and more of my heart by the minute, and his answer might be more than acceptable.

"Yer so different, love, and what I *feel* fer ye is different. What I have *always* felt fer ye is different."

113

I just looked at him and waited for his explanation.

"Yer intelligent. Not just educated, mind? *Intelligent.* When you dinnae get in yer own way, of course, yer instincts are usually right."

"Really?" I said, as I laughed at this compliment combined with a slight reproach. Then he kissed me sweetly on my right cheek.

"Yer *confident* in yerself in a way that I have not seen in any other woman I have ever met," he said, shaking his head at the notion and kissed me the left cheek as he whispered in my ear, *"and some men, fer that matter."*

"Yer *kind* and driven to help others, especially those in need. I admire yer genuine heart," he said as he kissed me on the nose.

"It matches yer own kind heart, Will."

He continued by saying, "And by Christ, ye make me *laugh!*"

I looked at him as he smiled sweetly at me. "Ye were *always* the woman fer me, and I will spend the rest of my life trying to *deserve* ye."

This time, he left his lingering kiss on my mouth. One that left me breathless. As I opened my eyes, his forehead was on mine as he whispered to me with his eyes closed, *"I have loved no one more than ye, Alexandra."*

I pulled back and smiled at him, and he waited for me to say the same. And he waited.

And the poor man waited.

Will pulled back further for a minute and said with a smile, "And ye, Missus, are supposed to say ye have loved no one more than *me!*"

"I was just thinking it through," I said, trying so hard not to laugh. He looked concerned as I took my time in my response. His eyes only grew wider and he sighed with impatience.

I finally said, "I mean between ye and Munro..."

"*Munro?!*" Sitting up now, startled at my words of another's name before he realized that there was only one Munro. "*Yer horse, lass?!*"

"Aye, Will," I said with a serious tone, looking him directly in the eyes, "Ye ken Munro is verra *special* to me!"

He knew then that I was teasing him, and he started kissing and tickling me as we both laughed together. I was laughing so hard as I fought to get away from him that I was nearly crying. Finally, I gave in to his flurry of kisses and said as I raised my hands over my head in surrender, "I give in! *I give in!* I have loved no one more than ye William Lachlan MacCrimmon! And I never will!"

We just stared at each other, and I bit my lower lip and he asked, "But?"

My face betrayed me again as I paused and then said, "But... my beloved Munro is gonnae be *broken-hearted!*"

I immediately pulled the linens to my face and started laughing so uncontrollably that I shook the entire bed. He could not help but bow his head in resignation to my chest and laugh with me.

"I believe Duncan is right! Yer a right pain in the arse, Alexandra Flora MacLeod. But I will love ye forever."

"Och Will," I said, pushing his curls from his forehead, "if you could have seen yer sweet face when I mentioned Munro!"

I kissed him, and I thought to myself that I liked this part of marriage. To be this close with someone that you can laugh with and enjoy each other as people—as friends—was something I never considered. I only thought about the formalities of a marriage between a man and a woman. Formalities of body and mind, all laced with obligations and duty. But I believe that friendship and laughter are the best part of marriage for me, so far.

+++

We finally left the confines of MacLeod House on Canongate and met Angus at the White Hart Inn in January, with wedded bliss still showing on our faces and made all the more evident by our inability to keep our hands off of each other. We were constantly connected. Our legs touching each other under the table, our hands on each other in some form of silent affection, or just looking lovingly into each other's eyes.

I missed my uncle but was glad to see Angus, who was off on the side, talking to Jacob—presumably about the whisky situation like his dearest friend. I took the moment to sneak sweet kisses with my husband. When Angus had secured the whisky and returned to the table, I said to the men before me, "I want a plan to go home when Duncan returns."

"Aye, it is time," Angus said.

Will spoke up and said, "I will work with Jonny to secure another horse and cart, if we think we need it."

"Aye, we will need it." Angus said. "E'en if just a few paintings, we cannae carry 'em all on yer sweet pony. We might 'ave to sell yer lass."

"Aye, Hettie has served us well from Glenammon, but we cannae take her to Skye," Will said. "But we should leave her fate to Jonny."

I spoke up and said, "Angus, yer right. I thought that ye should go to Glenammon to see if Duncan needs help to bring anything back from our list. It may take ye both more time to settle things there, but I would like to have a plan to leave."

"Aye," he said, downing one glass and pouring another. "I can leave in a couple of weeks. I already paid in advance with Jacob fer my lodging."

Will said, "That is only fair. Actually, now that I think about it. If Duncan brings back all the items we noted on the inventory list, then he might have secured his own cart."

"Aye, yer right, lad," Angus said, and I nodded in agreement.

"We will wait until ye return to decide about a cart," I said. "I believe we are *all* ready to go home."

We sat quietly for a moment before Angus spoke again, raising his glass to me, "Marriage suits ye, lass."

"How so, cousin?" I asked, meeting his glass in the middle of the table.

"Ye were always strong-willed, and now *yer a force*."

"High praise indeed, sir," I said to the man who fought for his country and his beliefs only to suffer for it in prison. And praise from a man I can suddenly understand. High praise indeed!

Angus left us alone for the last of the night to talk to his other friends he had made in the tavern. Living above the White Hart has been good for him, as he is much more comfortable here than in the grand house. You can see how much more relaxed he is, and it is not just the ale and whisky making it so.

"Will," I said, moving closer to him on the bench. "I sent Angus to Glenammon to bring Duncan back, but when they return, I want them both to stay in MacLeod House."

"Aye, of course!"

"I appreciate them giving us the space we needed after the wedding and respecting that the house is mine, but they should not pay to stay at the tavern when we have a grand house that can accommodate all of us."

"I agree, love. We will welcome them back and make our plans to leave for Skye as soon as we can."

"*Skye*," I sighed as I laid my head on his shoulder, thinking about the trip back home with my gallant knights who have all has proven themselves to be good company on this incredible and journey across Scotland.

"*Angus is right, ye ken?*" Will said in my ear.

"*Is he then?*"

"Aye, marriage suites ye, lass," he said, kissing the top of my head.

"Take me home, my love."

+++

Once we arrived back at MacLeod House, Will locked the front door behind us with the keys, and he suddenly picked me up and tossed me over his shoulder without any effort and began carrying me up the stairs.

"Och! Put me down!" I screamed as I hit his backside with my hands. I tried not to be sick as all the blood and whisky rushed to my head. "Will, put me down, *now!*"

"Ye hitting my arse like that is only rousing me more," he said, laughing at my protest. "And stop kicking so hard! I dinnae want to drop ye on yer head."

Missus Douglas had already prepped us for the evening, knowing we would be at the tavern, with bread, butter, almonds, and olives, along with whisky in our bedchamber. Instead of putting me down as I demanded, Will walked directly to the small table, grabbed a couple of olives, and just stood there. Olives in one hand and me in the other.

"William Lachlan MacCrimmon, *are ye eating?!*" I yelled, still upside down over his shoulder. His shaking was the first sign that he was laughing at me despite his mouth being filled with food. I almost laughed with him. *"Put me down! Put me down, now!"*

Finally, Will threw me full force onto the bed. I barely caught my breath because of the throw, and neither of us could help it. We were both in a fit of fierce determination.

"Ye brute!" I said half-heartedly, knowing the accusation would hit a nerve.

"Och, lass, ye have no idea!" he said as he loomed over me and placed an olive in my mouth before kissing me. He confessed in my ear, *"I love it when ye say my full name."*

"We will learn each other," I said, looking him in the eyes, acknowledging that he was telling me again what he liked. I had not been as generous with my preferences. Not because I did not feel like I could, but because he seemed to know what I wanted without instruction.

He pulled himself away from me, looked me in the eye, and with a wink, lifted my skirts slowly. He stared at me, and I smiled at him until he threw them over his head. I started laughing at the thought. I felt his whiskers against my thighs as he kissed them, and then his mouth and hands found new ways to make me cry out his name. It was then that I realized there was more to the connection between husbands and wives, between lovers, than I ever knew.

I laid across his chest as he held me tight in his arms. He raised one hand up to wrap his fingers around my curls. I should have told him at that moment how happy he made me, but I smiled thinking that the real

119

debt of gratitude I owed this night—the many before and those to come—was to the lass at the brothel, for she taught my husband well.

SEVEN
The Fount Of Every Blessing

MacLeod House
Canongate, Edinburgh, Scotland
February 1767

I could feel Will leaning over me, and before I could move, his soft lips were upon my own. My eyes opened to meet those of my love and with a sleepy smile and a stretch before he kissed me again.

"Why are ye here, love?" he asked me in a whisper, stroking my hair. *"Are ye unwell?"*

I looked to the ceiling before looking back at William and said, "I was *so* tired. I was reading and kept falling asleep in the chair before the fire, so I thought I would lie down for a minute. But I can see through the window behind ye that it is dark outside. That means I have been in bed longer than I intended."

William nuzzled my neck and kissed me again on the cheek. Keeping his warm face next to mine, I held on to him before I returned his affection with sweet kisses of my own upon his cheek.

"Please, stay with me for a moment," I whispered as I pulled him closer.

"Aye, but only for a moment," he said, as he rolled me over to the center of the bed so he could wrap himself behind me in his loving arms.

The truth of it is that I have been tired since Hogmanay and thought it was mostly because of the dark and cold chill of Edinburgh in winter. The lull of sleep called to me once again. Either because I had not completely woken or the new comfort of Will lying here with me, cradling me in his arms, and keeping me warm. It is all too enticing a proposition to stay here with him in blissful sleep. Nothing could pull me from this comfortable position now that I settled into his embrace.

We stayed wrapped together for a bit until he finally whispered in my ear, *"We should go. Missus Douglas has supper waiting."*

"Aye, I suppose we should," I said in resignation that we could not stay here together forever. Will stood up and waited for me by the door, his hand outstretched to take mine. I sat up and tried to stand, only to find myself on the edge of the bed once again. My head was spinning, and I could not focus. For a moment, I thought I might be sick.

"Are ye alright, lass?" he asked as he now moved toward me and grabbed my arm.

It took me a moment to gather myself before I said, "Aye, I think I just stood up from the bed too quickly. I am not sure I am yet awake, and my legs gave way. Give me a moment."

I finally stood and followed him down to supper. But I know that I did not feel like myself. Everything before me on the table looked and smelled revolting. I looked at Will and expected him to say the same, but he did not. I just stared at him while he ate every bite on his plate and seemed more than eager to finish everything on his plate and some of mine.

I took one bite, and I knew I would be sick. I excused myself politely but ran straight for the courtyard outside the kitchen, where I retched beside the stables. Will ran out after me and kept his hand on my back as I stood holding on to the stone wall, shaking and crying with both sickness and embarrassment.

"I am so sorry," I said, wiping my mouth and then my crying eyes.

"It is going to be fine, my love," Will said, as he picked me up and carried me inside. "Petey, lad, send for Doctor Tyndall, aye?"

The lad nodded to Will and ran out of the close immediately as Missus Douglas said, "I will bring cool water and a cloth for ye straight away, Missus."

+++

"I suspect yer with child," Doctor Tyndall said plainly and without actually doing anything.

We both did the calculation in our heads since the wedding and while early, it *was* possible. In the thrill of being newly married, I had not noticed that I had missed my courses in January and now February.

He then said directly before I could ask, "More than one woman has conceived on her wedding night. It is early days, and things can happen naturally to end a new pregnancy. I will send the midwife, Missus Malcom, to see ye in the morning. Ye will want to talk to her about it all and take her advice in preparation so ye and the child remain healthy."

I nodded my head in stunned silence. I never even thought I would be married, let alone a mother. This has all happened so quickly. As

Doctor Tyndall spoke to me, I only heard some of his instruction to stay healthy and to minimize the sickness I currently felt.

In fact, I heard nothing he said, until his last words, "I trust Missus Malcom will tell ye the same."

He stopped at the door and looked at me.

I took this as my cue to finally speak. "I thank ye, sir," I said, still in disbelief at the thought of a child.

He said at the door and said with a wink, "I will tell yer husband to talk to ye, Missus. Ye can deliver yer own good news to him."

"Aye, I thank ye fer that," I said, sitting myself up on my pillows and preparing myself for a conversation I never expected.

Doctor Tyndall opened the door and met William nervously standing in the hall. He shook his hand immediately as Will asked, "How is she, sir?"

"She will be just fine! Go to yer wife, man!"

+++

Will came into the room with a smile from ear to ear and I gathered he knew exactly what illness suddenly befell his new wife, having caused it himself.

"Ye can wipe that proud grin off yer face, William MacCrimmon!" I said as I folded my arms across my chest in a dramatic show of false anger.

He came straight to the bed and placed his hand on my belly and kissed me sweetly.

"I told Missus Douglas I kent immediately when I found ye in bed this afternoon, and she said she was exactly the same with wee Petey. We have been beaming downstairs."

"If by *beaming* ye mean drinking whisky in the parlor, I can tell," I said, wiping the edge of my mouth with my hand. I could smell and taste the whisky the minute he kissed me, and it surprisingly did not make me feel unwell. This child has MacLeod blood after all and should have absolutely no aversion to *uisge beatha*—the *water of life*.

We had not even talked about having a family. I am not sure if we were so focused on each other over the last few months that it never crossed our minds or if it was just an expectation of being married and that it would happen when it was supposed to.

I smiled at him and asked, "Are ye happy, then?"

"Aye," he said, kissing me once more, "verra happy. How do ye feel?"

"I feel better than I did an hour ago. But with this unexpected news, I must admit that I also feel a little *scared*."

"I understand," he said, sitting beside me and placing his arms around me. "Ye will be just fine lass and I ken ye will be a wonderful mother."

I sat up and looked at him now with worry in my eyes. "How can ye say that? I ken nothing about raising bairns or being a mother!"

Will hugged me tight. "Och, lass! Ye will be a natural. Think of the love and care ye have given wee Robbie and how ye have grown to love Petey while we have been here. And what ye dinnae ken, ye will learn just like every other woman has to when she has her own bairns."

"Aye, I suppose ye are right," I said, settling down again with my head on his shoulder.

"I can tell ye, I ken nothing of what being a good father means myself! If in doubt, I suppose I can just do the exact opposite of what my own did."

I held onto his arms around me tight as I said, "Och, Will! Ye will be a wonderful and loving father, because that is how ye are as a man and as a husband."

He kissed the top of my head in acknowledgement of my words, but said nothing. I grew up without my mother and father. William grew up in a home filled with violence at the hand of his own father. Neither of us had a perfect model of family life to rely on, but he was right. We will learn. We will love each other, and this child, and we will both learn. Being parents is just another thing in our married life that we will learn together.

I did not tell Will about what Doctor Tyndall said about staying healthy or that sometimes pregnancies fail on their own in the early days and weeks. I will save all of that for after I talk to Missus Malcom in the morning. Until then, I am going to sleep soundly in the arms of my husband and dream of the new life that just changed ours forever.

I walked out into the courtyard to the stables to see my sweet Munro. I felt better being outside of the house for a moment. Even the soot-laden air of the city felt refreshing after days in front of the fire in my chamber. The cool air brought some color back into my cheeks.

"Master Jonny, I just wanted to say hello to Munro."

"Aye! He has been missin' ye lass!"

"And I have been missing him!"

I walked to the last stall for my beloved and stood until he came to me. Once he placed his head on my shoulder, I stroked his nose and face and said, "I have missed you so much, my dear Munro. We have been here in the city too long, haven't we?"

I held his face in my hands and kissed him over and over before reaching back to his withers. Once I broke the trance with my beloved horse, I saw Petey standing at the door to the stables.

"Hello Petey, sweet lad! Do ye ken my Munro?"

He walked over to me, and I put my arm around his shoulder and introduced him to my horse. Munro came to the lad immediately, with his head bowed. Petey stroked his nose and smiled. He leaned in and hugged Munro's face. Munro followed with kisses on the wee lad's shoulders, making him smile and hug the horse tighter.

"He is grooming, ye lad. It is a sign of affection. My Munro already kens you are a verra important person here at MacLeod House." Petey just nodded and smiled at me.

"Have ye just been cleaning the walk this cold morning?" I asked, as he quickly nodded to me. "Can ye show me what ye do? I would verra much like to learn more about yer important job here."

Petey grabbed my hand and led me to the cistern at the side of the building, where he filled his two buckets that he keeps there. The first had a little soap bar in it that he lathered with a brush with rough and worn bristles and the second had just plain water. He picked up his buckets and motioned for me to follow him to the front of the house. He showed me how he uses the plain water bucket to clear the steps and walk and then the other to scrub anything he needs to. He ran back to the cistern to get more water while I waited for him at the front for the final rinse. He looked at me proudly standing in front of his handiwork. It has to be the cleanest walk and house steps in all of Edinburgh.

"Well done, lad! I kent there was a process here and think you have done an incredible job of keeping MacLeod House clean. It is a beautiful, sunny day, but I suppose that there is a different process for when it is too cold to wash or there is snow and ice."

He nodded and smiled. He motioned shoveling, which I took as clearing ice or snow from the steps on colder days, and all that goes with it.

"Aye, ye should be proud of yer work here, Petey!"

I forgot for a moment that I was mistress of this house. He wanted to please me, and my words of appreciation made him proud. He stood taller and smiled at me the whole time I spoke.

"Come with me, lad."

He followed me back around into the close and dropped off his buckets at the cistern. We entered through the kitchen where his mother saw us pass and likely wondered what we were doing, but said nothing to us. We walked straight across the hall to Father's desk in the parlor. I took four coins from the bottom drawer of the desk.

"The first two pennies are fer yer good work on the walk. I can tell ye take yer job seriously, and I am proud of what ye do each day. Ye should save them for something *verra* special."

He smiled at me and was almost giddy with excitement. He kept swaying from one side to the other as I spoke to him. I am not sure if this was because he was garnering praise from the mistress of the house or that he knew I had another two shiny pennies in my other hand.

"These two are just for *ye*. I want ye to buy yerself a sweet cake or a toy at the shop at the end of Canongate. Would ye like that?" I asked, as he nodded his head vigorously. I placed all the coins in his hand. "Ye have earned them, lad. Ye have earned them fer yer hard work!"

He stared down at his four shiny new coins with immense pride. I thought of my wee Robbie at Dunmara and missed having a bairn to love and care for. Now I will have my own and feel stronger and more complete every day. Perhaps I could be a good mother after all.

"Petey, are ye excited about school?" I asked, walking back to the kitchen with him. I knew he would want to show his new coins to his mother.

He nodded his head at me. While his response seemed affirmative at first, his head remained low, and he did not look at me. It was clear that he was not as excited as I was. In fact, I felt a sadness in his response and maybe even a little fear. He had to tell me he was willing, but nothing about his demeanor told me he truly was.

"Och, my love! Master MacLeod sent you to Braidwood's Academy because he thought it would be good for ye. I dinnae ken this place, but I ken *this*—education is verra important. It will change yer life! Ye will discover things ye never imagined. Ye can read, ye can write, ye can communicate with all of us, lad!"

Braidwood's Academy was intended specifically to help teach the deaf and mute. Petey is a smart, hard-working lad, and this should help him complete his education in an environment that meets his needs. The good news is the school is here in Edinburgh and he does not have to leave his home. He can go to school and return in the afternoon to be with his mother.

"All you have to do is *try*. Will ye do that for me?"

He nodded his head in agreement. He would try and that is all I could ask of this sweet boy.

+++

"Stay still, Peter Douglas!" Missus Douglas said loudly as the lad shuffled his feet while she put on his coat and smoothed out his hair with her own spit on her hand. "Do ye have yer books and quill?"

The boy nodded to her.

"I have put a bit of bread and cheese in yer bag, as well. But will have a hearty lunch fer ye, when ye return."

Jonny waited for Petey at the back door to take him to school by carriage. Missus Douglas kissed him on the top of his head. The lad looked at us all standing around him, nervous and overwhelmed. I walked to him and bent down on my knees so that we were eye to eye. He just looked at me. I put my hands on his shoulders and said, "Ye will be just fine. I am so proud! Ye told me ye would try, and ye are! Trying is the first step."

In a much unexpected move, he hugged me tight around my neck, and I hugged the sweet boy back. "Och, Petey! We will see ye the minute ye come home. In fact, I will ask yer mother this verra minute to save my lunch for when ye return. We can all eat together, and talk about yer day."

Will said, "Aye, we can eat together, Missus Douglas! A late lunch is fine for all of us on the lad's return."

Missus Douglas nodded in agreement with this plan and seemed appreciative of the support. I stood up and felt William's hand on my back as a sign of support. Petey left with Master Jonny to the carriage, and we all waved to him as he walked out of the back door.

+++

Petey returned in the afternoon, energetic and excited about his first day at school. He bounded into the dining room as Missus Douglas and I sat out food for lunch on the dining room table. Running straight for his mother, he had a huge smile on his face. I could not tell at first if it was that he had a good day or he was just happy to be home.

"*There he is!* There is my sweet lad!" Missus Douglas said, taking the boy in her arms and lifting him from the ground and kissing him over and over.

"Someone is as happy to be home as ye are to welcome him back, missus," I said, smiling as I watched them hold each other tight.

Petey quickly came to me and hugged me as well. It made me happy that he felt so comfortable with me. I have truly grown to love the boy during our stay here. We asked him question after question on his first day and he nodded positively at all of them. He pulled a book from his bag and brought it over to me to see.

"Aye! Yer first book of letters," I said as he flipped to the page with A's on it, and then B's he practiced today.

"That is fine work for a first day," Will said to patting the boy on the shoulder as he looked down at his work from behind us. Petey looked with pride at his work, and I looked at Will and thought that my beloved will indeed be a good father.

"This is a fine place to start! Petey, I want ye to use Master MacLeod's desk, ink, and quill to practice yer letters," I said. He just looked at me and shook his head. My guess is that parts of the house, especially the desk has always been restricted to the child.

"Ye have my permission and I can help ye if ye want. I ken my letters and can help ye practice." He relaxed and nodded his head in agreement before running back to his mother.

"Well then, it has been a most productive and exciting day! Thank ye for the late lunch, Missus Douglas. I think I would like to walk with Will to the White Hart this evening. No need for supper tonight. Please spend time with our new student and help him prepare for his second day of school."

"Aye, mistress! Thank ye!" she said, relieved to have the evening off. It was better for her to be with her son tonight than to tend to us.

Will said sweetly to the lad, "Petey, ye have survived yer verra first day of school and did so well. Day two will be *even easier!*"

The lad nodded to us both in agreement and gathered up his books and papers to go home. All I could think as I watched him is that Alexander MacLeod knew exactly what he was doing, and I know wee Petey will live up to his expectations.

+++

Sitting in the White Hart Inn, I watched Will talk with Jacob as he prepared our ales. I smiled at the thought of Will becoming a new father and wondered if he was asking Jacob how he was faring with a new bairn to tend to himself. Hilary delivered a lad named James. We have all taken to calling the blue-eyed darling *wee Jamie.*

"I was telling Jacob all about our new student at MacLeod House," Will said, sitting my ale pot before me.

"Aye! The poor lad was scared at first, but came home so happy! Father knew what he was doing, and it was a wonderful thing for Petey. Whether he ever speaks again, he will not be relegated to washing the front steps for the rest of his life. He can continue to learn, read, and explore the world around him."

"Not to mention, by being able to write, he can communicate without his own voice."

"That is exactly right, my love! This school and his education will be an incredible gift to him and his mother! I am so proud of him for going there on his own today. I am not sure I could have."

"Ye could! Ye have incredible confidence."

"I suppose, but if I have learned anything, being here in the city is that I was so sheltered on Skye. It would take more confidence than I have to attend a large school here in the city alone."

"I can see that, but ye were so loving and kind to him, and it is clear to everyone that he has grown to love ye as well during our time here."

"I *love* him, Will. Like wee Robbie, he is a special lad. I love his kind heart and his hard-working spirit. Did I tell ye that Missus Douglas told me that the boy turned mute after finding his own father dead on the floor of the stables when he was just five years old?"

"Och, no! Ye never told me that! Somehow, I just thought that the lad had always been mute."

"Aye, the story is tragic. Missus Douglas worked fer my father and left his employ to join her beloved husband, Sam, and work for the man who owned this house on Canongate before. When my father bought the house, she was so thankful. She had Petey and enjoyed working here, but Sam grew ill after one Hogmanay. She lost her husband suddenly and wee Petey found his own father stone-cold dead on the floor of the stables and the poor lad never spoke again."

"That had to be hard to understand at such a young age."

We sat in silence for a moment at the thought of such a thing happening. Losing the love of your life suddenly and the pain inflicted on a young lad so much that he has refused to speak for years. I cannot imagine what Missus Douglas has had to endure in her life.

133

"There is a *positive* here. Think about it! It is not that the wee lad *cannae* speak. *He refuses to!* It gives me hope that one day, he will again."

+++

EIGHT
The Intruder

Will leaned in to kiss me, first on the forehead and then on my mouth, waking me from the deepest sleep. Since finding I was with child, I have honestly never slept better. I suspect my husband has not either, as I am not as restless as before.

"Goodbye, my love. I will see ye before supper. Jonny and I will sell Hettie and secure the additional horses to help take us home after Duncan returns from Glenammon. He gave us instruction on the type of cart we need and what will get us across the Highlands."

"Come home safe to us, Will."

"Aye!" he said, smiling at me as he touched my rounded belly. We stared lovingly into each other's eyes, still in the blissful realization that we were soon to be a new family. Another unexpected love filled my heart with joy and my mind with the possibility of the future. My mind has so many thoughts of heirs of my own that will continue this line of MacLeods on Skye. Such thoughts made me want to do the best I could and to make them proud.

I sat up on my elbows and said with a pout, "I wish you didna have to go. Cannae we just have Jonny handle this fer us?"

I looked at him, hoping he would stay here in bed with me, but he was on a mission to rid us of all that was keeping us here. I respected his leadership. We *have* to leave this city. We *have* to go home.

"I ken, love. I wish I didna have to go, but I need to help Jonny lead the horses and the cart back. It is too much fer one man. But, it is an easy trip, I will be home soon!" He left me with tender kisses on my lips and then my forehead. We smiled at each other as he walked to the door.

Since the night at the stables, I have not been sick, but I cannot get enough sleep. I am exhausted doing nothing and decided this morning that I could stay in bed longer as a married woman with no occupation and in a grand house. What a luxury!

When I woke again and dressed, it was afternoon. I was determined to accomplish the beginnings of our exodus from MacLeod House and Edinburgh. I had a list to set aside my father's personal items within the house for transport, but we would sell the rest with the house. I had to make progress on this list before Duncan returned from Glenammon.

I opened the bedroom door to start my chores, albeit late, and heard an unfamiliar male voice talking below. As I walked down the stairs trying to place the voice, I found I was wrong. The voice was not talking. It was *singing!*

> *"Adieu, Dundee, from Mary parted,*
> *Here nae mair my lot may be.*

Wha can bear when broken hearted,

Scenes that peak o' joys gone by.

A' things ance were sweet and smiling

In the light o' Mary's e'e,

Fairest seemings maist beguiling

Love, adieu! Adieu, Dundee."

I walked straight into the dining room to find a man I did not know, with his muddy and broken boots propped up on the dining table, singing this dirge, and casually drinking our whisky. A lot of our whisky, in fact! He not only finished the whisky on top of the table, but had found the additional bottles stored underneath the cabinet.

The hairs on the back of my neck rose the minute I looked at him. He did not belong here, and he was a threat to me and anyone else in this house. He seemed all too comfortable where he was, seated at the head of the table, and drunk.

Knowing Will, Duncan, Angus, and Jonny to be gone, I frantically thought about what other men might be near the house to help me. In quick order, I realized it was just me and Missus Douglas and a wee lad under the age of ten. We potentially had Reverend Gordon across the street or even Doctor Tyndall, but I was not certain either could fare in a fight. Despite this knowledge, I confronted this intruder immediately with a boldness I feared I could not support for long.

"Excuse me, sir, do I ken ye?" I asked as I could not place his face, and he had the look—and smell—of a man who had been living on the streets for a long time.

His fingernails were black around the edges with dirt and filth and his face showed he had been in the elements of Scottish weather for a long time. He also had the clear traces of recently being beaten. His right eye was a distinct shade of purple and was nearly swollen shut. His lower lip was split in two and it seemed it had trouble healing. He winced with every sip of whisky seeping into the wound, and as he did, I could see the many chipped and broken teeth as his lips exposed them in his pain. Someone had fiercely beaten this man and perhaps more than once. He wore a wool bonnet that obscured half of his head, but I could only assume that it hid other injuries by the bluish-green bruises on his face and what looked like dried blood that had seeped through the cap itself.

His clothes were not distinctive. He sat before me in a wardrobe colored in all variations of the shade of brown, from the fabric to the caked mud and soot on his garments. I tried to muster every ounce of grace I could, as mistress of this house, and asked, "Who let you in without calling me to greet you properly, sir?"

I looked around over my shoulders for the unsaid 'others,' knowing we were alone in this part of the house. My goal was to remain hospitable and respectful and yet I grabbed the whisky bottle from his reach and poured myself a glass as if I were to join him.

"Door was open, weren't it?" he almost hissed, pointing his glass to the back, but never met my eye. He remained focused on his glass and what was in it. He returned to lightly humming his tune and trying to ignore my talking.

"Ye must have come in from the back then."

There was no way that the front door was unlocked. Perhaps Petey was washing the front walk, and he slipped in the close when the child was not looking, and Missus Douglas must have been out of the kitchen to not have been confronted by the man walking through her kitchen to the dining room. I also could not account for the fact that she could not hear him singing.

He looked as if he had been on the streets for a long while and was hungry, but still clearly strong. He was relishing in his access to free drink, which he was consuming at an incredible pace.

I did not see any outward evidence of a weapon, though, as my uncles had taught me, I needed to remember that he might have one concealed. This made him even more of a threat. I had to keep my wits, protect myself, and I had to protect Missus Douglas and Petey. I do not know how he did not see her and could only pray she does not come out of the kitchen if she hears me talking. This man thinks of me alone and for now, it is best that he continues to think that.

"Well, are ye here to meet with my husband, then?" I said, trying to impose the slightest fear that there was indeed a man in this house—or near this house—that could walk in at any moment. I did not say his name, in case this man knew who we were.

"I didna see any *husband*, Missus," he said, peering at me suspiciously through his goblet. "No, come to think of it, I didna see a man at all when I walked straight into the courtyard and back door of this fine house. Just a wee lad clearin' the steps."

He looked around but wasted no time in drinking what was left in his glass before reaching across the table to take the bottle back from me to fill it again.

Trying desperately to keep the conversation light and amiable, I said, "Are ye looking fer work then, sir? I am certain Jonny, our stable master, can tell ye what is available."

My mind scrambled to think about where Will and Jonny would be at this hour. Surely, they were on their way back, but with one or two extra horses in tow and possibly a large cart, it would slow them. I stared at the clock on the mantle, but I could not calculate the time at the moment. I only knew that I had to get this *horrible* man out of my house.

"I am not lookin' fer anythin' but the bottom of this glass and the warm fire, *fer now*," he said as he paused but added with emphasis, still not looking at me.

+++

The intruder had, in fact, read the falseness of my situation correctly and the coldness of his response made the hairs stand up in my neck again. I knew immediately that this man could do me and Missus Douglas harm. And likely intended to do just that. He was just biding his time with plenty of drink.

Undeterred, I said casually, "Well, I am sure my husband will be here shortly. Ye will both need some fresh bread and butter to go with yer drink, will ye not?" I asked in the calmest and most accommodating voice I could muster, "If you will excuse me one moment, please. I will grab both from the kitchen."

I placed a bread plate from the cupboard on the table and then walked slowly toward the kitchen to not cause him concern with a hasty retreat. He remained focused on his drink, and he did not seem alarmed in any way that I left the room. I suspect he knew I was not one to run from the house.

He wanted food. He wanted drink. And if food and drink were what I offered at the moment, this retched man would happily let me go to the kitchen in the hope of more of both.

I rushed into the kitchen just as Missus Douglas walked in from the storehouse. The timing could not be more perfect!

"Missus Douglas, stop what ye are doing now, woman!" Basket in hand, she froze as commanded. With urgency, I whispered to her, grabbing bread and butter as I spoke, *"There is a man in the dining room. He just walked straight into the house from the close. He thinks I am here alone, and that my husband is outside or on the way, and he needs to keep thinking that. I have bought myself some time."*

She remained frozen and just looked at me as I assembled my linen cloth parcel of bread. *"Ye have to go, Missus! Get help. Run like hell to the kirk for Reverend Gordon or the White Hart for Angus. Will should be close. Ye may even see him and Jonny on the street at this hour. Get a man here quickly to help me. My God, even Doctor Tyndall would be welcome!"*

"I dinnae want to leave ye here alone," she pleaded. As much as I knew it was a risk to be truly alone with the stranger, I knew we needed help.

"He could easily kill us both! Ye cannae stay with me. Take Petey with ye and ensure he is safe! He saw the lad on the front steps. Ye have to leave this house, now!"

I placed my hand on hers and gave her a slight smile of reassurance that this was the right action—this would be alright. *I knew it!*

She acknowledged the transfer of urgency between us by kissing my hand and ran out the back door. I looked back toward her with a silent prayer, and said under my breath, *"God, be with ye, Madam! And haste ye back!"*

I returned to the dining room, and said to the intruder, "Here is the fresh bread and butter I promised, sir. The creamy butter is fine! We make it here and it has the faintest hint of sea salt, much like they do in France."

Now clearly rambling unnecessarily, I said, "I have bundled it all up so it will keep on yer travels." I could see he had now found the wine in the room, after drinking all the whisky. "Ye may take the wine with ye, as well. But ye should hurry as we dinnae want any trouble here, *in this house.*"

The man looked again through his glass and said, "Again, I have seen no evidence of men at yer grand house. I walked yer stables, yer courtyard, and right in yer back door," he said as he raised his glass at the end in triumph over this. "I saw nothin' but *a wee lad.* And here I sit, my dirty boots on yer table, drinking yer whisky and wine... talking to... *just... ye.*"

The last part said with a disdain that made me shudder. I was on the verge of putting this man in his place and forcing him out of my house, but I let decorum, and the goal of a peaceful outcome guide me.

I made a mistake.

Just then, he broke his goblet on the edge of the table and came at me with the jagged glass. "Come here, pretty *lass!*"

"Sir, ye mistake yourself! I dinnae want to scream, but if I do, my husband *will kill ye!* Please, take the bread and wine and be on yer way! Again, we want no trouble in this house."

He called my bluff immediately, laughing at my request. *"Scream?"* he said, pulling himself closer to me as he raised the jagged glass to my neck. He shook his head at me and said with his horrible breath on my face, "I cannae believe there is a single soul in this house who would hear ye if ye did, *woman!*"

I saw no way out. I backed into the door to the room. I was stuck between the door and the man. With my back to the door, I tried to reach my right hand behind me to grab the handle, as he stroked my left forearm, wrapped in front of me and protecting myself across my chest.

At that very moment, he kicked the door open with his muddy boot. Everything went dim for a moment after the fall. Pinpoints of light scattered before my eyes. I slowly put my hand to the back of my head and felt the warm blood from the rough landing on the flagstone floor. My ears were ringing from the hard landing. I could not see anything. I could only feel his filthy and clumsy hands pulling at my skirts all while he kept the sharp goblet scraping my face and neck. The jagged edges of the glass cut into my skin every time I struggled against him.

Then, in a last plea for mercy, I whispered, *"Please! Please, sir, dinnae do this! I am with child."*

It was then that I succumbed to the darkness of the stone floor and the depraved act this man did to me with a force I had no ability to fight against. I woke again to the intruder standing above me. He threw the remainder of his goblet against the floor next to me, where it shattered into a million pieces. Some of the glass landed in my hair and on my face. He then stomped his tattered, muddy boot onto my stomach. Before I could catch my breath from the first blow, he kicked me once more as his last act of cruelty. I could barely breathe as he grabbed my face and made me look at him, with eyes blurred with tears and the darkness enveloping me again, for his last words.

"Thank ye for the hospitality, mi' lady. Yer husband is a lucky man."

I heard him unlock the front door, open it, and close it forcibly behind him.

As the darkness claimed me once again, I only know one thing for certain—*I did not scream.*

+++

NINE
The Peace Within The Fire

I do not know how much time passed when I finally heard William shout my name, bringing me out of the darkness on the stone floor. I opened my eyes to look at him as he lifted me up effortlessly. I could not focus my weary eyes on his sweet face, but melted in the comfort of his arms. Even if I could not say the words, I was so happy to be alive and to have him here with me. I wrapped my arms around his neck. I thought to myself that only William could save me from what I just endured. I held onto him as tight as I could.

"Alexandra! Can you hear me? I am here, my love," he said, as he carried me to our bedchamber.

I heard Missus Douglas say, "I will send for Doctor Tyndall straight away, Master MacCrimmon."

"No, Madam! Please send for Missus Malcom immediately!"

"The midwife?" she asked as she turned to him. It was then that she saw the blood on the back of my skirts, and she understood instantly that I took more than a beating in this hall today.

"Och, my Lord God! Straight away, sir!"

Missus Malcom was not much further than the doctor and while I could not say the words, she was my first choice at this moment as well. I knew the bairn was no more. I did not want Doctor Tyndall here. He would be no comfort to me.

At one point, I opened my eyes but only saw the ceiling. I could not bear to look at him, but I knew he was there. He took this as a positive sign when he saw me awake and blinking away tears.

"Aye! Stay with me, my love! We have called for Missus Malcom. She is on her way."

Will undressed me as far as he could bear. He wiped my face gently with a cool, wet cloth and tried to assess my external injuries. I could hear him talking to me, reassuring me. I could feel him stroking my face, picking glass out of my hair, and wiping away the hot tears that would not stop. I could not make them stop.

I shut my eyes again out of weariness and only opened them again to voices in the hall outside the room. He jumped up and said, "I think that is her now!"

Missus Malcom walked into the room with Will, and I heard him whisper about his assessment of my injuries. *"Alexandra has been attacked, Madam. Likely an hour or two ago, based on what Missus Douglas told me when she found us on the road as we returned from Leith. We bolted straight here to find my wife on the floor in the front hall."*

"Aye, sir," Missus Malcom said as she took off her cloak.

145

"I see a huge bump to the back of her head and the skin is broken and bleeding. I think she hit the stone floor, and she hit it hard. There are also cuts to her face and neck. I saw a shattered goblet nearby and that may be the weapon... he used." He continued, his voice softer but still barely taking a breath, *"I believe she has lost the..."*

This loving man could not speak the words aloud for them to be true. I felt for Will at that moment. These are the very words I could not speak myself and ones I did not want to believe. I knew the truth of it, however. We were so happy at the prospect of a new life and an unexpected family of our very own. A family that he and I both knew was no more. I lost the wee bairn on that cold stone floor after the intruder raped and kicked me.

I watched as Will collected himself, choked back his own tears, and focused on the task at hand, saying, *"We have seen that you have what you need by the fire. Please tell us if you need anything else. Missus Douglas and I are at yer service. I have not sent for Doctor Tyndall to be here to assess her other injuries. I felt this was more... important."*

Will breathed in for the first time, having told the midwife everything he could. She grabbed his unsteady hand and said reassuringly, "All will be well, sir. I can handle her wounds on top of the loss. If I determine we need to call Doctor Tyndall, I only ask that ye ensure yer wife and I have had the time we need before bringing him in."

"I believe I ken Alexandra's preference here. I will not call fer the man unless ye ask fer him. Ye have my word."

Midwives in Edinburgh were working with doctors, but there were still gaps in the hierarchy of medical care, especially for women. I cannot say the words to reassure him, but William understood my preference and was correct that I only wanted this woman here with me at this moment—this *horrible* moment.

"Alexandra and I will take care from here, Master MacCrimmon," she said, as she walked him to the door and closed it quietly behind him.

I love William for the devotion and attention he showed me here, but have to admit that I also felt a sense of silent relief that he left this room. I could not bear for him to be here any longer.

Missus Malcom drew the curtains to block any light in the room and to keep the heat of the fire that she stoked. While darkening and warming the room was often the practice of the midwife in childbirth, it was just as important in the ritual of loss. She checked the broth and hot water brewing in the pots hanging over the flames before coming to me.

"Now, my dear, I am going to start."

Missus Malcom walked me through the tending of my head wounds first and did so in the faintest of encouraging and soothing whispers. I remember thinking this woman was an absolute blessing and comfort.

Anytime I opened my eyes, I kept them focused on the ceiling or the fire. I never said a word to her or made a sound. But I know I felt warm tears stream across my cheeks into my ears as she tended to my wounds and then as she tended to the loss. At some point, I quit wiping the tears away. I let them flow freely and just held tightly onto the linens on the bed in fear and discomfort.

+++

"Ye are so strong and brave, my dear Alexandra! I am finished," Missus Malcom said softly as she wiped my sweaty brow and tear-stained cheeks once more with a cool cloth from a washbasin. She also helped me sit up and sip broth for strength.

147

"Ye have a horrible wound on the back of your head. Ye have a large bump there and the skin is broken and bleeding. I will give yer husband and Missus Douglas instruction on how to keep the wound clean and tended for healing. I have left a salve of lemon balm with a hint of wild garlic in it for ye. It smells to high heaven, but it will tend to yer wound."

She helped lift me up a bit and propped me up on my pillows as she continued her assessment. "The cuts on your neck and face are mere scratches. They are nothing. I suggest ye let them heal as they will. Just keep 'em dry."

I looked at her, hoping her words were true, and she said again, "Do ye hear me? They are *nothing*. Ye willna have any permanent scars or disfigurement. If ye need to, the same healing salve for the back of yer head will tend to them, if ye wish. It is just a matter of having the smelly balm right under yer nose." I smiled at her as she tried to keep things light for a moment. But we both knew that there was more.

"He kicked ye, aye?" she asked me. "Perhaps more than once, from the look of it." My eyes met hers and I nodded my head. I do not remember fully as I came in and out after the fall to the floor. But I know he did kick me at least once because I could not breathe for it.

"Ye will have an ugly bruise for a while on yer belly from this, but after tending to everything else for the loss, I dinnae see anything that tells me you couldna have another child. That is a blessing, is it not?"

I closed my eyes in silent agreement, with my tears streaming again. It was a blessing for the future, to be sure. But it was a future I could not fully comprehend while I was consumed with the pain of the future I just lost. When it was taken from me, all the hope and happiness I had left me in an instant. It all remains buried in my skirts and the stone floor in the hall below.

"In fact, the loss coulda been from the fall as much as the kick, lass. We will never ken! Ye will have to tend to yerself, as if yer having yer courses for several days. Yer bleeding may be beyond what would be normal at first, but look at me." I looked again at her on her command as she said, "The minute ye feel intense pain, or the start of a fever and chills, ye send fer me straight away. Do ye understand? Do ye understand me, Alexandra?"

She placed her hands on my face and a sense of urgency that I give her some sign that I understood the instructions she gave me. I just stared at her, and she said again, "This is important! Do ye understand what I have just said to ye? I will tell yer husband to watch for the same."

I nodded in silent agreement to her. I could not form the words of appreciation to Missus Malcom in that moment of her care and comfort, let alone say them aloud. I gulped in air and shut my eyes once more. I told myself that one day, I would acknowledge her kindness to me. Today is not that day. For now, I just need the warmth of the fire to overcome me so that I could finally sleep.

+++

Will, my constant guardian, sat with me for several days. This man talked to me, loved me, and brought me fresh flowers every morning that he refreshed in a porcelain vase on the table beside the bed. Where he found flowers in February was a mystery, but he did.

He brushed my hair after tending to my wounds at night, while telling me a tale about something that had happened in the house or town. He even read from the book of Shakespeare's sonnets at night to comfort me.

He was tender. He was gentle. But as much as I loved him for loving me, I could not look at him in the eyes or speak. I just stared into the fire, letting each flicker of the blazing orange and blue flames silently consume every one of the tears I should be crying.

I remember watching Will tend to the fire one evening and thought to myself, *'Please, my love, just pick me up off of this chair and toss my weary bones into the fire!'* He just kept talking and all I could do was drown him out with my new obsession of watching the dancing flames and listening to the crackles and pops of the burning wood. There is a power within the rhythm of the fire. A rhythm that can easily mesmerize you and lull you into its magical trance. I wanted to be part of the red-hot embers churning underneath, fueling the flickering flames above. Not unlike the place that I miss and love, Cairn's Point, where I could listen to the churning sea below for hours on end.

Will slept at the foot of the bed most nights if he did not fall asleep in front of his own fire in the parlor downstairs. He knew by the lack of acknowledgement from me I did not want his company in our bed. I did not want his touch as a comfort. He understood that rejection well enough from my coldness when he was near me. The wedge between us, driven by my silence and withdrawal, grew more with each day that passed.

One day turned into the next and it became easy to suppress my emotions along with my voice. I think his fear matched my own. Finally, one evening, he grabbed my hands so swiftly it broke the trance I had in the roaring flames of the fire. I looked at him and with tears in his eyes, he said, *"Please speak, Alexandra! Tell me what to do fer ye!"*

I looked at him briefly on his last plea and without an ounce of empathy to his own loss—of the child or me—I looked away again to cast the last of my emotion and tears into the blue and red smoldering embers just beyond his shoulder. He bowed his head in resignation on my shoulder, and then whispered in my ear a line from Shakespeare's *Macbeth*.

> *"Give sorrow words. The grief that does not speak*
> *Whispers the o'er-fraught heart and bids it break."*
>
> **Macbeth,** *Act 4 Scene 3,* William Shakespeare

I had no response that could give him hope, but the words he said produced the first tears that dared to escape the flames. He saw them fall one by one upon my cheeks. He wiped them away with his thumbs and kissed my forehead. He saw in that instant that I still had a heart within me that loved him and could be moved from the fire—even for a moment.

"Please come back to me, my love!" Will pleaded, kissing the top of my head.

I heard the door to our room open and close. I naturally kept my gaze on the fire, as I had nothing left to give my husband and I wanted nothing from him. I wiped my remaining tears from my face and thought of his ask. I hated for him to leave, but I also could not bear for him to stay. Despite his invocation of Master Shakespeare, I do not have the words for him.

I do not have the words for my sorrow.

+++

TEN
From The Darkness Emerged

I sat in the chair before the fire and read Sonnet 23 to myself for the hundredth time. There was something oddly comforting in Master Shakespeare's lament on love, silence, and his inability to write. My own silence and lack of communication consumed me, and I found myself reading this same sonnet multiple times each day.

> *As an unperfect actor on the stage,*
> *Who with his fear is put beside his part,*
> *Or some fierce thing replete with too much rage,*
> *Whose strength's abundance weakens his own heart;*
> *So I, for fear of trust, forget to say*
> *The perfect ceremony of love's rite,*
> *And in mine own love's strength seem to decay,*

O'ercharged with burthen of mine own love's might.

O! let my looks be then the eloquence

And dumb presagers of my speaking breast,

Who plead for love, and look for recompense,

More than that tongue that more hath more express'd.

O! learn to read what silent love hath writ:

To hear with eyes belongs to love's fine wit.

Sonnet 23, William Shakespeare

As I thought more about the Bard's words, I heard the door open and the floor behind me creak. Creaking floorboards were unavoidable in this grand old house, particularly on the second floor. I thought to myself this was just another reason to leave this horrible place! Every board on this floor seems loose, and it is more than I can stand today. I shut my eyes and breathed in resignation, assuming that Will had come back to talk to me for the evening. I looked up from my reading of Lady Margaret's book of sonnets and stared into the flames, bracing for my husband.

He is if nothing else, persistent.

When nothing was said, I turned around and saw the face of wee Petey peeking around the half-opened door, unsure if he should enter this darkened chamber of grief. I waved him forward with my hand over my chair, and he entered with a fresh bouquet in a small jug. The lad also had a small piece of paper with his own drawing of flowers tied around the top of the jug with string. I am certain his mother helped him, but I could tell this gesture was of his own doing. He was *so* proud. I smiled weakly at him in appreciation for his kindness.

He stood before me; his eyes were as mournful as my own. He placed two fingers on my lips and shook his head. I shook my head back at him. *No lad, I am not speaking,* I thought to myself. It had not occurred to me until this very moment that if anyone in MacLeod House understood me and my silence before the fire, it would be wee Petey.

He smiled weakly at me and then put the same two fingers to his own lips and shook his head. Together, in solidarity with our grief and pain, we refused to speak to others. We refused to hear our own voices because they would be laced with such pain that our hearts could not bear it.

When the lad hugged me tight, it was so sweet that I could not give my tears to the fire, and I cradled his head with one hand and tried to wipe my face with the other. I could not keep the tears from falling. My sniffles were the only noise I could muster in this moment.

He pulled back and looked at me with a smile. In some ways, I could feel his silent reassurance that I would be alright. I kissed the lad on the forehead, and he walked back out of the room. I do not know how long it will take us, but I believe we both will be alright.

+++

The door opened again, and I closed my eyes. Expecting Will for certain this time, I sat up in my chair to prepare for him. But the person who came in remained silent behind me once again. I turned back, only to see Duncan standing there. My head immediately dropped to my chest, and I broke down into loud, uncontrollable sobs.

William, still grief-stricken himself, slowly began closing the door so that we could have our moment. I tried to stop the emotion when Petey visited me, but now this was the time I could let go of all the pain I had willingly cast into the fire for so many days. My uncle had been at Glenammon House, and I while I needed him so, I could not find my voice to ask for him. Will must have read my mind, and while I have struggled with him since the intruder was here, I did appreciate him sending for my uncle.

"Och, my dear, lass," said Duncan, who ran to me and knelt at the foot of my chair, rocking me in his fatherly embrace. He let me sob and wail for what seemed like an eternity. Nearly a week's worth of grief, anger, and shame that I could no longer keep confined to the flames flooded my eyes and Duncan's coat.

My breath shuddered as I tried to steady and collect myself. When I could breathe again, I spoke for the first time in days in a whisper, *"I am so glad... yer here. I couldna..."*

"Aye, I ken. Will told me."

"Och, *Will*," I said with a look back at the fire and a wish to disconnect from my husband standing outside the bedchamber door. My unfair indifference over the last few days, now showing openly to another.

Duncan grabbed my shoulders and looked me in the eye. "The man is broken fer ye, Alex. I dinnae have to tell ye this! He feels..."

"Why do ye think I care what Will feels right now?" I asked blankly, interrupting his sentence, and staring again into the flames. I refused to look him in the eye as the last of my tears dried. I could already expect the scolding I was likely to receive. And a scolding I likely deserved.

"Ye dinnae mean that! Come now," his voice raising a bit at my open rejection of my husband.

"We have always been honest with each other, Duncan," I said, testing his resolve slightly. I snarled through my teeth in an anger that

155

Will did not deserve, but I did it anyway. *"I do! I do mean it!* He wants to act like nothing happened... sitting here talking endlessly and telling me stories day and night. It is almost as if he thinks I should just wipe my face, smooth out my skirts, and not think of the fact that I was," I said, almost choking on my breath and tears streaming from my eyes. "that I was *raped...* and beaten so in my home that *I lost our child!* He was supposed to *protect me!* His entire purpose of being here was *to protect me* and *he failed! He failed!"*

I refused to look at Duncan, but instead stared back into the fire and said, "So, tell me again all about how Will *feels!"*

Duncan let me have my moment of anger and rebellion, but said quickly and in his fatherly voice, "Ye have every right to be angry, but yer anger is misplaced, child!"

I am not sure that Duncan has ever called me *'child'* before, but his words and his tone just added to the anger I already felt. He was diminishing me and my feelings, and I would not have it! Pulling back from him immediately, I looked at him with resentment in my eyes and said, "Why are ye here, Duncan? Fer me *or fer Will?"*

"Now, that is my lass! I ken there is a fight in ye yet!"

"I am not fighting ye or anyone else," I said immediately in resignation, slumping back in my chair. If I was truly successful at anything, it was sulking. If Duncan thought I would have matured my way out of that with marriage, it was clear that I had not. It was also the one thing that my father and uncles would never allow me to do for very long.

His voice raised now, "Are ye not?! What do ye call refusing to speak and staring endlessly at the fire? What—or who—do ye sit in protest of,

Alex? Surely not those that love ye! And to answer yer question, I am here fer ye both! I *love* ye both!"

Only Duncan could cut to the heart of my emotional response like this and shame me in the face of my own misguided hostility. As much as I did not want to argue with him, he made me state my case aloud.

In half-sobs I said, "If we were not here in this miserable city, we would be happy... and this horrible thing would have never happened. Will was only sent here to protect me, and *he failed! He left me alone.*"

I was ashamed to hear the words, but there it was. In my admitting my own emotions, it was clear. I blamed Will, my own husband, for what happened to me.

"He left me alone," I kept saying the words, shaking my head and sobbing. *"He was supposed to protect me, but he left me alone. He left me alone!"*

"You ken that is not fair, lass," Duncan said, as he grabbed my chin to face him directly and broke my connection with the flames. "We *all* left ye alone. I swore an oath to yer father years ago and then Laird Graham before ye in his chamber, that I would keep ye safe and protected. *I failed ye* and I will *regret* it for the rest of my days! *I failed ye.* Not Will. But that is only part of your anger and emotion, is it not?"

"Why do you always try to read my mind, Duncan?" I said in exasperation, pulling his hands away from my face. Again, I tried to sink further into the inner folds of the chair I was sitting in. His words were breaking my heart that he felt he had failed me as well, but with my regained voice, I still kept fighting him.

"Why are your responses always in the form of a question, lass?"

"Stop it! Stop it *now!"* I almost smiled but yelled at him with an angry voice through my tears that were suddenly flooding my eyes, "Ye ken, I hate this *infuriating game!"*

"I do! But the *old question game* made ye smile for half a second, lass, so that means my teasing was worth it to see such a beautiful thing," he said as he gently wiped a remnant tear from my cheek.

I immediately grabbed his hand and looked him directly in the eyes and said softly as the tears welled up in my eyes again, *"Duncan..."*

"Aye, lass..."

"I have to ask ye... and *please* tell me the truth."

"I have *always* told ye the truth."

"Did my mother take her own life?"

The shock and pain on his face told me the answer before he said the words. "Aye, she did," he said slowly and removing his hand from mine and backing away from my chair.

I looked back to the fire for strength and to dry my tears before asking him directly, "Was it fer the loss of a bairn?"

"Och, Alexandra!" he said as he looked concerned for me before a small tear fell onto his cheek. "Please, tell me yer not thinking..."

"No. I mean, I thought about it. But... no."

My words lingered in the room as I turned my eyes back to the fire for comfort. Duncan moved forward to me, but stopped just before my chair and knelt down. I did not look at him.

I *could not* look at him.

"We have never spoken of this because I learned as a young lass that any mention of *her* caused ye and father pain." We sat silently for a few moments and then I paused before I said the next, looking at him, "What ye have confirmed also helps me understand why she has come to me twice."

"What do you mean, *she has come to ye*, lass?" he asked, sounding concerned, and rightly so. The thoughts of a departed soul visiting you could be seen as ominous, but it could also be seen as a sign that the person who says they saw such a ghostly specter has become mad. I looked him in the eyes now and said, "She has come to me twice in my dreams or delusions."

I hoped my choice of words told him I was not completely mad. At least, I hoped I was not completely mad. The tears flowed again. I kept my focus on the flames to calm myself. I knew that if I looked at Duncan in his eyes, I would be consumed by my own emotions and unable to speak.

"When I was lying on the floor in the front hall," I said, breathing in a large breath for courage while closing my eyes and thinking about that moment. "I felt the bairn leave me... and I *wanted* to die right there myself."

Through a steady stream of tears that had no end, I continued, "I tell ye uncle, that I wanted every ounce of my being—flesh, bones, and blood—to dissolve into the crevices of the hard stone beneath me so that no one would ever find me, and I would no longer feel the pain and sorrow that I did in that moment."

Duncan looked down as if in prayer and placed his hands on mine, knowing he was unable to speak to the loss I was feeling as a woman in any way. All he could do was show his love and support for me as my loving uncle.

"I *never* thought that I would love a man and have him love me back. Ye have watched me push people away for so long, but I didna ken how much I could love someone else not of my own blood family. I had such hopes for the future we could create together. And then..." I said as I choked back the tears, and haltingly shared the rest, "a *child*... another *love* that I never expected and never thought I wanted. *But I did! I wanted it more than anything!* And I feel as if they were *both* taken from me in an instant by a cruel act of violence."

I could see how the words I said impacted Duncan. My words hurt him, but he knew that I had to tell him the truth of what happened. We sat quietly together for a moment, as he let me finish sobbing openly into my own hands for the second time.

Then when I could speak again, I said, "I lost all sense of time after the intruder left, but at some point, I smelled the strongest scent of roses. Beyond any bouquet ye have ever had underneath yer nose, aye?"

Duncan nodded silently again as I continued, "The scent was *so* strong that it pulled me out of the fog of confusion and pain on that stone floor. Someone above me was gently stroking my hair. It was almost like my own head was no longer on the floor, but cradled in their lap. I couldna see who it was, but their touch and the smell of the roses comforted me. I ken without a doubt, it was *my mother!* I swear to ye, Duncan, while I ken it was not real, I could *feel her* as much as I feel yer hands on mine now!"

I stared intently into his eyes to make my point. He gave me a quick nod of understanding and held on to me. He asked, "And the second time?"

"I was just there," I said, pointing to my bed. I took a pause for a moment to look at the place of the memory I needed to share. "Days later, I woke out of a dead sleep from the strong scent of roses once again. When I looked up, she was sitting beside me. I stared at her for a bit. This was the first time I saw her, not just felt her. She was familiar to me and at the same time, not. Do ye ken that I do not fully remember my own mother's face?"

"Och, lass!"

"I wanted to just stare at her and try to reclaim any memory I had of her. She looked verra much like the face in the painting my father had at Glenammon House, so I *ken* it was her."

He nodded to me but said nothing as I cried again at the thought that I do not really remember my own mother and that only added to my sadness in telling this story.

"She started to talk to me in a whisper, and I could barely hear her. I looked into her eyes and even raised my head to try to watch her mouth to better understand her words. I believe she said, *'ye must live for your love.'* As soon as I called out to her, she was gone. I woke up in a cold sweat and tried to call out to her again to come back to me. Will was sleeping at the foot of the bed and was startled awake by my cry, but I could not tell him what happened because it was even more than I could describe. So I laid back down and sobbed into my pillow. He just held onto me and stroked my hair, trying to comfort me in his own way. I was overcome with the thoughts of what she said and worried that perhaps I had, in fact, gone mad in that moment."

Duncan remained quiet for a moment before saying, "I dinnae ken what I believe myself, lass, but that is Flora, to be sure."

He let go of my hand, stood up, and faced the fire himself. Perhaps he knew the strength of the flame as much as I did. I knew that this conversation would open old wounds, but it was long overdue. As Flora's daughter, I deserved the truth of her story. Flora's story was part of my own and I needed to hear it!

"Yer mother loved roses and any flowers to be honest! Rightly so, perhaps, considering her name," he said, with a smile in remembrance of her. Turning back and leaning in to share with me in my chair, "Ye may not ken this, but she often tended to all the rose bushes on the grounds of Castle Dunmara on her own. She loved them so. She wore roses in her hair whenever she could and even made her own scented rose oil. Every time she passed ye in the Great Hall. *Roses.*"

I smiled at this recollection and that my memories may be of my mother indeed. I believe this is also the first time I had seen him smile when speaking of her. His memories reinforced my own experience.

"You ken that lass had a line of suitors from here to Edinburgh before she chose Alexander?"

"Aye! My father said the same. I didna remember until now, but ye both spoke the very same words," I said as I smiled, thinking about a mother I barely knew and a father I missed dearly. She must have been a beauty! But Duncan paused for a moment to tell me the truth.

"When ye were just six years old, Flora and Alexander did have another child. A boy. James Douglas MacLeod. But the bairn came too soon and was not well. The wee lad died three days after his birth. His name is also at Cairn's Point."

I said softly through new tears, *"His name is not there."*

"It is if ye ken where to look," he said with a loving smile. Before I could ask where the lad's name was, he continued, "The birth itself was difficult on Flora and the loss, harder still. She was melancholy for many weeks after." Looking at me with tears forming in his eyes, he said emphatically, "Yer father did *everything* he could for yer mother. I promise ye that, lass!"

I breathed in and said above my own tears at the thought of her loss, "I ken he did!" I paused and said reassuringly, taking his hands, "I ken ye *both* did."

He did not acknowledge my last line, as he would have been only sixteen years old when she died, but they all grew up together at Castle

162

Dunmara. I know my mother and father were important to my uncle. I am not certain, but I believe Duncan feels some relief in finally sharing these memories with me and I am grateful to hear the truth of the story I had formed in my own imagination as a young girl and even further still this week.

"One afternoon, Alexander came back to the cottage they had on the clan lands to check on her and she was not there. Ye were seated in a corner of the room crying, having been left alone for Christ knows how long! Ye were frightened to be alone and ye were hungry. That is when Alexander told me to take ye to Lady Margaret. I did as he asked and joined him in the search for Flora soon after."

I gripped his hands in mine for the remainder of the story.

"We found her on the beach. We dinnae ken this for certain, but based on the marks on her face and body, we believe she jumped from Cairn's Point into the sea and likely died from the fall on the rocks instantly. I am filled with sorrow, *every day of my life*, to think of what would make her do such a thing! But I pray to God that it was quick, and she didna suffer any more than she already had," he said as his eyes filled with tears. "And I thank the sea fer bringing her back to us."

"I am so sorry, Duncan!" I whispered through my own tears.

"No one ever spoke the words aloud about Flora possibly taking her own life. Father Bruce, the kind soul he is, was willing to allow her to be buried in sacred ground at the chapel, and she was. Alexander wanted her name on top of the headland cliff. A cairn had been there for centuries, but it was a ruin. It was weathered and crumbling from its location due to the sea wind and pure neglect. He had it rebuilt and put the names of his wife and son on it. We often placed stones on it when we went there."

"I didna ken..."

"Like ye, Flora would sit out and stare upon the sea for hours. Next to the rose bushes she tended, that was a place of peace fer her right up until the day she died. I guess in the end it was the *ultimate* peace fer her."

I could only silently cry at his words. It *was* the ultimate place of peace for her. Duncan continued, "Alexander did not want to stand at a grave in a chapel to honor her. He did not want to remember her anywhere else. Cairn's Point was her place, and he only wanted to remember her there. I think it brought us all some comfort in a way that ye naturally found yerself there on yer own."

We sat together silently for a moment in honor of my mother and the sharing of her story. I was always drawn to the cliff, and I could not fully describe why. I was drawn to comfort and peace that were as much my own mother calling to me as the open sea. I also thought about the babe and the fact that my father's will said that I was his *only living child*. I had no idea about sweet James Douglas MacLeod when I heard those words.

I began to speak to him softly, his hands still in mine. "Duncan, ye asked who I am angry with... *and I am angry!*" I repeated it once more with conviction, shaking my head and yelling into the room to make it so, though my voice cracked at the last, "I am *angry!* First, I ken it is unfair, but I am *angry with Will.* He was supposed to protect me."

"Now, lass," Duncan started to defend William at first, but let me continue.

"But that is an easy answer. It is easy to place blame on someone else. But I deserve my own anger. I am so verra angry with *myself!* I am so *angry and ashamed!* I should have walked right out of this house with Missus Douglas and Petey to seek help and protect us all. Instead, I confronted the intruder *alone.* I thought I could talk my way out of danger and send him on his way with wine and bread. I kent better than to confront an unknown man alone. It was a foolish choice *that I will regret for the rest of my life."*

I paused for a moment to think about how much of my silence was my own anger at myself and not just a rejection of Will. I continued, "But I confess, I am also *angry with God!* I am angry every waking minute I have to think about... about what happened... and that I lost our child in such an act of cruelty. *What kind of God allows such a thing?"*

Duncan hung his head low. He had no words for what I was saying and even if he did; he was not going to interrupt me and my tears now. Neither of us were particularly religious, but we were brought up in the church with Father Bruce's teaching and guidance, and this was a rejection of the God of peace and mercy that I had always believed in. For someone who had no words for many days, I could not stop talking.

"I could have taken the violation and beating of my own body... but I cannae... *bear this,*" I said, as my voice was breaking more with the tears that followed. "I ken what my mother was feeling with her own loss. Just as I said about disappearing into the stone floor, ye want to let the pain consume you to the verra end, only so that you can finally be free of it. Part of me wants to do the same. *I have done the same!* Only I have thrown myself into the *fire* instead of the *sea.*"

He looked at me with pain at my words and said, with his eyes shining with his own tears, "Och, my dear lass! Ye dinnae have to bear this loss alone! Ye have me. Ye have a loving husband outside this verra room," he said, stopping as he caught my side glance at the door in my weakening resistance, but still resistance all the same.

Duncan would not allow me to be stubborn and resentful at this moment, and grabbed me by the arm forcefully. "By Christ, woman! That man standing outside that door *loves you deeply* and in a way I have rarely

165

seen in my life! He only wants to ken what he can do to help ye! But ye willna allow it! Ye have just told me that yer beloved mother left you a gift—if ye will listen to her! *Live fer yer love.*"

I said nothing back to his admonishment of how I have treated Will over the last several days, because I deserved every word. He was breaking my already broken heart, and his own tears made me shudder. I still could not find the words to respond the way I should. Sitting before him, frozen in the moment, my tears streamed down my face. I was still consumed by emotions that I cannot fully control.

"Can ye not see it, lass? Dear Flora is telling ye to find the hope and strength ye need and she is asking ye to do what she wished she coulda herself!"

Duncan turned himself back to the fire and continued his calm instruction, "Tell William everything ye just told me. Tell him what ye need him to do—or not do fer that matter. Let him help ye carry this burden. Alex, he is already carrying it in a way ye need to ken yerself. He has also lost a bairn and feels he has lost his wife. He is grieving ye, and he grieves *with* ye. Be honest with yerself and with Will, and I ken that ye can work through this together."

I remembered my uncle said something similar when Will asked why I did not love him... *I would need to be honest with myself first, and then I could be honest with Will.* I flashed a look of recollection his way and he read my mind instantly, as he often does.

"Aye, lass! True happiness starts with being honest with yourself first. You cannae maintain any relationship based on half-truths and unspoken words. And Christ above, Alexandra MacLeod, ye need to learn how to let the people who love ye *actually love ye.*"

I smiled at him and sighed, shifted myself upright in the chair, resigned to what must happen next. Duncan has always known how to tell me what I should hear, even if it is not what I want to. I wiped my face clear of tears with my hands and sniffled, "Aye, I do."

"Why do ye never have a handkerchief?" he asked as he handed me one of his.

"I dinnae ken," I said with a slight smile through my tears. I dried my face and wiped my nose with his always clean embroidered cloth and said, "Send Will in then, aye?"

Duncan kissed my forehead and stroked my hair. "For ye, my dear, anything! I believe the lad is waiting just outside."

I tried to wipe my face with Duncan's handkerchief and to further collect myself to be presentable to my husband as Duncan walked forward to the door. The cool air rushed into the room the minute the door was opened. It hit me and the fire. Duncan found William in a chair in the hall just opposite the room. I have no idea how long the poor man has been sitting there, as it feels as if we have been in this bedchamber for hours. I could barely hear them, but watched their exchange intently over the back of my chair.

"How is she, sir?" Will asked, standing up immediately on Duncan's exit from the room.

Grabbing the whisky glass out of Will's hand, he said, with a weary voice from our long and emotional conversation, "She is talking and waiting for ye. Go to yer wife, lad."

"Och, thank Christ!" Will said as he moved for the open door. He turned back, paused, and said in appreciation, "And thank ye, Duncan."

"Dinnae thank me yet! I didna say this was going to be an easy conversation."

He saw me looking at him through the open door over Will's shoulder and raised the whisky glass he just commandeered and winked at me. I nodded back in appreciation as Will shut the door between us.

ELEVEN
Resilience And Retribution

Will stood with his back to the door and remained there, holding tight to the handle behind him as I stood up to stoke the dwindling fire. The room was already warm enough, but I knew that if I was going to talk honestly with my husband, I needed to rely on the power of the flames once again. I needed my beacon of light and warmth to focus on when I needed to.

When I was done, I turned back to retrieve the poor man from the door. He had been watching me with such intensity that his hands could not let go of the handle.

"Are you beholden to the door, then?" I asked as I released each of his fingers and guided him by the hand to a chair in front of the now roaring fire.

He spoke finally and almost apologetically as he sat down, "I should have tended the fire for ye."

I immediately sat on his lap and placed my head on his shoulder. He seemed a little tentative at this approach as I have made a such a concerted effort to avoid any physical contact or conversation with him for nearly a week. He absolutely has a right to be uncertain of my attempt at being close when I have done nothing but reject him for days.

We sat silently for a moment in front of the fire. Will is such an imposing figure that it is quite natural to shrink in his presence and to allow his arms to swallow you up and surround you in his warm embrace. But, after such a disconnect, I could tell that he was uncertain what to do with me. I nestled in his arms and said into his chest, "There. It is warmer here than by the door, no?"

"'Tis," he sighed, burying his face in my hair, and kissing the top of my head over and over. His touch showing me how relieved he was from the pain and worry he had been feeling for days. I felt this man melt beneath me.

"I was right to send for Duncan then?"

"Aye, and I thank ye. I *needed* Duncan and could not ask it of ye. We had an emotional conversation that I will share. Fer now, I just want to sit here a bit."

Despite the physical trauma and loss, I wanted Will more than anything in my life. More than I did on our wedding night. He makes my skin hot and my mind race. I grew to know this man not just as my friend, but now as my husband, and I know that he loves every ounce of my being. I love him just the same. Opening my heart and living for my love will have to be something that I will keep working on, but I do genuinely love the man holding me in his arms.

As much as I wanted to tell Will everything that happened on that horrible day and all that I told Duncan, I really just wanted his strong arms to comfort me and a husband's physical connection so that I could regain the passion and joy I had once. The joy I had before the intruder.

+++

"Och Will," I sighed the words as the tears began to flow again.

"Please dinnae cry. I cannae bear it. I shoulda been here to protect ye and I will never forgive myself that I wasna," he said as he wrapped his arms around me tighter.

I wrapped my arms around his neck, kissed his cheek, and whispered in his ear, *"It wasna our fault."* I was trying to convince myself as much as him. "Will, I love ye with all of my heart, but we have some work to do for us to go forward and regain what we had."

"Aye, I suppose we do."

"That starts with everything that happened," I said, taking his hand in mine. I told Will everything I told Duncan. I held his hand the entire time, and he held mine. You know when you are connected and when you are not. This man, the man that I love, was with me for every word. He felt my pain, and he shared it. He cried with me, and he comforted me.

I stood up to move to the fire, mesmerized even more by the relief of bearing my heart to Will.

Live for your love.

My own mother's words were still ringing in my ears, and reminding me, along with Duncan, to challenge my own independent nature and continue to open my heart more to my husband. That starts with telling him the truth.

I told him of my mother, the loss of my wee brother, James Douglas MacLeod, and Flora ending her own life off of Cairn's Point. I told him of the grief the family endured after her tragic loss and the words never spoken about it, words I never heard until this day. I shared that she came to me twice and her words to me were to *live for my love.*

I tried to help him understand my feeble attempt to bury the pain and anger I felt in my silence and the flames of the fire each day since the intruder came to this house. He seemed to understand my method of coping and shutting off all emotion and that it was less about rejecting him and more about what I needed in the moment to control of my own emotions.

Through my tears, I told him honestly what the violation of my body, the beating, and the loss of our child meant to me and how I wanted to die on the stone floor immediately in the aftermath. He listened to me intently and naturally became visibly concerned with my descriptions and moved toward me when I openly shared the truth of contemplating my own death. I believe this was the hardest part of the recollection for him to hear.

"I am so broken for ye, my love," he said as he grabbed my hands and kissed each of them as the tears flowed from his eyes. "But, if ye hear nothing else from me this night... I couldna survive this life without ye here with me."

"I ken, and as much as I tried to push ye away, I couldna survive *without ye.*"

Will stood and moved next to the mantle for a moment and said calmly, but firmly, "When ye are ready, Alex, ye will tell me everything ye can remember of this intruder. I ken it will be difficult for ye, but I willna rest until *I kill him with my own hands.*"

172

"Och Will," I said, turning him to look intently into his eyes, and touching his cheek. I could see both the tremendous pain and love that made him say such a thing. He has fought the persona of being a brute for so long, but I believe that for the sake of my honor and for our shared loss, he would kill the intruder without remorse. "Revenge and retribution are not what I need from ye, as it will not truly heal our broken hearts. I just need yer love and I just need time to heal."

He handed me a small blade, with a silver handle that looked like interlaced hearts sheathed in ornate leather, and said, "This is a *sgian-dubh*. I want ye to keep it on ye at all times in yer skirts or yer bodice—somewhere ye can get to it. If ye ever have to protect yerself, and I pray ye never will again, ye will have it."

"Laird Graham has one, and Duncan does as well. I never thought I would need my own."

"Aye, and I do as well," Will said, showing me his own blade hidden in his coat. "I never thought about ye having one and I wish ye didna have to, but ye have to be able to protect yerself if we are not with ye, my love. Ye must keep it hidden."

"I understand."

I also wish that I did not have to carry a blade of my own, but I welcomed it just the same. I felt a renewed sense of power made of steel and sheathed in leather.

+++

I placed both of my hands on his cheeks and brought him down to my mouth. I was not ready to lay with him. I still felt wounded and scared. I was also still healing. I was ready to have him return to our room and no longer have to sleep at the foot of the bed or elsewhere. I wanted his arms around me for the rest of my days.

"Come," I said, standing and reaching out my hands to him. "It is time fer bed."

We got ready for bed silently. He reached out to touch my belly as I changed my shift. The blue and green bruises were healing but were still a visible and painful reminder of the beating I took that day and the loss that came as a result. The last time he touched me, we celebrated the new life that we created together. The ache of the memory pained me for a moment, and I know that he was still afraid for me. I always felt safe in Will's arms, and for a moment, I let go of all the painful thoughts and emotions that have consumed me.

Like the fire has for days, I let his touch erase my heartache and dull my senses. I was surrounded by love and would now reclaim the promise of our future together. All was not lost. I am alive and surrounded by love. I thought of Master Garrick's words and also felt surrounded by hope. I chose hope today.

"For the first time since that horrible day with the intruder, I feel like my heart and my mind match each other again."

"Och, my love," Will said, kissing the back of my head and held me a little tighter in his embrace, with one arm tightly around my shoulders and his other hand in my hair. After a week of not talking, I found I had more to say. I broke free of his arms, sat up, and turned around to face him.

"Will," I said as I looked into his eyes and spoke freely, "I am so *ashamed*! I tried to place blame fer what happened. First, on ye fer leaving me here alone."

He hung his head low, feeling his own shame and regret for leaving me alone and perhaps even remembering the state in which he found me.

"Then, I blamed myself fer not leaving the house immediately and confronting the intruder, because of my own careless thinking. And then, I blamed God Himself fer taking the child in a such a cruel manner," I said as I lowered my eyes at the reflection of the last several days and my own feelings of shame and misplaced blame. Will listened quietly as I continued to find the words that had been lost for too long.

Looking up at him with tears in my eyes, I said, "But it *isna* our fault. It *isna* God's fault. *None of it!* It is the intruder's fault and nothing more." He nodded in agreement, unsure of what to say. I paused with him for a moment and said, as I looked into his eyes, "I do have a request."

"Aye! Anything for ye, my love."

"I want ye to take me *home*. We started to plan our return to Skye many times, but we dinnae belong here in Edinburgh." I looked around the room and the thoughts of the memory within this house of my dear father and now the intruder was more than I could bear. The tears flowed again as my confession continued. "I admit that I became enamored with a grand life in the city. The father I did not really ken revealing himself to me every day. I have had a grand house and money in my pocket. I have been pretending to be something *I am not* here, and I need to put my focus and effort into our own lands, our own family, back on Skye. We have occupied ourselves here fer too long, and I am done. *Please,* take me home!"

Before I could continue, Will reached out to me, and stroked my forearm wrapped across my chest, tenderly in support and agreement. That simple moment of honest connection hit me as if I were struck by lightning!

175

Every nerve, from the top of my head to the bottom of my feet, was set on fire!

Every hair on my body stood on end! Before my very eyes were flashes of memories from the floor below. I could not even see Will sitting before me anymore. Just the images and reminders of that dreadful afternoon in the front hall.

I immediately jumped off the bed, standing before him shivering in my shift because of the cold air of the room and the shock of what that one innocent touch from my husband brought back to me.

"Christ, Alexandra! What is it? What did I do?" William sat up and yelled to me to take me out of the recollections in my own mind and bring me back to the present. "Did I hurt you, lass? *Alexandra! Can ye hear me?*"

I looked at him and could hear him, but could not truly see him. I could not speak, as my mind raced before my mouth could form a single word. Finally, I said, "We have to talk to Duncan... *and now*!"

I ran out of the door immediately with Will trying to catch up to me as he put on his breeches under his shirt, "I dinnae ken what just happened! Do ye *hear* me, my love?"

I ignored his questions and leaned over the banister to see if there was a light downstairs. I yelled for my uncle, "*Duncan!* Where are ye, Duncan?!"

"*Alex*, he is likely in his bedchamber at this late hour," Will started to say in an attempt to calm and quiet me when Duncan yelled to us from below.

"What is it, lass?" Duncan said, looking up with his whisky glass in hand.

Will finished the sentence he started with a smirk, "... or not!"

"Come with me!" I said, as I grabbed Will's hand and moved to the stairs. "Pour us a dram, will ye?" I yelled ahead to my uncle over the banister as we ran down the stairs together.

I had not been out of my room for nearly a week and slowed suddenly as I descended the last step into the front hall. Will, trying to keep pace with me, placed his hand gently on my back to try to keep me moving forward, knowing that the scenes of what happened on the flagstone floor might be before my eyes again. *And they were.*

It is all coming back to me *at once!* We made it to the parlor and Duncan handed us our whisky glasses, as requested. He looked at me and then Will for a sign of what was happening with such urgency at this late hour. Out of breath from the run downstairs, I said, "Ye both should sit."

I gulped most of my glass and stood before two men who by the looks of them, clearly thought me raving mad. I stood, shivering from both my emotional energy and the cold, inappropriately standing in my thin shift. I was barely able to set down my glass on the mantle due to my shaking hands before I grabbed a wool blanket off of the back of Duncan's chair and wrapped it around my shoulders. Now modestly covered, I turned back to the men looking up at me, wide-eyed with anticipation of my words to help clarify this late-night family meeting and my sense of urgency.

"What has ye so frantic, lass?" Duncan asked while looking side-ways at Will for a clue. Will raised his eyebrows and shook his head slightly as he sipped his glass, showing Duncan that he was uncertain himself about what brought us here in such a rush. "It is late."

"Will just retrieved a memory... of... that afternoon... when the intruder was here," I said almost excitedly, but then the realization of the pain came flooding back.

I left Will and Duncan to look at each other, again still confused but also a little concerned about my mental state. I could feel the conflict in my own emotions, but did not know how to temper my speech and voice. I was energized with the recollections before me, and my mind was racing faster than my mouth.

"Go on," said Duncan from the top of his glass.

"Will innocently stroked my forearm, like this" I demonstrated the motion myself on my own arm holding the blanket wrapped across my chest.

Will continued the story for me, "And she shot out of bed like she had just been branded with a hot iron!"

"Ye have that kind of effect on her, do ye?" Duncan said, laughing and drinking what had to be the latest of many glasses of whisky this evening. Will nodded his head slightly in agreement with my uncle.

"Ye two, let me ken when yer done, and I will finish," I said as I turned back for my own whisky glass atop the mantle and took it to fill again in the back of the room.

Still chuckling at his own joke and Duncan finally said, "Sorry! A wee joke." Looking at Will for support where there was none to be had, and tried to place the blame. "He set me up, fer it, Alex!"

I waited, surely with a stern face of disapproval, and Will finally said apologetically, "Please go on, my love!"

I shook my head, clearing the cobwebs from the memory as I said, "Do ye not understand? The intruder did the *exact same thing* to me! The intruder stroked my forearm just before he kicked the door down and I fell onto the stone floor!"

I was smiling maniacally at this memory and the energy the recollection was giving me at the moment. But soon realized that the two men before me were still confused and rightly concerned for the woman who was consumed with silence just a day before and now sharing such a memory of a horrible day with a smile. I realized that I was two steps ahead of them and would have to explain more.

Will said, looking at Duncan and then me as he sat in the chair next to my uncle. "I am so sorry to bring up these horrible memories with my touch. We are trying to follow ye."

"No, Will!" I said as I gripped the sides of my head to help slow down my words and share with them what I needed to. "Let me explain. *Let me explain!* There is only one other person who has ever touched me that way."

Now they both were intrigued and turned to me.

"Only one other *man* was so bold to touch me that way and it was not tender, as you were, Will. It was an unwanted touch. It was a *threat.*"

They both looked up at me with concern.

"Allan Calder!" I said as I held my hands wide, with the dramatic revelation of such news to the room much like my friend Grant would in his storytelling.

Will stood up immediately, enraged, and nearly spitting the name, *"Calder?!"*

Duncan leaned back in his chair, dumbfounded. I continued, looking into the fire again for strength. "I kept looking for something familiar about the intruder, but I could not place him. The man's face was swollen and covered by many cuts and bruises from a serious beating. He

179

had a rough beard. He was so filthy and weathered. He...," I said, looking back at them again for reassurance and starting to cry at the confession. "He was unrecognizable as the man with the blackened tar hair and pocked corpse we met at Dunmara. I also had no hints from his voice or speech. Some of his teeth were broken or missing from whatever injury befell his face. But now I *ken* it was *him*!"

Tears flowed from my eyes, and my audience of two sat in stunned silence. We were all quiet for a moment before I could speak again, and I knew that I had to help them understand.

"Och, Alex," Will said, touching my arm, "please dinnae cry."

"Calder made the same move at Father's office," I continued, wiping the tears from my face with my own hands. "Right after he showed me the marriage contract, and I told him the practice was no more. I did not realize it at the moment in the front hall, because I crashed to the floor so hard that I lost my wits for a bit. And then..." I stopped, intentionally not finishing the story we all knew, and placed my hands on the back of my sore head that was still healing.

"My love, the night we all met at the White Hart Inn, I specifically asked ye if Calder touched you or threatened you in any way. Ye didna tell us this part of the story! Why?"

"Yer right, Will. Ye did ask. I didna share that he touched me because I brushed it off as meaningless in the moment. A man's flirtation of no consequence. I only told ye of his verbal threat to me because... I didna see his being forward with me physically as anything more than what every woman has to deal with day in and day out. I see now that his physical actions were *also* a threat to me."

"Did ye not? *Christ above*, Alexandra! The man *touched* ye!"

"Alright, ye two!" said Duncan, trying to calm Will's anger and frustration that he had not dealt with Calder at that time—perhaps saving us all from this heartbreak. "What do we intend to do with this information?"

We all sat quietly for a moment, and then I stood up in front of my enraged husband. "Will, I told ye—just moments ago—that I didna need retribution. *I was wrong!*"

Looking them both in the eyes and seething with all the anger, pain, and resentment I felt, I said, "This wasna a random attack that unfortunately happens to too many women. This was *intentional!* This was *personal!* He said he would bring his *reckoning* upon me, and I suppose he did. But we will bring our own *reckoning* upon the head of Allan Calder!"

The room went cold and quiet, along with a small piece of my heart.

+++

The men before me sat quietly and still looked stunned.

I admit that I too did not know what to make of my own words. Duncan spoke first, apprehensively, looking between me and Will, "What ... do ye mean by that, lass?"

I shook my head to return to some sense of rationality. "I should be clear. I am not asking anyone to do anything illegal or immoral here."

Duncan leaned back in his chair again, clearly relieved. "I should hope not!"

"Did ye think I was asking ye both to commit murder on the streets of Edinburgh?"

Duncan nodded his head slightly as if that were in fact what I had done, as Will spoke to us both over his shoulder at the fire, "Does Calder deserve anything less?"

181

I grabbed the bottle again and started refilling our glasses with the last remnants of whisky. Duncan spoke to Will directly, "Come now, man! That isna who ye are."

Will put his head down in silent agreement with the assessment of his character, but I could tell my husband was contemplating his own boundaries on the concept of honor and justice when it comes to defending his wife and family. He defended my honor once before and committed to do so when he took his assignment from Laird Graham to deliver me to and from Edinburgh. He committed again for the remainder of his days on the day we were wed. Marriage has been good for him, and the prospect of a child was a blessing. I could imagine that the thought of Calder being the reason for him not having the family he desired was heartbreaking to him. I loved him all the more for his emotional response.

I spoke again, "We *will*, however, find this man, and set the full force of the *law* upon him. He should die at the end of the rope on Grassmarket or at least spend the rest of his life in a prison cell fer his crimes."

"Let us calm ourselves for a moment. A touch is not proof it was Calder. I believe ye and everything ye are saying, Alex. *I do!* But there is no proof he is the one that attacked ye," Will said, closing his eyes and in repulsion of his final words, "*and raped ye.*"

"And killed an *unborn* child," I added to the litany of charges against the vile shadow of Allan Calder, Esquire. Realizing that just as I said this, my own words and tone did not match my guidance of restraint. Will was correct. There was no proof that the intruder was Alan Calder.

I looked at Will and shook the last words from my head while a little flustered by this debate. "Then we will get him to confess! If I ken this man, he is quite proud of himself. Proud of what he did. I bet he has already told someone about his act of revenge."

"If we can even find Calder," Duncan interjected now, "and I dinna ken how we would. Until he arrived at Alexander's office, we couldna find the man in the city. And why would we not just let the man rot in the streets, as he has for many a month now? Ye said he was beaten, and weatherworn. The man has lost everything in his life, he has no income, no reputation, and he is not the type to survive living rough for long."

Now I was enraged. Not at my husband or my uncle, but at the situation. There is no way they could understand my feelings, not because they did not have love for me or have feelings of their own in the loss, but because they have never been where I am at this very moment—as a woman. A woman violated on the stone floor of her own home. A woman who lost a child in the process of cruel revenge. That is what it was—*revenge*!

I had to gulp the last of my glass for courage to say the rest. I placed the glass on the mantle, walked to Duncan, and took his hand, closed my eyes for a moment, and said softly with the conviction not just borne out of anger and rage, but the protection of my name and our clan.

"Because uncle, I willna go to my grave thinking that *this man*, this pathetic excuse of a man, beat and raped me in my father's own house. That *this man* took my child out of jealousy and spite. That *this man* enacted his own version of revenge on our family for his lot in life. Allan Calder will get what he deserves, and I will not rest until I see that *this man* gets that justice with my own eyes!"

Duncan and Will could not say anything to this emphatic petition for personal and righteous justice. I looked at them again and said, "Allan Calder betrayed my father the minute he put his hands on me and he tried to ruin my life and that of my family out of his own thwarted ambitions and jealousy. Ye warned me yerself about men with thwarted ambitions, uncle. *This man* will not succeed in his quest as long as I am alive."

Duncan was correct in his thinking; we could let the man rot on the streets of Edinburgh. But I could not go home to Skye without trying to regain the peace I need—the peace my family needs. There was a part of me that worried that Will or Duncan might kill Calder at first sight, and I have to admit I worried I might kill the man if confronted with him again myself. William just gave me a *sgian-dubh*—a black knife—to keep in my skirts should I ever find myself in need of protecting myself again.

So, I said this aloud for all of us, "We will find Allan Calder and we will honor my father and the name of our clan here. We are bringing justice to him but within the laws of Scotland. Do we understand each other?"

I raised my glass before me to them both. They met my glass and nodded in agreement and said, "Aye!" We all finished our glasses and went to bed in silence. The sun will be up in just a few short hours.

Before falling asleep, Will pulled me close and kissed the back of my head as he said, "I love ye. It has been a long and emotional day and we will talk more tomorrow. Sleep well, my love."

I think I said I loved him back, but I may have fallen asleep in the comfort of his arms before the words could leave my mouth.

TWELVE
When All Seems Lost

MacLeod House
Canongate, Edinburgh, Scotland
March 1767

The peace and justice we were looking for eluded us despite our extensive searches for Allan Calder on the streets of Edinburgh. At supper one night, I spoke to the men and said, "It is time for us to go home. I have said it many times over the last few months and ye let me stay here to try to find some justice, but I *want to go home.*"

The memories in this house linger and it is hard for my heart to find peace reliving the trauma every time I cross the stone floor of the front hall. I am exhausted looking in the face of every man on the streets or in the taverns of Edinburgh for signs of Calder. I am constantly filled with both anticipation and fear that *today will be the day* we find him and then going to bed at night devastated that it was not to be. Will gave me a faint smile of understanding and took my hand in his.

Our search was over.

Duncan spoke and agreed, "It is time. It will be a cold journey but, we have been here too long as it is."

"Too right, sir, and I worry about being away from Laird Graham any longer. He assures me in his letters that he is well. But I think he doesna want to worry me... with all that has happened here."

I could not speak of the intruder to Laird Graham, but I know that Duncan told him. His last letters to me have been so supportive and reassuring. He speaks to me gently as a father and guardian. He continues to message me with sonnets or Bible verses about finding strength and comfort in those we love and in the Lord's blessing. He *knows* what happened here.

When I have moments of uncertainty or fear, I twist the sgian-dubh slowly inside the pocket of my skirt. I bring it out to look at it during the day, reminding myself that I have my own protection if needed again. It is an unfortunate but necessary comfort. I could feel the sadness return, with tears beginning to form in my eyes. Will squeezed my hand in his as a tear fell on my cheek.

"Och, lass," Angus said sweetly to me from the other side of the table.

I am so fortunate to have these wonderful men in my life. They wanted to bring Calder to justice as much as I did, and they worry for me with the love and affection that runs deep within our family.

I looked at Angus and said directly to our advance man, "I ken it is close, but I would like to stop at Prestonfield House on our way back to

186

Skye. I would verra much like to talk to Master Garrick again before we leave this side of the country."

These men do not know what he and I discussed on our last visit. He was important in our travels here and I want to say goodbye to him as my friend. I suspect Will to ask me more about it, but this is what I want... what I need.

"Aye, m'lady! We may need a short trip at first to see 'ow we fare wi' the cart in any case."

"If ye will excuse me," I said, leaving my half-eaten dinner behind.

Duncan grabbed my arm as I passed him and said, looking up at me, "We will plan to leave in two days' time. Leave it to me and the lads."

I just nodded to him as I was afraid to speak. I ran up the stairs, fell onto my bed, and sobbed. I could try to tell myself that the intruder suffered the same fate as Mary and Wesley living rough on the city streets. That he was rotting in a pauper's grave with no one to know he was there and never to be heard from again. But not knowing the truth of it allows the specter of Allan Calder to haunt me every day from the shadows.

I do not know how I can stop being afraid of seeing him again, but perhaps leaving Edinburgh is the first step.

+++

Before our meeting with Master Forbes, I asked Duncan and Will to walk across the street with me to Canongate Kirk. We replaced the bouquet of flowers on Father's grave one last time and said goodbye. It was easier somehow knowing that he was at peace, and we were returning home to try to reclaim our own.

"Aye lad, where is Reverend Gordon?" I asked a young boy lighting candles in the sanctuary.

"He is just there, missus, in that room behind the door, writing his Sunday sermon."

"I thank ye, lad," I said, as William gave the boy a shiny new penny.

"Och, thank ye, sir," the boy said, staring at his newly acquired coin.

"Reverend Gordon," I said as I knocked and pushed forward the half-opened door to his chamber.

"Aye, och my! Lady MacLeod, this is a surprise," he said, as he stood up from his desk. His hair looked a little disheveled, and this was the first time I had seen him in glasses. I could not imagine having to write a new sermon every week. It had to be stressful, and the man's appearance showed me it was indeed a stressful task.

"Sir, our time in the city is at an end. We leave for Skye tomorrow."

He came around his desk and offered his blessing for a safe journey and thanked us for being so supportive of the kirk and its mission as he shook the hands of the men before him.

"Aye, sir, that is why I am here. I have received my inheritance and I would like to make this gift to the kirk," I said as I handed over a signed bank note for £100.

The look on his face made it all the more worth it as he said in shock, "Lady MacLeod, this is *most* generous of ye. *Most generous!*"

"Sir, I ask that ye use this *only* for the women and children's program and nothing else. It can be used for clothes, food, lodgings, or any work or education programs to help them get off the streets. But, unlike my father, I am not providing this for building repairs or gardens at the kirk."

"Understood, understood," he said to me, staring down at the banknote in his hand and then scrambling to another side of his desk. "Look here, we will record your gift in the ledger for the women's and children's program. Ye can see it is not the kirk's general register," he said, tapping another leather-bound ledger on his desk.

"Aye, I can see that, sir."

Looking over at the ledger even upside down, I could see that this was the program ledger and that this gift followed my own father's bequest from his will but also more than triples the program's current balance in an instant.

Reverend Gordon wrote my name and the gift amount and then asked, "Would you like to make this gift in honor or in memory of anyone?"

"In memory, if I may," I said calmly, but with tears starting to form.

"The name?"

"In memory of Alexander MacLeod *and...*" I said as I held my head high, and held back my tears behind my eyes through sheer will, "Mary MacAskill, sir."

I could feel Duncan and William looking at each other and then me, but neither man said anything. Once the names were recorded, I smiled at Reverend Gordon and shook his hand before leaving Canongate Kirk for the last time.

We all rode together in silence in the carriage for our last meeting with Master Forbes. I could tell that Duncan and Will wanted to say something to me about what they just witnessed but did not. Will just held my hand as we both looked out of the carriage windows. I fought the tears I had about what just happened and said a silent prayer for the women and children that may be helped in the future by Canongate Kirk.

Our duties today are to give Master Forbes permission to sell both of the houses. We have no need of them and cleared all of Father's belongings we wish to take back to Skye. Duncan also decided to sell a portion of his majority stake in the Glenammon Brewery, upon the agreement to build another one on Skye under his majority ownership.

I was disappointed not to see Elizabeth greet us at the door, as this might be my last chance to say goodbye to her, but Master Forbes welcomed us all with a broad smile.

"Master Forbes," I said, greeting him with my hand outstretched. "It is time for us to return to Skye and we are sad to leave, but ready to enlist yer help so that we can do so."

"I will be sad to see you all leave Edinburgh, but we will always be here to support you and Clan MacLeod," he said as he shook my hand and that of Will and Duncan and then ushered us into his office.

I wondered if he knew what happened, but he treated me the same as in our last meeting instead of as if I were about to crumble before him. I tried to muster up all the strength I had to conduct our business this day. I told myself these essential tasks were just getting us one step closer to home. We granted Master Forbes the power to represent me in the sale of both houses with the stipulations of the buyer retaining the estate staff at each house, as father detailed in his will.

"Sir, we brought ye the inventories for both houses and ye can see we have left nearly everything in them," I said, handing over the files. "We marked the items we are transporting back to Skye. Mostly paintings, bespoke dining porcelain and glassware that I wish to keep, treasured books, and some of father's personal items."

"I must say, this is an excellent accounting of each property. If I am fair to my friend, I may have to look closer to see if Alexander's estimate on the property valuations is accurate for each house. In my quick glance at this, I think Glenammon may be undervalued."

"Sir, that copper bath at MacLeod House on Canongate alone has to be worth something! If I could convince my uncle to put it on the cart to Skye, I would! It is a remarkable thing!"

Now, with the bank account in my own name, Master Forbes will continue to monitor staff payments on my behalf until the houses are sold. Due to the size of my account, I also have my own personal bank representative who will also keep me informed on the balance and I can message if I need money.

Master Forbes retains rights as my attorney, watching payments to staff, but cannot make any changes to the account without my signature. And until I am twenty-one, we cannot make any major changes without Duncan's signature, as well. The note I had today for Canongate Kirk and the money I have in my pocket were because Duncan approved the sums. He just did not know the full reason for my asks.

Master Forbes also had the contracts negotiated with Master Drummond, selling a portion of Duncan's majority stake in the brewery, and then establishing the newly expanded Glenammon Brewery—and eventual distillery—to be built on Skye. Duncan will retain a slim majority stake of fifty-one percent in that venture and proceeds will now go into his own account at the bank instead of mine.

"Master Forbes, ye were a powerful negotiator on this transaction," Duncan said, as he took the quill and signed all the contracts. I followed in signing as a witness.

"Aye," he said with a wink, "It is not my place to say, but I do not think Master Drummond was well represented on this contract. Your own account at the bank, Duncan, will be credited with the total sale of nine percent within a week. The amount of £2,000 is to be used as investment for the building of the operations on Skye. Your share of earnings from the brewery operations here will be placed in yer account directly, and ye will receive accounting for this distribution each month."

"Aye, I have seen Alexander's files and ken what to expect, even with this adjustment."

Master Forbes continued, "As of this day, Alexandra will no longer receive any income or payments associated with Glenammon Brewing. And I tell you, I cannot wait to hear more about the distillery."

"Aye! I was hoping that the Lady MacLeod might like to invest in my new venture," Duncan said, looking at me.

We all laughed, and I said, tapping him on the arm, "Let us see what ye build first, uncle!"

"I can confirm that all individual distributions against your father's will were completed since we last spoke, and I leave you an accounting of all payments here in your portfolio, along with all copies of the documents we just discussed and signed."

"Duncan, I am providing ye the final distributions for your sister-in-law, Sarah, and her son Robert upon your return to Skye."

"Aye, sir, I can complete that final task fer ye."

He placed the documents and bank notes in the portfolio, and we were done.

"Alexandra, I will keep ye informed on the sale of the houses, and will tell you that I have given members of the Advocate Society the first right of refusal before making them available broadly. If one of them does not buy, I just might."

I smiled and said, leaning in myself, "That makes me verra happy, and I expect ye will pay a handsome sum, sir!"

"Aye, and your inventories have made that clear!"

We got up to leave, and I went to the side of the desk and said as I took his hand, "Master Forbes... Campbell, yer so good at what ye do and I can see why my father trusted ye with his most important business and personal affairs. Ye have cared for me and my family the entire time we have been here in Edinburgh, and I thank ye. Ye have also become a most welcome friend and I look forward to working with ye more, as ye continue to represent me, my uncle, and Clan MacLeod."

"It is indeed my honor," he said, shaking my hand first, and then kissed me on each cheek. "I am at your service always, Lady MacLeod. Your father knew what an exceptional leader you would be, and from our very first meeting, I have seen proof of that myself."

He shook hands with Duncan and Will and escorted us all to the door. Just then, Elizabeth walked into the room.

"Elizabeth, I am so glad to see ye," I said, almost running to her and taking her hands in mine before we hugged each other tight. I was so thankful that I could say goodbye to her. "We leave tomorrow for Skye and... I just want to say thank ye fer helping my father, fer helping me, and fer being a most welcome friend while we have been here in Edinburgh."

I wish I could have talked to her about what has transpired over the last several weeks, but I suspect she already knows if for no other reason than a woman's intuition. I know she can see the pain behind my eyes. At least, I wanted to believe she could.

193

"Och, Alexandra," she said, holding my hands in hers, "I can say the same, but it has been my absolute pleasure!" And then, laughing through her own tears said, "I will write to you!"

"Please do! Please do, Elizabeth! And I will write ye back."

Master Forbes came around to us, and said as he took Elizabeth's hand in his, "It has been quite the romantic new year as I asked Mistress Hay to be my wife last week."

"And I said *yes*," she said, looking at him lovingly.

"That *is* a surprise!" I said, hugging Elizabeth immediately. I looked at Will and saw any remaining points of jealousy about Master Forbes leave his mind in an instant. "This makes me so happy—for ye both! When?"

Elizabeth said, "Not for another three weeks... mostly due to family traveling to the city. I know ye cannae stay, and I understand."

"Aye," I said, feeling sad to miss their union as they both were part of mine. "If MacLeod House on Canongate or Glenammon House can be of any use to ye and they are not yet sold, permission is granted to use as you need."

"Och, Alexandra, that is *too* generous," she said, looking at Master Forbes for support in this response.

"Aye, I agree," he said.

"Not at all! Ye ken that my father has seen to protect the wages and positions of his household staff until the houses are sold and they will be happy to support ye. This will be my wedding gift as I sadly cannae be here to celebrate with ye both, and ye have both been so kind to celebrate our own union."

Before I could take Will's hand in mine, Elizabeth hugged me again and said, "I will let you know if we ask anything of your houses."

"I will send word to Master Cameron and let Missus Douglas ken that if they hear from ye both, I have offered the houses as my gift," I said. "Again, even if just to house family fer the wedding, we are here to help and celebrate ye."

Elizabeth hugged me again in gratitude for my kindness and said in my ear, "Ye are a remarkable woman, Alexandra MacLeod. And an even more remarkable *friend*."

I pulled back, knowing that we needed to leave, and I said to them both as we walked to the door, "We will write, we will retain our counsel, and we will always be friends. Anytime ye find yerself on the Isle of Skye, my hope is that ye will stay with us at Castle Dunmara."

The happy couple nodded and smiled as Master Forbes said, "Aye, it could be good fer me to visit the clan seat I represent."

Duncan said, shaking Master Forbes' hand at the door, "We will have our final meal at the White Hart Inn tonight if ye wish to join us fer a dram, sir."

"Aye, we may stop by and join you for a farewell drink."

Once in the carriage, Duncan said, "One last stop, Jonny! It is time to say our final farewells at the White Hart Inn."

+++

THIRTEEN
Farewell To Edinburgh

We walked into the White Hart Inn and Duncan paused at the door to survey the room, as he always does. Jacob already knew it was our last night here and provided our family a large table in the back with oysters and whisky waiting. Duncan set to pouring our glasses as he stood at the end of the table and then raised his glass to me.

"First, Alexandra MacLeod, what ye did today at Canongate Kirk was not only a proud moment for me as yer uncle, but one of the kindest acts of charity I have ever witnessed!"

"Aye, sir," Will said, standing with my uncle and raising his own glass.

Angus put his own glass forward as he stood with the men, looking confused. Before he could ask, Duncan said, "The Lady MacLeod gifted £100 pounds sterling of her own inheritance to the Canongate Kirk's program for women and children on the streets of Edinburgh in memory of her late father.... *and Mary MacAskill.*"

"*Mary? Really?*" Angus asked, seemingly as shocked as the others.

"Stop it," I said, turning red with embarrassment at the display of appreciation and affection. I stood and raised my glass and met theirs so we could take a sip and said to them all, "Mary is an example of why this charitable program needs to be funded to help the many poor women and children forced to live on the streets. Mary got no benefit from it because we found her too late."

Will spoke and said, "I ken love, but she was never kind to ye, and ye honored her memory, anyway."

"Mary was a member of our clan and died on these city streets. Nice or not, she didna deserve such a thing. No woman deserves such a miserable fate."

Will walked around the table and kissed me in front of the others and said to me, "Yer kind heart is one of the reasons I love ye so."

"*Sláinte mhath,*" we all said together and sat back down.

We ate and drank the evening away. Jacob and Hilary ensured we never had to ask for a thing. Our glasses were always full, and our table had plenty of food. Master Forbes and Elizabeth did stop in to say one final farewell.

Elizabeth pulled me to the side as the men were talking and said as she held my hand, "Alexandra, ye have grown so much in the short time ye have been here in Edinburgh."

"I thank ye. We have been here too long, and I am *ready* to go home. But I am so glad we had a chance to become friends."

"*I know what happened, lass,*" she whispered to me, causing me to step back slightly on my heels and gasp for breath. She grabbed my hand and said, "Duncan told Campbell, as he sought help from the Advocate Society in finding Master Calder. I wanted to come see ye, but I did not know if I should. I did not want to cause ye any more pain, and I did not know if I should tell ye that I knew the truth about it. Duncan came to Campbell in confidence. It has hurt my heart so, not to support ye... as a woman and a friend."

"I cannae cry in front of these men again," I said as I turned us both to face opposite the table where the men were talking. I could not catch my own breath.

"Elizabeth..."

She touched her glass to mine and said in a calm tone and a smile, "Look me in the eye, lass. *Look me in the eye.*" I did as she asked, and the tears retreated immediately. "I am yer friend, and I swear to ye that these men *are* looking for Calder and will confirm if he is either captured or dead. I promise, ye!"

"I appreciate ye telling me this, and please tell Campbell how much I appreciate him not treating me in a different way today. Sometimes I want the kindness of a soft voice, but sometimes it *hurts* me to be treated like I am a broken vase on the verge if shattering at the slightest word."

"Aye, I can understand that. Ye are so verra strong and yer a woman I admire!"

We hugged each other tight as they prepared to leave the tavern. We had one last toast to their engagement and one of the few women I have ever been friends with walked out the door. It broke my heart.

It was our last night in the city, and none of us wanted to leave the tavern. As much as we all longed for home, we bonded together as family in our time together. I watched these strong, funny, and gallant men who took the task of escorting me here and back home safely, and I filled all the glasses and stood to raise mine to them.

In order around the table, I said, "Husband, uncle, cousin, my gallant knights, tasked with delivering me to Edinburgh safely on a solemn errand and who are tasked with seeing me back home to Castle Dunmara. I thank ye!"

"*Sláinte*," we all said together.

"The burden ye carry is almost no more," I said as I drank the last of my glass in one gulp and suddenly realized that the reactions on the faces of the men before me shifted. With everything that has happened with the intruder, my words landed poorly. I was trying to honor them and instead made them think that they would be rid of me soon—or even worse, that their fears were true—and that I was still contemplating negative thoughts of harming myself. Angus left the table quietly and Duncan stood and touched Will on the shoulder. We were left alone together.

"I didna mean," I started to say.

"Aye, my love," he said with his hand stroking my hand. "We are all just trying to support ye and sometimes we dinna ken how to do that the right way."

"I just meant about being home and obligations being completed. I see now that it sounded like I am a burden ye all are almost rid of. I am sorry."

Will smiled at me before kissing me, but still seemed tentative. You cannot read another person's mind and ye cannot read their heart and spirit. You never truly know what lies beneath what they show you. Realizing that some of this confusion was drink, and that I did not eat much tonight, I said, "We should go. First light will come early."

"Aye, it always does!"

Hilary brought the surprisingly still awake wee Jamie down for a soft cuddle as we said our goodbyes to our tavern hosts. I cradled the lad and talked to him about all he could be as the men shook hands and talked about the journey ahead. I could tell everyone was watching me with the child, considering my own recent loss. Despite the pressing stares on me with the babe, I was just in awe of the beautiful, blue-eyed darling grabbing his fat little fingers around my hair and talking back to me in coos and sighs. The lad had a lot to say to me, and I had a lot to say to him.

I handed the bairn back to his mother and gave her a hug. "Take care, my wee Jamie. Thank ye, Hilary, ye and Jacob have been a great hosts and have become good friends. Ye took care of my father and ye have taken care of his family, and we all thank ye fer it."

"Ye are most welcome! Jacob and I always tell each other we love seeing ye here. Ye are part of the White Hart family, and verra easy to care fer."

I looked at my rowdy, whisky-laden companions and said with a laugh, "I am not so sure about that!"

"Truly! We miss ye when yer *not* here. I am not sure what I am going to do with all the whisky I have on hand," Jacob said, laughing with me as he hugged his wife tight.

Duncan said, "Aye, save it, man! Let it age! If we find ourselves in the city again, ye can be certain we will be right here in this verra place."

Angus said something incoherent, but it sounded like it was a drunken lament about the early start tomorrow.

Will said, handing his coin back to Jacob to pay for our last evening, "Aye, ye have become good friends indeed and we are sorry to say our farewells. Thank ye again!"

"*But of course,*" Jacob said in his very best French accent to me with a slight nod of his head. Then he said to the four members of Clan MacLeod, walking out of the front door of the tavern, "*Haste ye back!*"

+++

The morning did come early, and I was struggling in the early glow of first light coming through the window to see my laces. Though I am certain part of my trouble was that I was still laden with drink from the night before. My hands could not seem to do what I wanted them to.

William came to help me and accidentally kicked one of my boots under the bed. I just sat down on the edge of the bed and thought about why we had to leave so early when Prestonfield was so close. Will bent down to retrieve my boot from under the bed.

Sounding serious, he said, "Alex..."

Upon his word, I opened my sleepy eyes as he handed me the wooden box we have been looking for all this time.

"The wooden box! Will! Ye found it!"

"Aye," he said, handing it to me. "I reached for yer boot, and it was just there under the bed and open."

I went through the contents and said, "It has everything he mentioned except his gold watch and the pearls. I dinnae ken why I never thought to look under the bed! Look under there again. Perhaps it fell on the floor, and those items fell out."

"I see nothing else under the bed. Lass, it was like it was thrown under the bed fer it to be open like that and not have things scattered about."

"*This whole time!* It has been here *the whole time* and we find it on our last morning here." I took his hand and looked him in the eyes as I smiled and said, "Father *wanted* us to find it!"

"Aye, love! He did."

We gathered the last of our things and went down to breakfast. I placed the box in front of Duncan and Angus already eating at the table.

"The wooden box?" Duncan asked, "*How...?*"

"If ye can believe it, Will just found it under our bed," I said, still beaming at the thought.

"Well, that is a stroke of luck!"

"It was open, but two things are missing from what Father listed in his letter—his gold watch and the pearls. We looked everywhere but didna find them."

"Well, this will have to do, then. At least ye have yer mother's ring and yer father's clan broach and plaid."

"Aye, this will have to do," I said, as I placed my mother's plain silver band on top of my own wedding ring and smiled.

This will have to do.

+++

We stood together in the courtyard and said our farewell to Angus as our advance man once again to prepare for our arrival at Prestonfield House. Everyone is as equally sad to leave MacLeod House on Canongate as we are happy to return to Skye. Angus gave Missus Douglas a huge hug and a wet kiss on the cheek. The woman blushed at such affection, but I believe Angus grew on her a little in these past months. Jonny and Duncan secured the last of the items on the cart and they tucked away the wooden box in my garment trunk. Will stood, holding the reins of our horses.

I said my first goodbye to Master Jonny with a smile, "Dear sir, ye have been a fine stable master and I thank ye for taking care of us with all those late-night carriage rides and for caring for my beloved Munro."

"Aye, ye have been no bother, missus. It has been so nice to have a task and it has been my honor to serve ye as I served yer father."

Will and Duncan followed with their goodbyes and handshakes to the man. I turned to Missus Douglas and said as I pulled the keys from my skirt pocket as I said, "I must return these to ye now as I am no longer the mistress of this house."

"Och, my lady," she said with tears in her eyes. She understood more than anyone here how this trip has changed me, how we uncovered my father's life here, how I found love, and how I survived unimaginable loss. She has served as another mother figure in my life, and I am so grateful to her. I have grown to love her.

"I thank ye fer taking care of all of us so well," I said, hugging her. "I will never forget yer kindness and patience with a house full of people fer so long and I will never forget the healing power of fried ham and tatties at breakfast."

We all laughed as Duncan and Will both agreed and extolled the virtues of her cooking, especially after a night of drink. "Remember Elizabeth Hay or Master Forbes may reach out if they need the house fer their wedding guests."

"Aye! I have always liked Mistress Hay and will do as ye ask."

I knelt down to look into the eyes of a quiet and sleepy boy and said, "Master Petey, remember lad, how important school is fer ye. Keep working hard there! Yer in charge of that front walk and I want ye to keep making MacLeod House the envy of *everyone* that passes by on Canongate. Ye never ken! If ye keep up the good work, the King himself may ask ye to tend to the walks in front of the Palace of Holyroodhouse."

The lad stood up tall and nodded to me. He hugged me tight as I slipped all of the remaining coins from Father's desk into his coat pocket. He heard them all and smiled the biggest smile I have ever seen and just placed his hand instantly over the pocket in anticipation.

Missus Douglas stepped to me and, with a kind touch on my shoulder, said, "I have watched ye grow here, Mistress Alexandra. I ken ye never thought to have a grand house in the city, but ye have been a fair mistress at MacLeod House. Ye are surrounded by men and family that love ye, and yer father would have been so proud of the woman ye have become here."

"I thank ye, Missus Douglas. If any of ye find your way to Skye, I hope ye will stay with us as Castle Dunmara, so that we can host ye as dear friends of Clan MacLeod."

"It is time, my lady," Duncan said, as he sat up in the cart and took the reins of the horses.

Will and I mounted our horses, and Petey ran to open the gate to the close. We rode out of Crichton's Close onto Canongate and the tears this time were for all the things I was leaving behind. Some good and some bad, but there is no doubt that the time spent in Edinburgh changed me. I carry things from this city and not just what was on the cart driven by

Duncan before me. I am carrying all the love, friendship, and even the pain in my heart back home.

+++

FOURTEEN
Prestonfield Revisited

We could have stopped a little further afield than Prestonfield House on our exodus from Edinburgh, but we expected to make some adjustments along the way due to the extra horses and the cart. I also wanted to talk to Master Garrick.

Sir Alexander sent word by messenger that we were most welcome to return and personally welcomed us heartily as he had months prior in front of the grand house—now as friends, not just as guests.

"Sir Alexander," I said as Will helped me off of Munro. "It is so good to see ye again!"

"Aye, Lady MacLeod," he said, taking my hand from Will, "ye are a vision for an old man's eyes! And Master MacLeod, ye are most welcome again here at Prestonfield."

"Sir, ye remember William MacCrimmon," I said with a smile and my hand behind Will's back.

"Of course, Master MacCrimmon," he said, shaking Will's hand, "ye are most welcome again, sir."

"Sir Alexander, Master MacCrimmon is my husband now."

"Well, I will reproach ye for not inviting me to yer wedding later, Missus," he said with a sly wink and smile, "but this is cause for a celebration indeed! We will not only welcome ye again to our home, but we will also celebrate such a fine match with only the best wine and whisky this night! My hearty congratulations to ye both!" He kissed me on the cheek and then placed his hand on Will's shoulder and shook his hand as a gentleman.

"Thank ye, Sir Alexander," Will said.

"Will, I need a moment with Munro before ye take him." Will stepped aside so that I could have a moment with my beloved horse.

"Och my darlin' Munro," I said, stoking and kissing his nose. "We are one day closer to home. Thank ye for getting me this far, my love."

Munro nodded his head to me and nudged my shoulder.

"He is a fine-looking horse," Sir Alexander said.

"He is a Highland pony and has been a gallant escort on this trip, I can assure ye, sir," I said as I smiled before Will took my beloved to the stables.

Sir Alexander took my hand under his arm and escorted me into the house as the men secured the cart and retrieved our bags. I looked around the fine hall, remembering the first time we arrived at the grand house.

"Please come wait by the warm fire until yer men are done," Sir Alexander said, escorting me into the parlor. "Despite the sun, there is a chill in the air today."

"The warm fire is welcome after a short day's ride. I fear our trip may be slower due to the cart and the cold this time of year, but we are all ready to go home to Skye. We couldna stand to wait any longer."

There is a chance that Sir Alexander may know what happened to me at the house on Canongate if the Advocate Society had been informed as Elizabeth said, but he has not let on in any way. His response to my marriage told me that. Even if he is not aware, I am certain he can see the conflict behind my eyes between newlywed bliss and the pain of loss and grief. I still see the same myself every time I look in the mirror.

"Yer rooms are ready, and we hope as comfortable as last time," he said, interrupting my thoughts before the fire.

"Och, sir! I told my travel companions how much I enjoyed staying here and yer company. While I did not want us to be an inconvenience to ye and Master Garrick, ye were both an important part of our journey to Edinburgh, to my father's life, and I wanted to say our farewells."

"Lady MacLeod, ye and yer family are most welcome," he said, handing me a glass of claret. "I told ye, it is nice to have a woman in the house again. Ye also bring youth and happiness back within these walls."

"Yer wife and children are not back from Pembrokeshire, then?"

"No. Sadly, all the children fell ill at the same time and delayed their departure. But they are recovered and on their way home as we speak."

"I am glad to hear it! Sir, will Master Garrick be able to join us for supper this night?"

"I believe the man is out in the stables directing the accommodation of horses with yer husband, but aye, he will join us."

I smiled at him and nodded as I sipped my wine as I said, "That makes me happy. Yer son was verra kind to me on our last visit, and I have much to say to him in appreciation."

+++

Will joined me in our bedchamber, which is the same as I had last time. He stayed in his own room on our first trip to Prestonfield when Angus vacated the small, shared room for accommodations elsewhere. He seemed pleased to share in the comfort of the grand room I had.

"How are ye, my love?" he asked as he stood behind me in front of the fire. He wrapped his arms around me and kissed the back of my head and my neck. I just shut my eyes and thought about how such a simple question has become difficult to answer on any given day.

"I am glad to be here and look forward to talking to Master Garrick at supper," I said. I am certain Will is wondering why this was my response, but he said nothing and waited for me to share more on my own.

"When we were here last," I continued, while rubbing my hands over his arms around my waist for comfort. "Ye may remember that we walked into the parlor together before joining ye and the rest of the men."

"Duncan and I agreed that it was kind of ye to walk with him because of his limp. Whereas all of us ran straight for the whisky in the next room!"

I smiled, thinking that moment of kindness, and frankly a kindness we all deserve, was an important fer me. But I said with a smile, "I thought ye all were drawn in by the harpist."

"Aye, she was bonnie," Will said with a laugh in my ear. "But nothing can pull a man to a room like fine whisky and Sir Alexander has the finest I have ever tasted!"

"Master Garrick and I had a conversation that means more to me... *now*," I said, my voice shaking a little. I wanted to say *'after the intruder'* but I knew that with those words, Will would worry for me even more.

"A conversation?"

"Aye, about his experience at Culloden."

I am certain Will was more confused than ever, but he relaxed his arms slightly. "It was actually Master Garrick who was *kind to me* that night, and I want to thank him fer it."

I turned to my husband and kissed him. Now, with our arms around each other, he moved his kisses to my forehead and held me tight in his embrace.

"Will," I said in a whisper as he kept his forehead to mine, "if ye can ensure I have a few moments with Master Garrick, I would appreciate it. I suspect I can just walk with him again to the parlor like we did last time, but if ye need to move everyone to the room ahead of us, I would be grateful."

"Aye," he said. I did not say the words, but I will tell Will more after the conversation. I made no promises at this moment. I want to talk to Master Garrick first.

Will brought me my fine blue dress from my chest, and we prepared ourselves for supper. I sat in awe as he shaved and thought about how handsome he was. I watched his hands carefully manage his straight razor across his own jaw and neck. He caught me staring at him in the mirror and smiled with half of his face covered in soapy lather back at me. I smiled and looked down, almost embarrassed that he caught me staring at him.

I welcomed his tightening of my own laces as a loving husband should. When we joined everyone else downstairs, we were met with a hearty celebration and toasts to our marriage.

+++

"Lady MacLeod," Sir Alexander said as he walked toward me, raising his glass. "I said this when ye were here last, but ye are indeed a *vision*. To the Lady MacLeod and her husband, Master MacCrimmon!"

"*Sláinte*," we all said together. I smiled at this show of affection and held Will's hand tightly in my own. He sweetly kissed me on the cheek and released me to the arm of our host, who seated us for supper. I was so happy to see Master Garrick already waiting for us at his seat at the table.

Much like last time, the food and drink were magnificent, and I engaged the most with our hosts, though now with Will seated across from me, participated in the conversation more. I did not even notice Duncan and Angus as they seemed to hold court with each other at the end of the table.

"I have not arranged any music this night," said Sir Alexander as he started to move us all to the parlor, "but in continuation of our celebrations, I hope ye will all join me in across the hall for some fine Scottish whisky."

We all nodded in acceptance of his invitation.

"Master MacLeod," he said to Duncan as he walked ahead to lead us out of the room, "I have found a new whisky from a small private maker near the River Spey. They rarely make batches for anyone but their laird, but let me buy casks on the side and yer gonnae love it!"

Will winked to me as he walked out of the door, and I saw that was my chance, much like last time, to let the men run for the promise of drink so I could talk to Master Garrick on the walk across the hall. The men cleared the room quickly as I waited for my friend at the end of the table.

"Ye didna have to wait fer me, Lady MacLeod," Garrick said as he offered me his free arm, with his cane in the other.

"Aye, sir, I did. Yer the reason we are here this night," I said, taking his arm. He looked at me, confused by my words. I stopped outside the door to the dining room and turned to him as I said, "Sir, when we were last at Prestonfield, ye told me about yer experience at Culloden."

He nodded in remembrance of our conversation, and I continued, "I appreciated the words ye said about being confronted with death and wanting *nothing more than to live*. I thought that was a brave and honest admission, and one that I have thought about many times since."

He smiled at me, but still looked confused by my confession as to how anything from his experience at the Battle of Culloden could remain with me.

I tried to steady my voice and emotion. "I was attacked in Edinburgh, just after I found out I was with child."

"Och, Lady MacLeod," he said, placing his hand over mine, still wrapped around his elbow. I appreciated his sympathy and the fact that I did not break down into tears at the memory of it.

"I lost the bairn and I have since not been able to reconcile the pain of life and loss with the comfort of death. I wanted to ask ye if ye ever had the same thoughts or if ye went straight from cannon fire to wanting to live?"

I tried to correct myself as I could see his face change upon my words, and perhaps reassuring him and much as myself, I said, "I am not thinking about ending my life, sir, but I am *constantly* thinking about the pain I feel. I tell ye that recovering from what happened remains verra difficult fer me. Sometimes I think about hurting myself and as much shame as that brings me to admit... ye are the first I have admitted that and said the words..."

"It was not instant, Lady MacLeod," he said, interrupting me softly as he reflected on his own memories. "I cannae imagine what ye have gone through with such a tragic loss, but I hope yer husband is a comfort to ye. Yer uncle..."

"Aye sir, Will tries," I said, "and my uncle and cousin, of course. They are all fine men and try to help me. I am comforted by them every day."

Master Garrick thought about his words and said thoughtfully, "I told ye I went to the battlefield prepared to die." I nodded my head to him, remembering his story. "Then I had a choice to make. And ye have a choice to make, Lady MacLeod. It is that simple. Something about that cannon fire told me that I should choose to live for myself, fer my father, and fer the hope that I could find love again. Ye *have* to do the same."

Suddenly, I thought of the memory of my mother at my bedside saying, *live for your love.* It is a choice.

"Ye have to hold on to the love within yerself and with the love that surrounds ye, so that when ye make the choice that the pain ye feel is not worth losing the people ye love and who love ye. It is only then that ye can see where new hope and happiness lie ahead. I believe that each choice in the positive leads to another."

213

I nodded as I took in his words.

"Lady MacLeod, I will be honest and tell ye that ye may have to make this choice many times over, and in many ways. I did myself. Sometimes those decisions will be small, like just getting out of bed one day and sometimes they will be large, like not hurting yerself like ye said ye have thought about. I can tell ye that there will be times ye are plagued by yer loss, but ye must look for yer hope on the inside and to the people *that bring ye hope.*"

I smiled and nodded at him. His words were correct. I had not thought about it, but I was indeed making small and large decisions each day to hope. It will be a choice I have to make—*every single day.*

"Yer young and newly married, and I can tell yer husband loves ye dearly because his eyes are never off ye, lass," he said, leaning in and making me blush slightly. "Ye have to choose to let that powerful love between ye give ye the hope ye need, and I believe hope will overtake the feelings ye have that are consumed with thoughts of pain and loss."

I smiled at him but said nothing, as his words were as painful as they were profound.

"I am thinking of remarrying myself," he said, trying to show me how he has embraced his own new hope.

"Och, Master Garrick! That makes me verra happy to hear such good news!"

"She is a widow-woman on our lands. She has no children, and she is kind. My father does not yet know and may not like the match, but she makes me happy. I believe I can make her happy."

I just smiled at him at the thoughts of new love and new hope.

"I mean no offence to the loss ye feel now. Ye will *always* feel it, I am afraid. It is not the same, but I will always have this mangled leg, this limp. A constant reminder of what happened on that bloody moor, but ye will find new happiness to replace some of the pain ye carry. Even if the injury is not seen to others—ye will carry it. In its stead, I have found a new happiness and a new hope. I wish the same for ye."

He kissed my hand, as I said smiling at him and thinking that our stop here was important for me, "Thank ye, sir! I wish ye and yer lady much happiness, as well. Truly, I do!"

It is my hope, and it is my choice. One that has become increasingly difficult to make. Master Garrick is correct. The choice feels different each day, and I will have to make it several times over in many ways. Some small and some large. But the choice is *mine*.

"I thank ye again, sir, for your wise counsel. Ye have proven that our stop here at Prestonfield House was needed. Should we join our supper party?" I asked, smiling at him. I have more to figure out for myself, but I am restored in some way. I knew being here would be valuable for me. Master Garrick has made me think more and I appreciate his advice.

He nodded to me, and we continued our walk together in silence. William and Duncan looked at us as we were last to join the group, but said nothing. My tears were immediately replaced by a smile as I left Master Garrick's arm and joined that of my husband on the side of the room for many whisky toasts in our honor.

I held William's hand tight all evening, and he knew that I would tell him eventually how Master Garrick tried to help me and how I would have to think more about how I can *choose hope*.

+++

FIFTEEN
The Last Miles Before Home

Our long journey home to Skye is almost at an end. After a week on the road, we neared the final stop on the outskirts of Mallaig. Skye is but a ferry barge away from us and we will return to Castle Dunmara tomorrow.

We had to book a separate passage just for us, our horses, and our cart. My travelers seemed excited about finishing the journey and their obligation to Laird Graham. This time, Angus got all the rooms at the tavern, and our traveling party was thrilled at the thought of sleeping in front of a warm fire and being only one day's ride from home.

Our journey back to Skye has been slower due to the cart. While much colder this time of year, we have been fortunate to make our way through many dry and sunny days. The fine weather allowed us to enjoy more of the beauty of Scotland. Crossing the glens and rounding the lochs revealed even more of a land that I have grown to love.

Months ago, I would have said that there was nothing more beautiful than the view off of the cliff at Cairn's Point, and it *is* beautiful. But Scotland has other wonders that make me proud. Duncan told me that was part of my lesson on this trip—to learn more about our beautiful country—and I have. I have learned to appreciate the quiet beauty of Scotland's natural wonders, the changing landscape, and the genuine kindness of its people.

"My love," Will said as he wrapped his arms around me, "ye have been so quiet the last few days. Are ye unwell?"

I just shook my head, signaling that I was not unwell. I could not tell him what was in my heart and mind. I did not have the words. I could not tell myself as my own emotions have been unsteady. The trip home has shown me that my mind is still consumed with all of pain and ghosts I have brought back from Edinburgh.

Somehow, the closer we got to Skye, the more painful the memories of Edinburgh became. I thought it would be the exact opposite and that the pain I felt would fade as soon as we left the city. The regret of leaving Edinburgh with the matter of Calder unresolved, the tragic loss of Mary, and an uncertain fear of returning home as a different person have started to consume my thoughts. I want nothing but to be at Castle Dunmara, but I am afraid to be there at the same time.

I have thought much about Master Garrick's words and struggle with my own choices between the pain of *loss* and the comfort of *hope*. It is a choice, and I have found it one that I am making so many times in a day. So much so that I am exhausted. I am exhausted by choices.

"Are ye ready fer supper?"

"Aye," I said softly and in resignation, that I cannot avoid having supper with my gallant knights. What I would rather do is crawl into the bed and go to sleep, but I cannot tell Will that.

We walked down to join Angus and Duncan, who were already consumed by whisky and laughing with new friends they made in the tavern. Will and I sat together as the barmaid brought us a hearty stew and ales. I could feel his eyes on me as I mindlessly pushed meat around my plate.

This was one of my conscious choices today. I do not want to eat.

"Will," Duncan yelled loudly as he sat next to the man and put his arm around him. "Angus and I want to thank ye man fer marrying Alexandra so that we could return to Dunmara without a security plan every night! We have slept like wee bairns on our trip home!"

Angus and Will knew that my uncle crossed the line with me in this instant, as they said nothing and did not laugh with him. Will looked at me with narrow eyes, either trying to gauge my reaction or willing me not to say anything back to my uncle. He could see my face showed the hurt of Duncan's words and with hurt, anger was surely not far behind. I could not believe he would say such a thing! Duncan sat there and continued to laugh at his own joke... *alone.*

"Aye, uncle," I said angrily through my teeth, "I imagine a good sleep is essential when ye insist on drinking enough whisky to fill yer boots every night."

They all looked at me in shock that I would be so bold and disrespectful with my words, but I was angry, and I did not care who heard it. I abandoned my still full plate, took my ale pot, and left the men in stunned silence at the table and returned to my room alone. This is another one of the choices I made this night and I have to admit, it felt good.

+++

I undressed for bed and was thankful to have a few minutes in the room to myself. I accidentally cut my right hand with my knife when Duncan was talking nonsense, and I was tending to it when Will walked into our room. He was respectful of my feelings and undressed himself in silence.

"Did ye hurt yerself, love?" he asked, seeing me trying to stop the bleeding from my hand with a clean cloth.

"I accidentally cut my hand with my knife. It is just a scratch."

He kissed me on top of my head and said as he tenderly helped me tie a piece of cloth around the wound. "Duncan feels great sorrow... fer what he said to ye. He and Angus hit the whisky too early tonight. They are just so glad to be close to *home* and started celebrating... *too soon.*"

I just looked at him, wondering why he was excusing Duncan and such behavior toward his own wife. But I was also focused on the word *home. We are almost home!* Yet, I still cannot figure out why I do not share in the same excitement they all have. We have been gone too long and this should be a happy moment for me, as well as the men. But I seem to have lost any ability to be happy on our return. I keep reminding myself of what Master Garrick said, and that it will take time, but I feel immense sorrow and even fear as we march toward the gates. It has been difficult each day to make choices that bring me back to love, hope, and happiness.

"Talk to me, Alex."

"I have nothing to say to ye, *Will*. Duncan was drunk and rude, and I will forgive him because I always do. I always will. But this night he hurt me, and I didna believe I could hurt anymore."

"Och, my love, what is it?"

I could not answer his question. Part of me did not want to say the words aloud, and part of me resented it. He knows exactly *what* it is, but does not want to really speak of it himself. Will kept his arms around me as we tried to sleep, but my mind would not cooperate, and I kept moving. It started with my feet and then I tossed and turned with all the thoughts I could not control.

"I am so sorry," I said in a whisper into the darkness of the room. I know my restlessness is keeping Will awake, because he keeps trying to still me with the weight of his hands on my hips or holding me tight. He said nothing, but kissed me softly, and gently on the back of my head.

+++

First light came early again, as it always does.

We all rode together on our final miles to Dunmara Castle. We no longer needed Angus to serve as an advance man, and the four of us set out on the last of our journey together. This part we all knew, and the destination needed no preparation.

Much like our departure, they placed me between Duncan and Will on our ride. Will looked at me with a faint smile and rode ahead to speak with Angus. Duncan took his place closer to me. We looked at each other but said nothing.

Duncan spoke finally, "I shouldna made a joke like that at yer expense, and in front of the lads. Yer our lady, and I had no right to say what I did. Fer that, I am so verra sorry!"

I looked ahead, focused on the back of my husband's head, as he took a small glance back at me. These two must have coordinated this well-timed apology so that Duncan could be forgiven before we arrived within the castle gates. He kept talking, and I didn't say anything back to him.

"I didna mean what I said last night. I am happy fer ye and Will and it has nothing to do with security plans and sleep! Ye ken that, lass! Ye ken how we have talked. I was a drunken fool on too much whisky, and I am verra sorry to hurt ye with my careless words."

"Aye," I said with a half-smile and a nod to my head that my uncle was absolved, and I was done with the conversation. I know he did not mean to hurt me, but I also know that he does not know how hurt I am. I ran my fingers over the painful cut on my hand from my accident the night before and thought about all the scars and wounds I carry with me back to Dunmara.

The unfortunate moment with Duncan was just one more wound for me to heal.

+++

SIXTEEN
Arrival At The Gates

Dunmara Castle
Isle of Skye, Scotland
March 1767

**Just as I left the gates of Castle Dunmara months ago, my
return was also in tears.** We are all *finally* home. I felt more and more
uncertain of my emotions as we rode across Scotland, but the minute I
saw my home, relief overcame me.

So much of me has changed in the last seven months and I just want
to be the young lass in Father's painting, seated at Cairn's Point and
oblivious to the world outside these castle walls. I am here with my
husband. I am here with a stronger sense of family, with Duncan and
Angus by my side. But I am also here carrying the burdens of loss and

fear that continue to haunt me and that I cannot seem to keep from my thoughts.

"My darlin' Munro," I said as I stood before my beloved in the courtyard as I placed my cheek on his own. "Ye have been an absolute gift to me this entire trip. Ye are my love." He nodded to me and nudged my shoulder with his own signs of affection. He nibbled at my shoulder in his attempt to love and groom me. I let him love me as I loved him back.

"I hand the mighty Munro back to ye, sir," I said as I gave the reins back to wee Robbie with a slight bow to Castle Dunmara's youngest stable hand, who seems to have grown taller since we left.

"Welcome home, Lady MacLeod," the boy said as he leaned into me for a warm hug. As expected, I placed my hands immediately in his hair.

"We have a lot to talk about, lad."

"Aye, cousin! I was verra happy to get yer letter."

"Och, I was verra happy to send it to ye."

"Ma reads it to me every night, but I keep it in my pocket always," he said, tapping his coat. "Are ye *really* married?"

"Aye! I am. Are ye happy fer me?"

"If ye are happy, then I am." I could tell that he had some sadness at the thought of me having a husband, but he did not say another word about it.

"Ye ken William, Robbie! Ye are already good friends from the stables," I said, introducing them again as Will joined us. The boy just looked at me and Will but said nothing. His face just gave me a look of resignation and perhaps a little embarrassment at the thought of me being married. Will handed his horse's reins to him and, like anyone else on the grounds, took his own opportunity to touch his glorious hair by patting the top of the young lad's head.

I turned to give Munro another kiss on his nose and said, "Yer journey and yer duty is complete, my dear Munro."

Knox and the grooms came out of the stables to help Robbie with the horses and the cart, and I walked straight into a swarm of welcomes and congratulations from the crowd gathering in the courtyard.

Knox just placed his hand on my shoulder and said, "We are glad yer home, my lady."

"Thank ye, sir!" I said with a weary smile. "I am verra glad to be back at Dunmara."

I looked at my wee Robbie once more and said so that Auld Knox could hear my direction, "Munro is mine, do ye understand, lad? Ye will work him and groom him, but he is his lady's alone. No other can take him. Ye made a fine match, Robbie!"

"Aye, my lady," Robbie said with a pride that he had made the right choice for me. I have not only learned to ride my beloved, but grown to love him. He was mine alone!

"Welcome back, Lady Alexandra," said a teary-eyed Missus Gerrard, hugging me tight. "We set yer bedchamber fer ye and Master MacCrimmon. Many happy blessings to ye both! This marriage is such a wonderful and unexpected surprise!"

"Aye, thank ye, Missus Gerrard," I said with a hand around my husband's back. "Master MacCrimmon has been a wonderful and unexpected surprise indeed."

"Yer past supper tonight, but ye both come down to the kitchen anytime and I will see yer fed. We have plenty set aside."

Will said with all the charm he could muster, "Aye, missus! I have missed yer cooking."

I smiled at him for his kindness and as the woman turned red upon his compliment. He had already won Missus Gerrard over once, and here he was charming her again. She put her hand on my face and gave me a faint smile as she brought her kerchief to her nose and walked back into the castle. Robbie took the horses and Duncan was giving Angus and the other men instructions on where to deliver the items on the cart.

I yelled to him, "Duncan, if ye can have the Dunmara painting, the Ramsay portrait, and the trunks with both the clan papers and my dresses sent to my bedchamber, we can sort the rest later."

"Aye," Duncan said to me. "Ye heard Lady MacLeod, lads! I will pull items she asked fer and ye can put the rest in my bedchamber fer now."

The rest was mostly an assortment of other paintings, books for the school, and the custom porcelain dishes and glasses rimmed with gold. Duncan and I both took a set of linens from the house on Canongate, as they were so fine. I smiled again, thinking to myself that if I could have brought the copper bath to Dunmara on this cart, I would have! I am going to have to figure out how to replicate that wonder here on Skye.

I walked slowly through the Great Hall. The last time I was here, I was a different person. As glad as I was to be home, I was also sad. I ran straight to the back stairs to my bedchamber alone. All the way, I thought about being the Lady MacLeod and now a married woman. Our return to Dunmara means that I have to assume my old life. All the while, nothing feels the same. I am not the same.

+++

The men delivered the items I requested, and William found me staring out of the window at my beloved sea and the promontory of Cairn's Point. I was wondering how and when I could escape my guardian to go there. William placed his arms around my waist and kissed the back of my head. He knew that something was wrong and tried to comfort me in his loving arms.

"Will," I said, leaning back into his chest and giving myself to his warm embrace, "nothing feels the same here."

"I understand. Ye have had to deal with a lot of change in a short amount of time."

"We all have, but it is more than that. I feel like everyone is treating me less like myself. It is like I am a piece of glass, ready to shatter at any moment. It makes me feel... broken. I am in many ways, but I dinnae want anyone else to treat me like that. I want to be treated the same as I was... *before*."

He held me tighter and whispered in my ear, *"I ken, love, but ye are not the same as ye were before. Please, tell me what ye need. I will do as ye ask!"*

I wrapped my arms around his tighter and whispered back, *"I need to go to Cairn's Point. Even if ye join me there, let me have a few moments alone with my family."*

"Aye, take yer time," he said, kissing me on top of my head and letting me go.

I grabbed my cloak and headed for the door, where I stopped and said, "Actually, come to think of it! I should see if we can see Laird Graham first. We need to show our respect to him and allow him to bless our marriage in person. If I dinnae return, it is because he has already retired for the evening, and then I will go straight to the cairn."

Will looked at me in a way that told me he understood, but I could also feel his apprehension about me going to the cliff alone.

"Ye can see me from the window there."

I do not know if that eased his concern and worry, but I had to say the words. Laird Graham had already retired for the evening, so I walked alone to Cairn's Point. I missed the destination, but I also missed the walk to it. I smiled, looking across the courtyard and the walk up the rocky hill. I looked back down to the courtyard and now felt more at home.

When I arrived, I looked first for the inscription at the very back for wee James Douglas MacLeod in the dying light. Indeed, the lad was there. I said a prayer for the brother I never knew as I ran my fingers over his name carved in the weathered stone. I said a prayer for Flora, who jumped to her death here after losing her son. A small rosebush was also there behind the cairn. I never noticed it hiding behind the stones before. It was small and while there were no flowers at this time of year, I smiled at the thought of spring roses in celebration of my mother.

Laird Graham had Father's name added while we were away and after I ran my fingers over his name, I sat myself on the cold, wet ground. I thought about the family I lost and the family I dearly missed.

My beloved sea was before me as I sat before the cairn with a new sense of peace. I closed my eyes and breathed in the cold, salt-laden air I had been longing for. My parents and brother left me too soon. I spoke silent prayers into the crashing waves below. I missed this seat and was more comforted here in the memory of loss than in front of the fire at MacLeod House.

Will gave me the time I asked for and then came to retrieve me from the wind and the cold. He comforted me while I mourned for my family and our own loss. He rocked me in his arms and whispered to me in my ear, *"Cuiridh mi clach air do chàrn."*

I looked up and recited the Gaelic back to him, *"I will put a stone on your cairn."*

I cried, and he kept rocking me in his arms and stroking my hair. He said, *"Some wounds take longer to heal, my love."*

"Aye! They do."

As we walked back down the hill together, I wondered if my husband might be afraid that I was still melancholy from the loss of our child and that one day I might pitch myself over the cliff like my mother. He just held my hand tight and guided me safely home as I thought more about his words.

Some wounds *do* take longer to heal.

+++

"I told ye, my bed at Dunmara was bigger," I said with a smile as I stroked the hairs on the chest of my husband.

His fingers began wrapping themselves around my curls and he said with a laugh, "Aye, and if I sleep soundly this night, I will believe ye!"

"Will!" I yelled, looking at him now, wide-eyed at his admonishment. He smiled at me, but I believe he meant what he said. I am not sure the man has had a restful night of sleep since we married and, for that, I was truly remorseful.

I lifted myself to kiss him once more and his hands moved up under my shift onto my back. "This is *our* home now. I want ye to be happy here. The last few months have been hard for both of us, but I want us to be happy here. I *need* us to be happy here." *I need to be happy here.*

He whispered, *"I dinnae ken how I cannae be happy where ye are."*

+++

SEVENTEEN
Celebrations And Secrets

Will and I walked into Laird Graham's darkened bedchamber together to see the man sitting up against his pillows. Despite being in his bed, he looked happy and healthy. His greeting to us was warm as I rushed to hug him and sat by his side. Seven months apart was too long, and I missed his calm disposition and fatherly affection.

A smile spread across his face as soon as he saw me. "Och, Alexandra! My dear! *Yer here.*"

"Aye, sir! I am here," I said as I grabbed his hand in mine. "We arrived last night, after ye retired, and we didna want to disturb ye."

"I thought I was imagining yer voice in the stairwell," he said, as he turned and looked at me with glassy eyes. This was the first sign to me he was not well.

"I have missed ye so, my laird! I never thought that going to Edinburgh to settle everything fer my father would us take as long as it did!"

"Duncan was just here and said the same words to me, lass. I ken that ye all encountered more of Alexander than expected on this journey."

"Aye, that is true. I thank ye for giving me the opportunity to discover more him on our journey. Coming back this time of year was not ideal, but not as hard of a trip on our return despite the cart and extra horses. We had the gift of fine weather on our journey. And I believe we were all so ready to be home that our sheer determination moved us forward across Scotland."

"Aye! But ye gained a husband along the way, lass!" he said, smiling with the pride of a father to both me and Will.

I leaned to him, tightening my grip on his hands, and said, "Ye ken better than anyone that I tried my best *not* to have one."

"She did that, my laird," Will said with a laugh.

"And let that be the only thing the lass fails at, Master MacCrimmon!"

"My laird, ye gave yer blessing for us to sign the marriage contract and to be married in Edinburgh," I said as I took Will's hand in mine, "but we are here to ask that ye give us yer blessing before us."

Laird Graham smiled at me on this moment of respect for his position within the clan and our family. "William is a fine man, and one I never thought I wanted or deserved. Thank ye for agreeing to our union. I have also brought the signed copy of the marriage contract, if ye want it, sir."

"No Alexandra, keep that fer yer own. I give ye both my blessing fer a long and happy marriage," he said as he reached his other hand to Will, who took it gladly, while gripping my hand tighter.

"William, lad, I ken ye are not granted any title or influence here beyond becoming a member of the Fine, but I ask ye here, as yer wife's uncle and guardian, that ye love and care fer *our daughter* fer the rest of yer days."

"Aye, sir! I made my commitment before God in Canongate Kirk and ye have my commitment fer the rest of my life. I love Alexandra. I always have and I always will."

"Ye have another role here, lad, and that is to help yer wife navigate the changes that are coming to us on Skye. Yer support will be most important to her as she serves Clan MacLeod."

"I take this responsibility and duty to heart, sir," Will said as he shook the hand my uncle was still holding. "Ye both have my commitment to this task. I will always do the best that I can for Clan MacLeod, my laird, and my lady."

I smiled at them both and said through my own tears, "We have brought ye two paintings, sir. The first is one was commissioned from an artist in Edinburgh of Castle Dunmara and Cairn's Point. It is most incredible, as Father must have told the artist from his own memory fer it to be so perfect."

Will brought the painting forward for Laird Graham to view.

"Och, it is fine! Look at our beautiful home! Look at Dunmara! Is that ye or Flora at the point?"

"Consider it us both, sir."

We looked at each other and paused for a few moments of thoughts on the comfort of home. I know they restored the old cairn after my mother's death and the painting reveals me as a young lass before the stones as they are today, but felt comfort in knowing that we both loved being on the promontory. Father's memory of home should represent both me and my mother. It was *our* place.

"And the second is a portrait Father commissioned with Master Allan Ramsay himself."

"Aye, Master Ramsay, who painted my father?"

"The verra same man, sir! He is a lovely man and a talented artist to the Crown. More than that, he was a friend to my father. The Advocate Society that Father helped create, framed the portrait for our family as a gift in honor of his memory. They presented it to us when we were there."

Will brought the painting forward and turned it to the laird who had the same reaction we all did. Tears welled in his eyes, and he could not speak. I understood what he was feeling. The portrait was an incredible likeness of Alexander MacLeod. One that still stirred us all.

"Master Ramsay said that he only had two sittings," I said trying to contain my own emotions and give my uncle a moment in his own grief, "and that he did not finish it because he felt like it represented that Father left us too soon and his life was unfinished."

"It is a fine painting and looks so like Alexander did in this life. Master Ramsay is a talent. Lass, ye should keep this one, and ye can decide where ye want to hang it in the castle. But this should be yers, not mine."

I nodded to him in this direction and then to Will, who held onto the painting to return it to our chamber until I could think more about where to mount it.

"I will leave ye both here to talk," Will said as he kissed me on the cheek and said with a respectful nod to my uncle. Then he walked out of the door and closed it behind him. I appreciated Will knew to give us this time together after being apart for so long.

"Will is going to see about getting his position back at the stables with Auld Knox," I said, explaining Will's departure, though I probably did not need to.

"Aye, the man needs to have an occupation, and I am certain Knox will find a place fer him. He respects William as an honorable man and yer husband doesna strike me as the sort of man to commit to an idle life with nothing to do."

"No sir! He likes to have a task and, like wee Robbie, loves the horses."

After a moment of silence together, he said with a smile, "I trust ye, lass, on the choice ye seemed so determined *not* to make in yer life."

"Will won a heart I was determined not to give... to anyone."

Laird Graham just kept smiling at me. I can only assume that, like Duncan and my father, he never bought my protest against marriage for a second.

"Is he kind and supportive to ye, lass?"

"Aye sir! Will is kindhearted and verra gentle," I said, laughing and somewhat embarrassed to say such words before him. I also thought about how blessed I was to have this amazing man in my life. His actions toward me have always been loving and kind. "He lets me be stubborn and argue when I have moments of fierce independence. He makes me feel confident, and he makes me laugh."

"Then ye have met yer match, lass."

"Aye, sir, I certainly have! And perhaps he met his!"

"Is Missus Gerrard preparing the wedding celebration I ordered on yer return?"

"I believe so, but I have not talked to her about it yet. I will spend time with her this afternoon in the kitchen if I am not interrupting supper preparations. It is to be tomorrow night, aye?"

"Aye! And I have instructed Auld Knox to carry me down the stairs if needed. I must be there with ye!"

"I would be verra disappointed if ye were not beside me at the head table. Duncan did a fine job giving me away at the Canongate Kirk on my wedding day, but I missed ye and I want to celebrate with ye."

He smiled at me but said nothing. I paused for a moment and asked softly as I looked down at my diamond wedding ring and spun it around, "Does Missus Gerrard ken what happened to me in Edinburgh?"

He sat silently on my question for a moment, and I looked up to see a look of concern. He knew I was also asking him to confirm he also knew what happened in Edinburgh. And I was.

"I only ask ye because it feels different here and not just because I have been gone for so long or that I am newly married on my return."

"Aye," he said, taking my hand in his. "When Duncan told me, my heart broke fer ye. It broke for ye *and* William in a way I cannae describe. I told Missus Gerrard because ye had been in the company of only men on yer journey, and I wanted ye to have the support of a woman. Lady Margaret is no longer here, and I wanted another woman—one who has been important in yer life—to support ye when ye returned, if ye needed it. I told her just the day before ye arrived, so her understanding is new, and it is simple. I gave her nothing more than the words that it happened."

"Aye," I said. I understood why he felt the need to tell her, but wished he had not, all the same. "I dinnae challenge yer decision. It just helps me ken how to behave and to better understand why I feel like the air has shifted at Castle Dunmara since I returned. But then I ken I am not the same lass that left the castle gates months ago."

"Ye can expect that she told her husband, but I dinnae ken that fer a fact."

"I can expect that. She and Auld Knox are verra close."

"Sarah and, of course, Robbie dinnae ken."

"Thank ye fer that, sir."

We sat silently for a moment before he said, "If I am doing right by ye as yer guardian and yer uncle, I would encourage ye to talk to Missus Gerrard. Ye are surrounded by men that love ye, that is verra clear! But there is another understanding that can only come from another woman. I wish Lady Margaret was still here fer ye, lass. But Missus Gerrard has cared for ye yer entire life *and* is a midwife. I ken she will be a fine comfort."

I smiled at him and nodded in agreement, "Thank ye, sir!"

"Of course, ye should also lean on yer faith and Father Bruce."

Laird Graham does not know how I tried to blame God for this at first, but I could see that Father Bruce could be a source of comfort. I am just not sure how much I want to keep talking about the intruder and the pain that seems to have grown since we left the city. I am struggling more and more every day and cannot understand why being home has made me even more anxious than I was in Edinburgh.

"And finally, ye can always talk to me and Duncan. We may struggle as men, but we love ye and have committed to care fer ye, as yer uncles and guardians. I ken ye are married now, but I will *never* completely give the responsibility of yer care solely to yer husband until I am dead and gone."

"I thank ye, uncle," I said with a weak smile back to him as I thought my husband was probably looking for all the additional support he could. I also needed to acknowledge the love and support I had around me. Sometimes I feel alone with my grief, but for everything I fear and worry about, deep down I know I am loved.

+++

I walked into the kitchen and found Missus Gerrard hard at work for supper. I could see the start of a large cake on the center table.

"Welcome back, my darlin' lass," she said with an enormous smile. I felt all of her warmth and part of me felt glad to be back home and the other part of me was still afraid.

"I just met with Laird Graham, and I wanted to see if I could be of any help for the celebration," I said, as she handed me a piece of warm and buttered bread. I put my hand up and shook my head.

"Since when do ye turn down bread and butter, Alexandra? Has the big city of Edinburgh changed ye that much?"

I was as surprised as she was, but I have not eaten a thing since we left the tavern in Mallaig. I just do not want to eat. I came home determined to ask how we could add fried ham to our breakfasts, but the task no longer seemed important. I said nothing to her of Missus Douglas' healing breakfasts.

"Lass are ye well?" She asked, looking concerned as I stared at the fire roaring behind her, mindlessly rotating the blade Will gave me in the pocket of my skirt.

I smiled and changed the subject to my original ask, "Aye, the celebration?"

"Och," she said, "Master MacCrimmon will now have a seat next to ye at the head table going forward. It has been set for days anticipating yer arrival. Tomorrow, we will have a fine supper and then have a toast to ye both from Laird Graham. And of course, Angus and Duncan have seen to us having plenty of wine, whisky, and ale for the party."

"Of course they have," I said with a smile. Angus and Duncan will always ensure we have plenty to drink—celebration or not.

"We will have music fer dancin'! We will have the cake! It will be a fine cèilidh—one the clan hasna seen fer a long while!"

"I will wear my wedding dress so ye can see it, and I will have William wear his new coat. We will dress in our wedding finery."

"Och, that will be so lovely," she said as I could see a tear forming in her eye. "If ye need my help to dress, the lasses ken what I expect fer supper. I am just in charge of finishing this cake."

I smiled at her offer and said nothing of taking her up on it. I suspect I can enlist Will on the buttons though he may resent the task as he knows what it takes to undo them after, having already suffered the tedious task once before.

"I understand ye ken what happened to me in Edinburgh," I said, as my tone turned solemn from the talk of wedding celebrations.

"Aye, lass," she said as she came around the corner of the table to me and wrapped me in her arms. "The laird told me so that I could be here to support ye in any way ye might need and having been sent off with a group of men, that is."

"Aye, and I have no mother to guide me."

"My darlin' lass. I will be here however ye need me to and if ye ever want to talk..."

"No missus," I said abruptly, cutting off her words. Trying to correct myself, I gave her a weak smile. "I mean, I just want to be treated as I was before. I am *not* broken."

I could not tell by her reaction if she knew with weak words that I was lying to us both.

"Ye are not, Alexandra," she said, putting her kerchief to her nose. "In fact, ye are the strongest woman I ken."

"I have to tell ye about Mary MacAskill," I said, intentionally changing the subject.

"Dinnae tell me ye saw her in Edinburgh, lass!"

"Aye!"

"Well, I bet that was a shock for the miserable lass to see a band of MacLeod kinsmen standing before her after being banished with her *beloved* Wesley!"

"Mary is *dead*."

"She is *not*! Alexandra! *She is not!*"

"Aye! That horrible Wesley took her all the way to Edinburgh, got himself killed outside of a tavern near the docks in Leith, and left the lass penniless and living off the city streets."

Missus Gerrard turned white and sat her knife down to steady herself on the table. She lowered her head as I continued describing the tragedy of Wesley and Mary to her.

"She came upon us begging in a tavern and, like ye said, was as shocked to see us as we were to see her. I tried to get her to go to the Canongate Kirk, as they have a program fer women and children living rough on the streets, but she didna go. The lass was found floating in the

Nor' Loch just days later. We dinnae ken if she drowned herself there, as the spot is where many a person does end their life, or if another left her there."

"That is the worst story I have ever heard," Missus Gerrard said, bringing her kerchief to her nose again.

"Aye, it is. I struggle with the thoughts of the last we saw of her and that I may have to find my courage to tell her mother of her fate."

"Och, my dear lass! This is where an already dreadful story becomes even more so. Mary's ma couldna bear her only child leavin' her and then being banished from the clan lands, no less! The poor woman died last month of a broken heart. She kent she would never see her babe again!"

I could not imagine a worse story myself and said with a weak smile, "Then I have to have hope in the belief that they are together again in heaven. Is that not what Father Bruce teaches us?"

"Aye, we can have that hope," she said, once again bringing her kerchief to her nose and dabbing her eyes again before she resumed her work cutting the bread loaves before her.

I bowed my head at the thought of such an unfortunate tragedy, all because of the sweet talk and lies from a horrible lad. I do hope Mary and her mother are together again as a family in heaven above. And perhaps if her spirit wants it... she is with Wesley as well.

+++

Will and I sat at the head table in our wedding finery and everyone else was dressed for a rare clan celebration. The entire room seemed thrilled to have a fine feast, drink, and dancing ahead of them tonight. The sound of the and the music playing throughout our supper made the night feel even more festive.

Missus Gerrard recruited wee Robbie to help her decorate the Great Hall with beautiful greenery and candles, making the room look not unlike our own wedding reception in the city. She must have spent the entire rest of the day decorating the cake sitting on the stand just below us. It was stunning! I had the gold-rimmed plates and glasses from Canongate delivered to her so that she could set the head table with our newly acquired Edinburgh finery. It was also a small way to include my father in the celebration.

"Yer not hungry?" Will asked as he noticed I was just moving food around on my plate.

"Not really," I said, putting my cutlery down. I changed the subject immediately, asking, "How was Auld Knox this afternoon?"

"Och, my love! I meant to tell ye that he welcomed me back with open arms."

"That is wonderful!" I said, as I took his hand in my left and raised my wineglass with the right. I do not think that as both the husband of the Lady MacLeod or his own history with Knox Gerrard, Will had any reason to be concerned about finding a position. William belongs in the stables. He loves his work, and he is good at it. That is where he should be.

He met my glass and kissed me on the cheek and then whispered in my ear, *"We are home."* I just smiled at him as I was struggling to feel at home, but I could not put my feelings into words. I just repeated his words.

"We are home."

Duncan nudged Will's shoulder and said to us both, "The laird is going to speak now. Ye might want to fill yer glasses, but ken he will make ye both drink from the quaich."

241

As William tended our glasses, we watched Laird Graham slowly rise from his chair. This silenced the room almost immediately.

"Clan MacLeod! I welcome ye this night and trust that ye have had yer fill on our bounty of food and drink!" The room erupted immediately in applause to support Missus Gerrard and her celebratory feast.

"Hold Fast!"

"Hold Fast," the room said in response.

"Over seven months ago, my niece and heir, Alexandra Flora MacLeod, left the comfort of her home at Dunmara to attend to the estate of her late father, my brother, Alexander, in Edinburgh. First, we must raise our glasses to honor the dearly departed."

The entire room said together, *"Sláinte mhath!"*

After a sip from his glass, he continued, "A band of travelers accompanied her, including her uncle, Duncan, our cousin, Angus, and a young man who defended her honor in this verra hall." The room murmured upon the recollection of the tales of *'William, The Brave'* and *'Wesley, The Banished'*.

"I didna ken when I sent this brave and honorable lad to see her to the city and back safely, that I would spark a love match," he said to a bit of laughter in the room.

William gripped my hand and smiled at me. My uncle unknowingly sparked a love match and one that I treasure more than anything. I also thought about Master Garrick's words again for a moment about choices. While I could not seem to settle on it, I felt like I was choosing to love. Not just hope.

I love Will, but I know I cannot completely love him while I keep carrying the silent burdens and torments that I do. My mind and my heart seem to separate themselves at times. Now that we have arrived at

Dunmara Castle, I do not know how to stop it. I do not know how to tell the man I love that I am struggling. I have tried to be so strong. I do not know how to deal with the pressure to recover from Edinburgh. I do not know how to take on the additional pressures as Lady MacLeod. I do not know how to tell him I need his help.

"But here he is, my new *son*, William MacCrimmon," Laird Graham said as he raised his glass to William, who raised his in return and in respect. I moved my hand to Will's shoulder as Laird Graham continued, "Ye were our kinsman already, William, but now I welcome ye to our family and ken that ye will love *our daughter* as much as we do."

"Aye, sir! Ye have my word, my laird... and my lady," Will said as he kissed my cheek. The hall erupted in its support. Even Duncan smiled at us in congratulations and patted William on the shoulder.

"My dearest Alexandra, our lady, every member of Clan MacLeod celebrates yer union and supports ye and William in yer new life together. We celebrate ye both this night!"

He walked to us with the quaich and offered it to Will first, then me. We both drank from it. He followed and drank the last of the whisky it contained sealing his agreement and approval on our marriage.

"*Sláinte mhath!*" Laird Graham yelled across the Great Hall, raising the empty quaich.

"*Sláinte mhath!*" said the room to loud cheers and applause.

He looked at me as if he wanted me to say something. I was not prepared for a speech but should have known that as the Lady MacLeod and his heir, I would be expected to speak before this room. I was uncertain of what to say for such a moment and slowly sipped from my glass as I tried to buy myself some time to think about my words.

"My laird, William and I thank ye fer yer blessing upon our marriage and for this fine celebration. Missus Gerrard, once again, ye have outdone yerself," I said, looking for her in the room and then raising my glass when our eyes finally met. "I am in awe of the wonders ye create and ken that we are all looking forward to this beautiful cake ye have placed before us."

The room immediately sounded its agreement on the anticipation of the cake and perhaps even more the drinking and dancing to follow. William took my near-empty glass from my hands, filled it, and handed me back a full glass of wine as I was talking. I said, smiling at him and then the room as I took my glass back, "Well then, if that is not a sign of true love and devotion, I dinnae ken what is!"

The hall erupted in laughter, and I bent down to kiss my husband for his kindness as the clan before us began roaring. As both of our faces turned red, I put my hand on his shoulder and turned back to the room.

"I left on a mournful journey with three men who pledged to their laird to see me to Edinburgh and back. I return to Castle Dunmara with an *uncle* who has become even more of a dear friend." With a smile, I raised my glass to Duncan, and he was now fully absolved of his mistake just days before. He nodded and raised his glass to me in return.

"A *cousin* I have grown to love and have even learned to *understand*." I raised my glass to Angus as he and some near him in the room laughed loudly in appreciation for the struggle of talking with Angus. "If ye need to understand what Angus says, I can tell ye, drinkin' whisky helps." The room laughed again as Angus raised his glass and said something incoherent, instantly proving my point before the entire room.

"And I left with a *friend* and honorable defender that became a *husband*," I said, raising my glass to Will. He stood up next to me with his

244

own glass in hand and his arm around my waist. "Thank ye all for celebrating our marriage this night! Let us toast once more, have some of this fine cake, and start the dancing! *Sláinte mhath!*"

"*Sláinte mhath!*" said the entire room.

Will kissed me once again, passionately on the mouth, to rousing cheers in the hall. All I knew is that I was ready to leave this room with him this minute, but we were going to have to eat cake and accept all the congratulations from the members of the clan.

The music started up again and Missus Gerrard directed us to stand near the cake as she handed us the first piece. I took a small bite and told her it was the best I had ever had, and it was. But after a night of only drinking wine, it was too sweet, and I could not finish it. I sat the plate back up on the head table with the unspoken promise that I would finish it after our duty here was done.

Will and I stood next to the cake table as the kind and generous members of the clan came to shake our hands and wish us hearty congratulations. Some left us with beautiful flowers, homemade jams and butters, sweet drawings from the children, and plenty of marital advice.

Plenty of marital advice.

It was all overwhelming. I began to feel anxious and looked around corners and in groups of men for the face of Allan Calder constantly. I dreaded seeing him and kept thinking that any moment, even here on Skye, I would. I do not understand why at this moment of celebration the man I despise more than anything keeps occupying my thoughts.

+++

"Lady MacLeod, I welcome you back to Dunmara Castle and congratulate you on this very special occasion," said a man with a very

245

formal English accent as he took my hand in his. He was fair-haired and had serious brown eyes. He was tall and thin with the build and smooth hands of someone who has never worked hard a day in his life.

"Thank ye, sir," I said as Missus Gerrard handed him his slice of cake on the side. Suddenly it came to me. "Och, are ye Master Harmon?"

"James Harmon, at your service," he said, nodding his head. He seemed much younger than I expected, yet still had the rigid coldness of a typical school headmaster. I knew it was him!

"Well, sir, yer on my list of people to talk to upon my return. Welcome to Castle Dunmara and Skye!"

"I thank you very much," he said formally as he bowed his head.

"William, Master Harmon is our new educator," I said as they shook hands with this introduction. "He arrived here at the castle while we were in Edinburgh."

"Congratulations to you, Master MacCrimmon," he said, shaking Will's hand as a gentleman.

"We welcome ye to Dunmara," William said, shaking his hand back. "Ye have been here for how long now, sir?"

"Since the middle of August."

"I am certain my uncle, let ye ken of my intentions for the school when ye arrived." Will looked at me as he does not know of my ask about educating girls on our clan lands. That portion of the agreement with my uncles was never announced in the Great Hall and we have not discussed this topic together.

"He did, indeed. I am not certain we are of the same mind on the topic, Lady MacLeod, but I will be most happy to talk with you about it now that you have returned."

This answer incensed me but the fact that I have had only drink this night did not help the tone or manner of my response.

"Then are ye saying to me Master Harmon, that no lasses are being educated on our clan lands?" I could feel William's hand on my back to steady me and temper my rising anger that was surely evident on both my face and in my tone.

"No, Lady MacLeod," he said, looking me directly in the eye, "but please let me explain. Laird MacLeod told me I was to work with you on a plan for such an expansion of education. I have an opinion here and drafted a recommendation, but we agreed not to make any changes until you returned to Dunmara."

I leaned back into William's hand, hoping he would take me from this moment and this space, or at least know that I was overreacting. I tried to calm myself, though what I wanted more than anything was another glass of wine.

"Then I thank ye, Master Harmon, and my laird, for giving me the respect to have my wishes heard now that I have returned."

"I look forward to speaking with you again soon, Lady MacLeod. My happy congratulations to you both on this day," Master Harmon said as he walked away with his cake.

Will said nothing but kept his hand on my back as we received our remaining guests.

+++

The last of the revelers were still dancing and singing. Neither Will nor I were fine dancers but were persuaded to go out on one song early on to encourage others. We made it through part of the way but began to laugh so hard at our inability that we removed ourselves and set out on the mission to find more drink. As the room thinned out, Duncan tried to celebrate us again with a whisky toast in the corner.

"Yer speech was fine, Alex! Ye ken yer a natural speaker, so I expected nothing less from ye. I tried to find Angus fer this toast to the weary band of travelers, but I cannae find the man."

"Och, he is under a hedge or a woman at this hour, uncle," I said rudely and without regard for my station or general decorum.

"Alex! That is horrible!" Will scolded me for my crass response.

"We are all friends *forever*," I said, putting my drunken arms around them both as much in gratitude as to hold myself upright. I could feel the tears start.

"Och, no lass," Will said, before he quickly corrected himself. "I mean, dinnae cry."

I could feel William's hand on my elbow, trying to steady me. They both gave each other a look that showed I was done for the evening. And I truly was.

Duncan said, as he and William moved me toward the back stairs. "Yer fine, my dear. We are *all* friends forever. And we will save our friendship toast when we can share it with Angus. He deserves to be here with us."

I could not speak the words, but he was right. We would wait until the four of us could be together to celebrate our friendship, kinship, and love when I am not drunk.

+++

When we finally cleared the hall and said our thanks to everyone left, William and I returned to our room, where I immediately fell on the bed,

248

swimming with drink. William was also but stood before me as he began lifting my skirts.

"*No*," I said in a whimper.

He waited for a moment and asked as he began moving his hand up my thigh, "No?"

I breathed in deeply and raised my hands over my head in resignation and whispered, "*Aye.*"

"That is what I thought ye said," he said with a smile and dove underneath my skirts. I fought him at first and laughed at the thought, but even in the dullness of too much drink and too little food, his attention felt good.

"I love ye, Will," I said in his ear when he resurfaced from my skirts.

"And I love ye, my darlin' lass," he said before rolling on his back.

"Did ye just try to avoid the buttons?"

"I did, but I ken the devils are waiting fer me."

I rolled over and said, "They are. Please get me out of this dress."

Once he removed me from the lovely, handcrafted prison of a wedding dress, William and I found our way into the bed, ready for sleep.

"What did we think of tonight?" I asked, sitting myself up on my elbows looking at him lying next to me, and feeling a lot more sober than I was when we entered our room.

"I thought it was a fine celebration and a great honor to ye on yer return as the Lady MacLeod. But to have Laird Graham say such kind things and call me *son* was incredible!"

"That *was* a lovely moment," I said, kissing him quickly. "I hope ye feel that yer part of our *family* now, Will. Not just a member of our *clan*... not just our *kinsman*."

"Aye, I felt that from ye, Duncan, and Angus when we married, but tonight, I felt it from Laird Graham himself. I was nervous sitting at the head table, but felt most welcome. And lass," he said, twisting my curls around his fingers as I pushed his own curls away from his forehead, "yer a natural leader!"

"How so?"

"To show yer respect to yer uncle, cousin, and husband before the Great Hall was not only kind, but it was a stroke of brilliance. The clan saw yer *heart*." I just looked at him as he continued, "A respected leader has many moments to show their intellect or to show their judgment and fairness before the clan. Some leaders show their cruel ambition that may have people follow them out of fear. But when a leader can find a moment to show their heart—and aye—even their humor that can make that leader not just *respected*, but *loved*."

I forgot Will did not hear my speech before the Fine and kissed him before saying, "Thank ye, sir. Ye are an excellent support for *this* leader."

"What did we think of Master Harmon?" I asked as I nestled myself in the bend of his arm and stroked the hair on his chest.

"I thought he was... *verra English*."

"Aye," I said, softly in agreement. This is the first time I have heard him say such a thing and knew that Master Harmon was going to have some work ahead of him to win us both over.

"It is late," Will said, politely telling me that this conversation was over for tonight. I smiled up at him and agreed by promptly extinguishing my candle when he did the same.

Neither of us said anything else on this topic, but before falling asleep in his arms, my last thoughts were that I am going to have to battle

Master Harmon to educate lasses at Dunmara. No matter what it takes, I will summon all the strength I have left to see that it is done.

+++

GRATITUDE

Completing one novel seemed like a feat, but to have prepared the first three books in a historical fiction series, plus a contemporary romance novel, was not only thrilling... it was overwhelming.

I learned a great deal along my journey over the last several years about Scottish history and culture, the generosity of the human spirit, my own writing style and process, and some of the positives and pitfalls of self-publishing. This adventure started as a journey of self-discovery and for my own mental well-being. I am so grateful to have had the gift of time to follow my dream and finish what I started.

I would like to acknowledge **Dr. Bruce Waltke and his wife, Elaine.** I got to know this amazing couple at **Matts' Rotisserie and Oyster Bar in Redmond, Washington**. Bruce is a well-known and respected Christian biblical scholar and professor. From the moment I met him, he was immediately a friend. He is a kind man—filled with peace and light. Miss Elaine faded from us in dementia over the years, and we lost her on 2 September 2020. This lovely couple touched my life in ways they will never understand. Bruce is the complete inspiration for Father Bruce in the *HOLD FAST Series.* And it is a name he told me that his friends at church often call him.

I returned to Scotland in November 2021 and stayed again for a month to complete my books. I would like to thank everyone I met along the way who made my story even better or just lifted my spirit. That starts with everyone associated with **Glen Dye Cabins and Cottages, Aberdeenshire.** I survived the great Winter Storm Arwen on 26 November 2021 with my new friends at Glen Dye and spent seven days in my incredible 300-year-old cottage with no electricity! I took every moment during that adventure—making my own fires to stay warm, making tea or food on the gas stove lit with matches, and warming water each morning to bathe—quickly! It was all a lesson in thinking about living in Eighteenth Century Scotland and I hope that it shows in my novels.

Even though I had more modern conveniences than Alexandra had, it was a new perspective for me and one for which I am forever grateful. I will say it again! It was an *adventure*—and that is exactly how I took the experience! I thank my hosts who did everything they could for me to be comfortable and safe.

The descriptions of the storm at Glenammon House in *A STRENGTH SUMMONED* are based on my own experiences and I hope they place my books on the shelves in my beloved *Bothy Cottage* where I spent many hours writing and editing this series on two separate trips to Scotland.

I met a new friend, **Dr. Brian Fleming,** on this same trip at **Bar Prince, The Balmoral Hotel, Edinburgh.** He was so kind and gave me his copy of *Scottish Culture & Traditions During the Late 17th and Early 18th Centuries* by Norman C. Milne. A book signed by the author, no less! Little did he know that the next day I would miraculously survive my drive through the storm to my cottage near Banchory and spend the next seven days without electricity. I read that book from cover to cover (more than once!) by candlelight and in front of my welcome fire. It helped me provide the detailed descriptions to my incredible designer, **Jared Frank,** for the cover art for both *A*

STRENGTH SUMMONED, Book 2 of the *HOLD FAST Series* and *RAISE YOUR SHIELD*, Book 3 of the *HOLD FAST Series*.

I must also acknowledge my new friends working at the pub at the **Burnett Arms Hotel, Banchory, Aberdeenshire.** The pub had power eventually! It easily became another respite on my journey where I could work during the day and recharge all of my devices for the evening ahead. But I also recharged my spirit, as my new friends were a tremendous support for me.

On this same trip, I had the chance to visit **Dunnottar Castle Stonehaven, Aberdeenshire** which serves as the original inspiration for Castle Dunmara on the Isle of Skye. Pictures do not do the castle ruins perched upon the seaside cliff justice. On a cold and bright November day in 2021, my visit was a dream come true! While there was no raging sea beneath the rocks that day, it was exactly as I dreamed it would be. I tried to imagine where Cairn's Point, the Great Hall, St. Margaret's Chapel, and the old stone wall would be if this were on Skye. This visit made my fictional castle real, and it was an emotional moment.

I would also like to thank the hard-working staff at the **Bosville Hotel in Portree, Skye** and **Prestonfield House, Edinburgh.** Each person I met along the way made my stay special during a tough time in the hospitality industry and encouraged my work on these books.

Every visit to Scotland reminds me I am *home*. On each of my trips, I crossed all parts of Scotland with a cheering section wishing me well, willingly connecting me with others, and helping me in any and every way they could. Many of my edits and additions were from these incredible people and places on my journey—not just academic research. One day, I hope to make my stay permanent.

+++

ABOUT THE AUTHOR

Cynthia Harris is the author of *HOLD FAST*, her debut novel and the first installment of the historical fiction *HOLD FAST Series*. With *A STRENGTH SUMMONED*, she delivers the second novel in the series. She is also the author of her first contemporary romance novel, *Fun & Games*. All of her novels are available in paperback and Kindle versions on Amazon.com.

Cynthia built a career in storytelling. From leading advertising and marketing strategy for some of the world's most recognized consumer brands, international news organizations, and major league sports teams—to leading internal and external communication strategy and speech writing for technology, human resources, gaming, and entertainment executives—words have not only been her passion, but her livelihood. With her novels, Cynthia now focuses her time on finding and sharing her own voice.

As a proud graduate of The University of Georgia, she made a home in the Pacific Northwest over sixteen years ago. She keeps her gas tank full and her passport current, so she can escape to the incredible places near and far that allow her to revisit history, fuel her creativity, and find peace. But Scotland is calling, and she is currently looking for a new home in the country that she loves.

FROM THE AUTHOR

Thank you for reading! But don't worry! Book 3 in the *HOLD FAST Series* will follow closely behind this one. You can follow the rest of Alexandra's story and her growth as Lady MacLeod.

If you liked *A STRENGTH SUMMONED*, Book 2 of the *HOLD FAST Series*, I'd appreciate a quick review on Amazon, so I know how to improve my books, and know what you want to read from me in the future. Your review also helps other readers discover my work.

If you want to preview some of my writing, get sneak peeks of future work, or learn about my journey as an author, visit me at cynthiaharrisauthor.com or follow me on Instagram at cynthia_harris_author.

Cynthia Harris Novels

Fun & Games

HOLD FAST
Book 1 Of The HOLD FAST Series

A STRENGTH SUMMONED
Book 2 Of The HOLD FAST Series

RAISE YOUR SHIELD
Book 3 Of The HOLD FAST Series

Printed in Great Britain
by Amazon

15366151R00161